THIRD

PARTY

Sarah Himebauch

Acknowledgements

As always, I have to extend a big thank you to all of
my family and friends who always support me in all
of my endeavors.
To my Parents…all four of you,
Thank you so much for always believing in me
To Alexis… my best friend,
Thank you for always supporting my passions,
including writing. Thanks for the hours you spent on
proofreading.
To Andrew… the love of my life,
Your support and love mean everything to me.
And to my Grandparents,
I love making you guys proud.

1

Riley

I stood there, watching in silence, as they lowered my sister's casket into the ground. They began to shovel dirt on top, and all I could hear were the guttural sobs coming from my mother. My father's face remained mournful as he held my mother while she wept.

I couldn't cry.

My sister was my best friend in every aspect of the word, but today, on the day of her burial, I was unable to cry.

I knew what everyone was thinking. They thought I was cold, or emotionless, simply because I didn't choose today, or this time and place to display all the emotions that are raging inside me right now.

It was suicide, or that's what they tell me. However, my sister was never someone who would have done something like this. She was free-spirited, kind, and loved life. She was always busy seeking life's new adventure.

Someone killed her.

I hold no doubt in my mind that my sister was murdered. The doctors, the medical examiner… even my parents believed it to be a suicide.

My sister was found in her car, overdosed on pills.

I don't know if it was the shock or the grief, but my parents failed to realize that Daisy wouldn't even take so much as an aspirin, let alone down an entire bottle of Oxycodone.

Daisy also would have never tried to kill herself. If she was ever feeling down or upset, she knew that I was there for her. But Daisy never really got upset. She was always happy, someone who looked at the world and life as "a glass half full".

The burial was over, as I felt distant relatives pass by me tapping me on the back and doling out hushed apologies. It was all the same, and I couldn't even muster the energy to properly thank them.
I feel dead inside.

It's been a week to the day since I found Daisy in her car. She was parked at the local grocery store lot, and I was tipped off about her car from one of the grocery store workers. She hadn't come home that night, or better yet, she snuck out of the house without us knowing. We didn't even realize she was gone until I saw that she hadn't slept in her bed that night.

And I haven't been able to get the image out of my head since.

I know my parents think it's foolish of me to hold out hope for a different explanation. Anything other than suicide.

It just doesn't make sense. Despite the number of times I have spoken with a trail of doctors, I can't possibly fathom that my sister would take her own life.

I have a gut wrenching feeling she was murdered, and while part of me hopes I'm right, the other half desperately prays for my deduction to be wrong.

We were twins... Daisy and I.

Both tall with curly red hair, and bright blue eyes. We were a carbon copy of one another, the only thing separating us was the clear personality differences.

I was shy, and reserved, while Daisy was the life of the party, making friends anywhere and everywhere.

I wish you were here Daisy. This isn't right without you.

"Come on Riley." My dad squeezed my shoulder lightly, in an attempt to usher me inside for the dinner portion of the funeral.

I snapped out of my thoughts and began walking with my dad right by my side, who no longer was holding my mother up.

I glanced at the banquet room, and saw my mother leaning on her sister Ava. My aunt was always so wonderful to Daisy and myself, and she was really close with my mother as well.

Thank you for being here for her.

"I'm sorry pumpkin. I know how hard this day is for you." My dad tried to comfort me.

"I just don't believe it, and you shouldn't either." I pushed out of his grasp and headed in the doors when we reached the room.

That was cold.

Yeah, well on a day like today I find it difficult to extend niceties to everyone. I'm mourning. Give me a break.

I want to go home.

"Riley dear, how are you?" My great aunt Dorothy waltzed over, a flute of champagne being pinched between her long red nails.

"Fine, thank you." I tried to walk the other way, but she caught me by the arm.

"Well dear, we were all worried about you. You didn't cry once."

Is she serious?

Once more I tried to walk away, desperately trying to avoid saying something I would regret, and once more she caught my arm.

"Hiding your feelings never fares well for the soul…"

"Take your fucking hand off me, now." She made an audible gasp, covering her mouth with her other hand, and I snagged the attempt to free myself and head the other way.

My mother was staring at me, wide-eyed, obviously a witness to the entire spiel.

"I'm sorry mom. She wouldn't stop pestering me." I didn't want to upset my mother any more than she already was today.

Why couldn't people learn to take a step back, and quit pushing, especially when it was none of their business? Just because I held back the urge to sob and throw myself into the hole with my sister, didn't mean anything. I was dealing with my emotions in my own way.

And by dealing with them, I mean avoiding them like the plague. But that was none of Dorothy's business.

"I know baby. She has always been nosy. Don't let it bug you. Are you okay?"

"Yes. Are you?" I reached out and squeezed my mother's hand in an act of comfort.

"No, but I will be. Thank you for being here my sweet Riley." She kissed my hand and was pulled away by another needy family member.

I scanned the room, desperate for someone of consequence to speak too. If I was caught again standing alone, I was sure to be subjected to an errant family member's prodding questions. I looked all around and spotted someone.

Cora.

I made a beeline for her, and upon seeing me, she rushed into my arms, squeezing me in a death grip.

Cora was my best friend since I was younger, and also really close with Daisy as well.

"I have been looking everywhere for you! Where were you?"

I didn't reply, but rather pointed a long finger towards Dorothy who was now pestering my father.

"Ahhhh." Cora gave a knowing nod, followed by a smile.

"Let's get out of here, please." I practically begged my friend.

"You got it." She snatched her purse off the seat and together we headed towards the door, which was now being halted by my father.

"Where are you going Riley?" He didn't seem upset, but genuinely curious.

"Cora and I were going to get out of here. I just can't be here dad."

"Okay, well I will let your mother know. I'll see you at home later, I love you." He pulled me in for a hug and kissed the top of my forehead.

I grabbed Cora's hand and we ran out of the stuffy building, down the grass hill, and towards her car.

She unlocked the doors, and we both climbed in, buckling our seatbelts.

"Where to?" Cora asked, hands positioned on the steering wheel.

"How about the lake?" I smiled, as it was one of our favorite places to go… all three of us- Daisy, Cora, and myself.

"Sure thing." She revved the engine, and put her foot on the gas, peeling away from the funeral site.

The drive to the lake was calm, filled with the comfortable silence Cora and I basked in. That was one of the reasons we were such solid friends. Sometimes there were moments, where you didn't feel like talking- not because you were angry or upset… but rather because the silence is much more welcoming. This was one of those times.

And Cora understood that.

Finally, we arrived, and she snagged a spot just along the tree line. The walk down to the water was always a little bit of a hike, but the view once you reached the bottom was absolutely spectacular.

I wish Daisy were here to see it.

My mind was constantly running rampant with thoughts of Daisy. It ranged from memories of us playing at the lake when we were younger, to our petty fights, to finding her that day.

I don't think I can ever forget that.

"Are you coming, Riley?"

I was lost in my thoughts, and when I looked around, Cora was already halfway down the hill. I started jumping over the branches and logs, climbing over rocks, and pushing leaves and bushes out of my way.

I nearly lost my footing over a wobbly rock but was able to steady myself on the edge of a tree.

I hobbled the last few feet until the start of the small dock.

The forestry brought you to a teeny tiny dock, where we would bring chairs and snacks to sit for hours on end, just admiring the water, the sounds of nature, and each other's company.

This is where we should have come to honor Daisy.

I understand that my parents were adamant about keeping Daisy one and whole, so they decided against cremation. However, I knew my sister best. We were twins. If she were going to die, she would have wanted her ashes scattered over the lake water.

So, she could spend an eternity at her favorite place.

My mood was somber, but I felt comforted to be at a place where I felt most connected to my sister.

Why did you do it Daisy?

…if she even did it. I still wasn't convinced.

Cora and I took seats on the dock, beside one another.

"So how are you holding up and be honest with me Riles."

Horrible.

"Not bad." I replied, hoping my friend wouldn't see right through me.

"Riley…" Cora warned.

"Fine. I feel like a piece of me is gone. She was my other half, and to be quite frank, I don't know how to live without her. She has literally been with me since I have been on this Earth, and now I feel like I am going at it alone. I feel like I am facing it by myself."

"I know that Riley. It's normal. She was your twin sister, and you guys were so close. But, don't for a second feel as if you don't have anybody by your side to get you through this. I'm here, always."

"I know that. Thanks." I squeezed her hand.

While I appreciated the sentiment, it simply wasn't the same.

Daisy knew things that I never told anybody, including Cora.

"Why do I feel like you're holding something back?"

"I just… I don't think Daisy killed herself. She wouldn't."

"Riley, you heard them. It was suicide."

"Yeah, I know about the pills. Why do they automatically assume Daisy took them willingly?"

My best friend gave me a look, one I couldn't really decipher.

"I know Cora, I know. But, something about it doesn't seem right. That's all." I continued.

"If you really feel that way, I'll help you look into it."

"Promise?" I held out a pinky.

Trivial, I know. But it made me feel better.

"Promise." My best friend hooked her pinky with mine.

2

Cora

Did I think Daisy was murdered?

No.

Would I help my best friend in her wild goose chase until she felt better?

Of course.

Daisy was also my best friend. We all three had a powerful dynamic, one that started when we were kids. The lake had become one of our favorite places, because we all three shared a love of tranquility and quiet. The lake wasn't very populated, especially the patch where we went.

The dock itself was one of our little hidden treasures, and when Riley had requested to go there, I thought it was because she was seeking a spot where she could feel close to her sister.
Especially on a day like today.

The mood that hung in the air at the funeral services today was that of a somber one. I was surprised at how well their mother was able to hold it together.

I know they always say that parents don't have a favorite, but anyone could see that Daisy was Anne's favorite child... and that doesn't go to say that she didn't love Riley. It's just that Anne and Daisy were always two peas in a pod.

In fact, Daisy got along well with everybody she met. She was incredibly spunky, outgoing, and pretty much the opposite of Riley who was quite shy and could be incredibly soft spoken. Knowing Riley for years and years, I knew that deep down she had a fire in her.

I can't believe Daisy is just gone.

Her death was a shock that left waves in our town. Her suicide was news for not just our towns but a few over as well. Everyone who knew Daisy felt lost, guilty, and were left wondering... could I have done something more?

I know this feeling all too well, as it has been the one going through my mind ever since it happened. Riley was the one to find her sister, but she called me right away before the police or even her parents.

I didn't see the scene, and I find myself incredibly thankful every day. I don't know if I could live normally with that image seared into my mind.

Truth be told, I was a little nervous about Riley. She seemed to be processing Daisy's death well, but then it turned into being a little too well. Since her sister passed, I have yet to see her cry once. I know Riley isn't big on public displays of emotion, but surely her sister's death would be an excuse. *Wouldn't it?*

Today when she rushed me out of the funeral, I hoped it was because she wanted to finally talk, clear the air, and have somebody to vent to about all the emotions I knew she was keeping pent up inside. *Wrong.*

She thinks her sister was murdered, and now I have agreed to help her chase a trail that is simply not there.

Daisy was also my best friend, and if I were to truly think that she was murdered, I would be looking for the killer day and night. Riley has become too overwhelmed with her grief, that she has clearly allowed it to cloud her judgement. While we all like to think that we knew Daisy well, and that she would never do something like this… it simply wasn't true.

The sad truth is that the happy go lucky girl that we all knew and loved seemed to be dealing with demons that she felt she couldn't overcome, and unfortunately took her own life.

How do I explain that to Riley?

I have no clue what to do and I feel like I'm stuck between a rock and a hard place. I don't want to completely rain on Riley's parade, because that could drive a wedge between myself and the only friend I have left. But if I don't say anything, am I just buying time until Riley realizes the truth and completely breaks down?

What to do…. what to do.

The drive back to Riley's house was far from quiet. Ever since I had pinky swore to help her find out who Daisy's "murderer" was, she had been talking a mile a minute about all her suspicions. "Okay Cora… chew on this- where was Daisy's phone? They never found it."

"I don't know Riley, maybe she left it somewhere in case you tried to call and stop her."

"Or, someone took it." She looked at me bright eyed, hoping I would agree with her.

This is crazy, Riley.

"I don't think so Riles. Come on, that doesn't even make sense."

Riley, clearly irate with my lack of understanding, turned to the side with a loud sigh. "I thought you wanted to help me Cora."

"Riley… I do. But honestly, I don't think this is the way to help. This is only delaying the inevitable." I looked at my best friend, who for the first time since the news of Daisy's death, actually looked broken.

"And what would that be, huh?"

'You're seeking out anything that will prevent you from having to deal with the fact that Daisy is gone, and she is never coming back. I don't mind helping you ever… you know that. But I don't think that this will help you in the long run. Daisy's gone, and I don't want you to kill yourself on the inside because of it."

I was met with silence, and I took that as a good sign. Riley was always one who needed to stew on things for a while, before ultimately coming to the right choice or decision.

I was right, but I wasn't sure if I wanted to be. There was no real "right" choice in a situation like this, and my only goal was to help my friend properly grieve for someone we both lost.

We pulled into her driveway, and she got out, shutting my car door without another word.

I watched as she slowly climbed the brick steps up to the familiar mahogany home. *We always joked that it matched her and Daisy's hair.*

I thought she might want me to come inside… like usual. But she unlocked the door and went inside, closing the door behind her without a final glance. *Well… that settles that.*

Hopefully after she thinks about what I said for a while, she might reconsider her course of action. Daisy's death was absolutely tragic, and I know I can speak for everyone when I say that we all wish we did more.

Nothing that Riley does will bring her back, and Daisy wouldn't want her to punish herself this way. I don't want her hurt, and I am at a loss about what I should do.

I threw my car into reverse and slowly backed out of the driveway. My long hair hung in my face, and I made a mental note to get a haircut soon.

Right as I almost cleared the driveway, a red car flew by nearly nailing the back of my car.
Idiot.

I continued to slowly back up until I was on the street. I put the car into drive, and slowly started forward when I saw Riley's parents coming towards the house in their car.

They slowed down and I rolled down my window.

"Hi hon. Is Riley inside?" Her dad smiled at me, and her mom looked like she was hanging on by a string.
Poor Anne.

My heart broke for her, as I knew that this must be nothing short of unbearable.

"Yeah. I just dropped her off."

"How is she?" Her mother looked optimistic and I started to struggle mentally with what I would say.

Truth… or a carefully orchestrated white lie?
Lie.

"Better, I think. We talked a lot about it." I cheerfully smiled as a cherry on top to completely sell my act.

"Good, thank you so much. Please hon, come by soon." Their window rolled back up, and I continued on to my house.

As I drove further and further away from their home, my mind remained on one person- Riley. What the hell was I supposed to do?

There was really only one thing I could do- and it was a tough pill to swallow.

I had to help her track down someone who didn't exist.

Should be a walk in the park.

3

Riley

Watching my friend pull away from my house felt like a weight slowly being lifted off my shoulders. After our lake trip today, I felt so defeated.

After Daisy, Cora was really my best friend.

I had thought since they were also friends, that she would agree to help me with no questions asked. She didn't have any questions, but instead a lot of "insight" and "advice" that I didn't ask for nor need.

I don't know which is worse.

So now I feel like I can't even talk to her about this, and once again, I feel alone.

You should be here Daisy. It isn't the same.

I know my sister didn't kill herself. One of the main reasons, is because I knew her inside and out. The bright and infectious personality she carried in her life wasn't a façade, it was who she was. She was someone who lit up whatever room they walked into, and who never had someone say a single foul word about her.

Not only that, and it might sound incredibly dumb, but we were twins. I felt things that she was feeling, even before she chose to confide in me about them. We were connected, whether we liked it or not, and since I found her in that parking lot- I have had a gut-wrenching feeling lingering around.

My sister was murdered.

And I didn't plan to rest until they were found.

I didn't know the who, what, or how. Right now, I was working on the "why".
Why would somebody kill my sister?

Maybe she was in trouble. Maybe someone was threatening her. We had separate bedrooms, but I couldn't bring myself to step foot in there since she died. It feels like I'm violating her space, despite the fact that she always was welcoming to everyone in her room.

I knew that I would need to push those feelings aside in order to achieve the greater good... finding the killer.
If there even is a killer...

There is. I just feel it in my heart and in my bones.

I took a seat on my bed and laid back. The comfort was a welcome refuge to the dark hole I had buried myself in all day. I felt incredibly defeated, and mentally exhausted. I didn't go too far out of my way to put on a good face, but rather kept a few emotions at bay.

I didn't cry at the funeral. I didn't want to.

Those people were family, sure, but they didn't really *know* Daisy- or me for that matter. Of course, I wouldn't want to bare my soul for them all to see.

Before I could even continue to wallow, I started to sob. The tears came and kept coming. I pulled my pillow over my face to silence the cries, because I couldn't really deal with the parental pity right now.

I heard the front door open, so I ripped myself away from my sob fest momentarily to lock the door.

I needed to be alone, even if it was just for a few minutes.

I want to mourn my sister in private.

Cora didn't think I was coming to terms with my emotions following my sister's death, but that was far from the truth.

I knew what I was feeling.

Ever since the passing of Daisy, I have felt like there is a now very prominent, and very large, hole in my heart. It's one that can't be patched with tuna casseroles from the neighbors, or sympathy hugs from strangers. It was only one that my sister could fix, or better yet- understand.

I felt like I had run out of tears, and soon came the pounding headache. I grabbed the bottle of Advil off of my nightstand, grabbed two, and dry swallowed them.

I took a swig out of my water bottle and got into pajamas. It was the middle of the day, and usually unacceptable to lounge around, but my sister died. So, everyone's opinions on anything I did from now on could go to hell.

I laid my head down on the soft down pillow and let my mind switch into overdrive.

"Honey?" My mom was knocking at my door.

I peeled my eyes open and looked around my now very pitch-black room. I switched on the bedside table lamp and sat up.

"Yeah?" I replied, still very groggy.

"We have some food if you're hungry."

"Be right down."

The good news was that my blistering headache faded, but the hurt in my heart lingered. *What's new?*

I threw on a pair of my slippers and pulled my hair back into a messy bun. I unlocked the door, opening it, and grabbed my phone.

I started down the staircase but decided to send a quick text to Cora.

Riley: I'm sorry about earlier. Rough day.

> *Cora: You know I understand. See you tomorrow?*

Riley: Of course.

I smiled to myself, pleased with the way I handled things. I was still a little bit irritated at the lack of reaction from Cora when I broke down all my findings- well, lack thereof.

But still, I couldn't really go about cutting off friendships with the only friend I actually had.

I was immediately greeted with the sweet smell of Mrs. Abbot's lasagna from next door. She had brought a catering sized pan last night, and I was pretty sure we would have leftovers for weeks. "Hey hon, dinner's being served right now." My dad shot a sweet smile as he loaded a heaping pile of lasagna onto my plate.

My mother was already seated at the dining room chair facing myself, so I took a seat. I seized the opportunity to survey the spread of food, which seemed uncharacteristically large.

My heart sank.

The amount of food wasn't unusually large, but only seemed so because we were missing one person.

Daisy.

I looked across the table at my mother, who seemingly looked as if she had come to the same realization that I had.

Daisy was never coming back.

My mother has always held a strong bond with Daisy and I, but she always seemed to click more with Daisy. The question was… who didn't? Daisy was bursting at the seams with a bubbly personality and bright outlook on life. Her energy was absolutely infectious.

I on the other hand, was slightly more reserved and while I did have a genuine love for life, it wasn't always as easily palpable as it was with Daisy.

My mother wiped a stray tear from under her eye, and I felt even worse than I did two seconds ago… if that was even possible.

Even if Daisy was murdered, and I found evidence, it would never heal my mother. It truly wouldn't heal any of us, because one thing remained true: The truth wouldn't bring Daisy back.
But it would bring her justice.

And that was what I held on to.

"How was your day hon?" My dad finally took his seat and turned to me with a forced smile pasted on his face.

"It was okay. Hard." I tried to keep my composure, but anytime someone asked if I was okay… I felt like I was about to break in half.

My mom finally looked up from her untouched plate long enough to hold steady eye contact with me. It was undoubtedly an awkward exchange, one that lasted several seconds. Before long, she smiled. A genuine smile. I reached across the table, took her hand in mine, and squeezed.

Despite the monumental progress made with my mother, the dinner continued on in a comfortable silence. Usually our dinner table was bursting with laughter and conversation before Daisy's death, but at this point I would take anything over having to "talk about my feelings."

Yeah, because that would be horrible.

After I felt too full to eat any more food, I excused myself and headed up the stairs to my room. On the way up, I lingered by Daisy's door, desperate to go inside.

It felt wrong… like I was violating her space.

Of course, I knew deep down that my sister always had an "open door" policy. But she was gone. And now I was left to deal with the ruins.

Despite all of that, I pushed open the door. The window was open, and the room was cold. I felt a shiver down my spine and took that as a sign that I should leave. But… I didn't want to. Daisy's smell lingered in the room and it brought tears to my eyes. I sat down on her bed taking her pillow in my hands.

I inhaled, and the smell of the coconut shampoo she always used flooded my nostrils.

God, I miss you so much.

I squeezed the pillow tighter and tighter, and soon felt a sharp poke in my hand. Naturally curious, I turned the pillow over and discovered that there was something in the pillowcase. I slid my hand down and grabbed what felt like a card.

I pulled my arm out and sure enough, there was a small envelope addressed to "D".
Daisy.

It felt wrong to open Daisy's mail, and this was something she probably wanted to be kept private, ergo the inconspicuous hiding place.

I couldn't help it, and opened the envelope, pulling out a dark red card with only a rose on the front. I opened the card, anxiety blooming in my stomach over what I was prepared to read.

There was only 5 words.
The lake. 10 o'clock. -T

4

Cora

I woke up this morning, nervous, and also anxious. I had been woken up from the sleep I desperately needed, due to an influx of incoming calls from Riley.

Apparently, she had found some evidence that Daisy was murdered.

A part of myself is scared that Riley truly did find evidence, and that Daisy was actually killed. And the other part of me fears that Riley is going off the deep end.

She only just opened up to me about all her feelings surrounding her sister's death. Like the good friend I try to be, I listened, and tried to offer her my two cents.

Two cents she didn't want or need.

Well, I know that now. So, in order to try and patch things up with Riley, I have made a vow to listen more, and offer her my complete undying support regardless of how crazy I may think she sounds.

She asked to meet this morning at the local breakfast joint. It was one of our favorites as well as pretty much everyone in the town of Calder.

I dressed myself slowly, perhaps hoping for a way to postpone this conversation I was about to have. I mentally prepared and reminded myself once more to keep an open mind, and to try and support my best friend regardless of how crazy I may think she is.

I opted for jeans and a sweater, given that it was chilly outside today. I glanced at the clock and saw that it was 8:30 in the morning. Perfect. We decided to meet at 9, and that gave me enough time to do my hair since it wasn't really agreeing with me this morning.

I turned on the straightener, praying that the tool would help me in the slightest with taming my extremely frizzy hair.

I walked down the hall to the living room, where my mom was cooking breakfast. The savory smell of bacon wafted through the room, and I physically felt my stomach rumble.
Bacon is my favorite.

I mentally scolded myself for agreeing to go out to breakfast. My mom wasn't the most amazing chef in the world, but if there was one thing that she could make well- it was breakfast.

My mom created the most delicious French toast I had ever had, and it was all thanks to a family secret that she swore she would take to the grave. My mom was making her own famous scrambled eggs, which were taken to a new level with the onions and garlic she added beforehand.

Weird? Yes. Delicious? Without a doubt.

"Hey sleepyhead. You're just in time for my famous breakfast." My mom said in a singsong voice, a clear indicator of the wonderful mood she appeared to be in today.

The French toast will do that to a girl… it's that good.

"I would love nothing more, but I promised Riley I would go out to breakfast with her."

"At Amma's?" My mom made a shrewd face, as if Amma's diner was unable to hold a candle to her cooking.

"Yes… and stop making that face. Their French toast doesn't compare to yours, but Riley is going through a rough time right now, and I really want to be there for her." I cracked a half-smile, knowing that my mom would be more forgiving of my breakfast betrayal if there was a good reason behind it.

"I understand, but you're missing out!" She laughed and waved her spatula back and forth.

My mom turned around and embraced me in a hug before I had the chance to walk away.

"Be careful okay? I love you." My mom planted a kiss on my forehead, and I seized the opportunity to make a clean getaway to my bathroom, where I could begin to work on my mane.

The straightener had finally warmed up enough to the point of use, and I started in on my hair. I had my music playlist on full volume, attempting to get myself in a good mood and mindset for the day.

Daisy always loved music too and swore that it was the cause for her bright and electric energy in the mornings. I had never met a morning person quite like Daisy. Not only could she get up at the ass crack of dawn with a smile on her face, but she was able to run on little to no sleep at all hours of the day. *She was amazing.*

I finally exhaled, not realizing that I had been holding my breath the entire time. My chest felt tight, and I took a seat on the toilet. *I miss you.*

I really did. All the time. Riley was my best friend and would always be. Daisy brought lightheartedness, and fun when times weren't all that happy. She brightened the moods of the people around her and would have been so necessary and vital in a situation like this. Riley and I were falling apart, and I tried to continuously remind myself to pull it together long enough to be there for Riley. *Help her first, and then work on healing yourself.*

Despite the closeness and my strong friendship with Daisy, Riley was her twin sister and I knew how deeply this affected her. Daisy's death shook the entire world on its axis and completely crushed Riley from the inside out.

She never showed it though, and I now knew just why that was.

She was channeling all those feelings and energy into a manhunt for a killer that wasn't there. I knew in my heart that when she finally realized that, and all the investigating and searching ended, she would be forced to deal with everything she was trying to avoid, and it would kill her.

What do I do?

All I knew to do was to be there for my friend, and that's what I would do. I was actually interested to see what kind of information she had, or what evidence she supposedly found.

What if Daisy really was murdered?

And by who? She wasn't. I knew it.

I finally finished my hair and stepped back to admire my handiwork. It was amazing what burning your hair over and over again would do.

I unplugged the hot iron and ran into my room to grab the rest of my things. I needed to pick Riley up, and it was 8:45. She only lived five minutes away, so I sent her a quick text giving her a heads up.

Cora: About to leave. Are you ready?

> *Riley: When am I not? Lol, see you soon!*

I swung my purse over my shoulder and started off towards the front door. I waved goodbye to my mom and stepped outside.

Yeah, the sweater was probably a good choice.

I gasped audibly when the cool morning air hit my body. It was freezing and sent a cold shiver up my spine. I found myself eternally grateful for bringing the sweater this morning. My car would need to warm up a little longer than usual this morning.

I unlocked the driver's door and climbed in, starting the car.

Why I thought leather seats would be a good idea... I don't know.

The leather seats were ice cold and I felt goosebumps forming on my arms and legs. I let the car run for about five minutes, and then cranked up the heater as I reversed out of my driveway and started on my way to Riley's house.

Like I originally thought, I was there three minutes later. I checked the time... 8:56.

I guess my time management is something to pride myself on.

I opted out of doing my usual honk, because I knew some of the neighbors wouldn't be too keen on hearing that early in the morning. Instead I texted Riley to let her know I was here.

She must have been waiting at the door to hear from me, because within seconds she was out the door and sprinting to my car.

She yanked open the passenger door and climbed in.

"Holy shit! It's freezing!"

She had the same sweater on that I had chosen this morning, except she accessorized hers with mittens. Riley's hands always tended to get more cold than anything else on her body.

"Nice sweater." I laughed, and playfully pointed at mine.

She had only then realized that we had matched unintentionally and broke into a fit of laughter.

I started towards Amma's diner, my stomach rumbling louder than ever.

I was a champion eater and needed to eat first thing in the morning to start my day right. I was starving.

We pulled in and got out quickly, neither of us wanting to spend another minute in the freezing cold.

Upon walking in, we were met with warm smiles from Amma herself who was not only the owner, but a waitress.

"Hi girls, take a seat anywhere." She motioned to the rows of empty booths.

Riley and I shuffled into our favorite booth by the window. She looked like she had something to say but was hiding it.

"Spit it out Ry."

She didn't say anything but slowly pulled something out of her purse and slid it across the table towards me.

"What is this?"

"Read it." She looked insistent.

The front of the envelope said D on it.

My heart clenched in my chest, and my palms began to sweat.

You don't even know what this is yet. Stop freaking.

I don't know why I was suddenly so nervous but found myself struggling to stay cool. I had thought Riley was bluffing, but the fact that she had found something proved otherwise.

I began to open the envelope but was thankfully saved by the waitress who had sauntered over to our table in the midst of my mild panic attack. "Hi, what can I get you ladies to drink?" She smiled, and her eyes flicked down to the envelope I had clenched in my palm. Her eyes jumped back up at me, and then she looked at Riley as a sad look spread over her face.

"You're her sister. I didn't even realize. You would think I would, given that you are twins." The waitress addressed Riley as if she had known her whole life.

"I'm sorry, do I know you?" Riley seemed just as confused and taken aback as I was.

The waitress chuckled and extended her hand to Riley.

"I'm Allison, but everyone calls me Allie. I knew Daisy, she came here a lot by herself. She was really a sweet girl."

A pained look took over Riley's face, and I reached under the table to give her free hand a reassuring squeeze.

Riley's eyes darted to me, and she smiled. She turned back to the waitress who was all smiles. "Sorry. It's still a tough subject." Riley shrugged with her apology.

You don't need to apologize.

"I understand. It's been hard for everyone, and I can't even imagine what you're going through. Daisy and I had gone to a couple movies together and she was always making me laugh, even when I didn't want to."

The waitress laughed, and she picked up her pen and paper.

"Now what can I get for you guys?"

We ordered two cokes, and two blt's with fries when she later returned with the drinks. Allie was really sweet, and even though it may have been hard to talk about everything with someone she didn't know, it seemed to have helped.

I knew Daisy had a lot of friends, so it didn't surprise me that she befriended someone from the diner. She came here a lot, and unlike Riley and I, Daisy had no problem doing things independently-even if that meant eating alone.

Riley tore into her sandwich as if she hadn't eaten before. It was good to see her eat, because she refused to eat anything for a few days after she found Daisy.

We finished our food, and I felt the surge of confidence that I desperately needed to open the letter. I yanked the card out and flipped it open to read the contents inside.

It was only a few words.

The lake. 10 pm. -T

Who the hell was T? I looked to Riley for an explanation, but my friend only shrugged as she popped her last fry into her mouth.

"Who is "T"?"

"No clue. But we're going to find out who wrote it." Riley looked determined, and I knew I had to help her.

"This isn't dated, so we don't know if it was the night she died, or a month before that." I tried to figure out the timeline, and mentally work through who could have sent this.

Riley opened her mouth to speak, and she was interrupted by the awkward silence that came when our waitress walked up to the table and stared open mouthed at the open card in my hand.

"What's that?" Allie gawked.

I tried to put it away, but to my surprise, Riley took it from my hands and handed it to Allie.

"See for yourself," Riley said nonchalantly, pushing her red hair out of her eyes.

Allie stared at the card in her hands, then looked back at Riley, a blank look clear on her face. *Yeah, I'm confused too.*

After what seemed like an eternity, Allie finally opened the card to read the minimalistic content that await inside.

It was only one sentence, but she stared at the card, clearly reading and re-reading the card over and over again desperately trying to make sense of everything.

"Do you know who sent this?" Allie handed the card back to Riley, confusion plastered on her face.

"Nope. Just someone who apparently goes by the letter T." Riley shrugged her shoulders, tossed the card on the table and took a swig of her drink. *Don't shut down Riley.*

"And this was sent to Daisy? Maybe it was that boy." Allie offered some new insight.

Both Riley and I nearly spit out our drinks.

Daisy never dated. She was well liked by everyone, and that didn't exclude the boys by any means. Daisy expressed time after time that she didn't want to waste precious moments of her youth "tied down to someone", as she poetically put it.

"What guy?!" Riley and I looked at one another, then at Allie who was taken aback by our outburst.

"Oh, I figured you guys would have known. Daisy was always going on and on about this guy she met to me. She never did tell me the name though."

Just then Allie was called away by another customer, and Riley and I were left to piece through these new bouts of information ourselves.

Daisy was seeing someone?

Was that someone "T"?

Riley started to grab her things, and started rushing out of the restaurant, dropping a twenty on the table to cover our food.

I pulled money out of my wallet, leaving it for the tip, and grabbed a napkin and a pen from my purse to begin jotting.

As I ran after my best friend, I handed the napkin to Allie.

"Here's my number. If you ever need to talk, I'm here." I offered her a small smile before dashing out of the restaurant.

I looked around and zeroed in on my car. I know I locked it, but I wanted to be sure. I ran over to the passenger side to see if she was in there, but she was nowhere to be found.

Where the hell could she have gone?

Then it hit me.

The lake.

I started jogging off to the left of the diner, heading straight for our spot next to the lake that was only a few minutes away.

5

Riley

I had barely reached the dock before I collapsed onto the ground in a fit of waterworks.

I know that I stepped into this mess of trying to figure out what happened to my sister willingly, but I already felt as if I was in over my head.

Allie was able to tell me new information about my sister.

Information that could be of great use if my sister was actually in fact murdered.

So why did I feel so bad?

Because she knew something you didn't.

Hit the nail right on the head.

It wasn't solely because we were twins, or sisters in general, but I had always believed that Daisy and I could confide in each other about anything and everything.

I would have listened.

I would have wanted to know.

So why would she spill details about what probably happened to be the first boy she ever liked to some diner girl, and not to her sister?

Maybe she didn't trust you.

I buried my head in my knees and covered my ears. Doubtful that it would do anything besides force me to feel completely isolated from the outside world, but it was worth a shot of an attempt to bring me some sense of peace.

I raised my tear-stricken face from my legs and stared out at the tranquil waters. They were still, untouched and untainted by man. I wish my life were like that.

I heard sound, and it wasn't me. I turned my head slightly to the left, not fully turning myself around.

I knew who it was.

Cora.

"Took you long enough." I cracked a small smile, and for the first time in a while… it felt genuine.

My best friend always knew where to find me, and what to do… I hope.

Cora took a seat next to me, pulling me in for a hug and leaning to whisper in my ear.

"I know you're hurting. Please talk to me."

"What should I say?" I looked at my best friend.

"The truth." She squeezed my arm.

Before I was even able to open my mouth and respond, I fell into yet another fit of tears. Holding back all my emotions surrounding Daisy's death for this long only delayed the inevitable. Now for the first time, I was allowing myself to express and fully feel all the emotions.

And it hurt like hell.

When I ran out of tears, and my best friend's new blouse was thoroughly soaked, I raised my head up and looked her in the eye.

Like word vomit, everything I had been harboring for so long, on top of what I felt about today's encounter and new information came spilling out one after the other.

Each truth that came out granted me the euphoric feeling of having heavy weights lifted off my chest, slowly, one by one until I could breathe again…

You can breathe again.

Cora didn't speak much but allowed me to pour all my feelings into her, with her absorbing and taking in them all- no questions asked.

"None of this is your fault. I have no doubt in my mind that Daisy was planning to tell you all of it. Do not let yourself feel any guilt. Daisy was your other half, and it is more than normal to feel sad. Please do not bottle it up inside any longer. It's killing you Riley."

I sat and stewed on the smart words of my friend and used those uplifting sentiments as strength to pull myself off the ground, and to do something I would never do.

I started off full speed towards the lake, fully clothed, before jumping off the edge of the dock into the freezing, and now unperfect water.

And I had never felt more alive.

I felt the ground beneath my feet, and using my newfound strength, pushed up with all my might until I soared up to the surface.

My head came popping out, and I couldn't help but to allow myself to dissolve into a fit of laughter. I felt so weightless, so free, that there was not a single thing anyone could say or do at this point to make me feel otherwise.

The look on my friend's face was one of confusion, but it was only momentarily, because before I knew it, she was running straight for me.

Cora cleared the distance in the air over my head and came splashing down a few feet from me. Her head popped up right away and she too joined in on the laughs.

I closed the remaining distance between us and pulled Cora in for a tight hug, as we both tread water.

"Thank you." I smiled.

"Always." She pulled away and then splashed me in the face.

"Last one out buys coffees!"

I started swimming towards the dock, and reached up for the edge, swinging my body onto it.

I loved swimming as a kid, as it was the only athletic thing I liked, and there was no way Cora would have beat me or even come close to competing against anything in water.

I think she knew that, because she took her time to reach the dock, and pulled herself up patiently.

While I had felt relieved, and lighter than I had since my sister's death, I was suddenly racked with exhaustion.

It must have been the complete unloading of all my emotions that really did me in today, but one thing was for sure- I needed a nap.

"Raincheck on the coffee C? I need a nap."

"Me too!" Cora smiled and we both started heading back to the car still parked at the diner.

We were still sopping wet as we reached her car, and the other diner goers in the parking lot were giving us funny looks. Usually I would care, but today I didn't. No one would bring down my mood today.

Just then, Allie emerged from the diner. She had her keys in hand and looked tired as well.

I knew serving wasn't an easy job. My mother did it to put herself through college, and she said it felt like backbreaking work sometimes.

"Hey Allie!" I yelled at her, forcing her to tear her eyes up from her phone which was glued to her face. *Just like Daisy.*

Her face lit up, and she jogged over to us. She reached the edge of Cora's car, and she finally realized that both Cora and I were wet from head to toe, so naturally, she looked shocked.

"What in the world did y'all get in to?"

"This spot that we all used to go... with Daisy."

Those last two words tasted like acid coming out of my mouth.

"The lake, right? Daisy told me about it."

Now it was our turn to be surprised. Cora and I shared a small look of shared confusion, and maybe even a hint of betrayal? That spot was ours, and only ours. The fact that Daisy felt close enough to share it with Allie... well, hurt.

"I'm sorry. I said something wrong, didn't I?" Allie looked apologetic and reached out to squeeze my hand.

I could see why Daisy took to her. Allie seemed like an empath to me, a genuine one.

"No, you did nothing. It's me."

Maybe this was a chance to be close with my sister even after she was gone. While Daisy and I were close, she clearly had parts of her life that she didn't want to share. Maybe hanging out with Allie would reveal some things I may have wanted to know.

She wasn't awful to be around either. Actually, she was really kind.

"Hey, take my number Allie, and we can hang out sometime."

She pulled her notepad out of her pocket along with a pen and handed both over to me.

"Sure thing!"

I scribbled the number out and handed everything back to her.

"See you later Allie!" Cora and I both waved to her as we got into the car.

"Bye guys!" Allie waved back, and I thought this friendship thing might not be half bad.

6

Allie

Ever since the diner encounter this morning, I couldn't stop smiling. Daisy and I had become extremely close in the past few months, and ever since news of her death broke, I had felt lost.

Seeing Riley today took me back for a second. I knew Daisy had a twin, mostly because she always talked about her sister and how much she loved her.

But to see Riley in person was a completely different thing.

Yeah, they were twins, but my god it was like a carbon copy of Daisy. The only thing different would be the personality, maybe.

Riley seemed more reserved, which was something I had already had an inkling of when Daisy was telling me all about her sister.

Daisy didn't deserve what happened to her.

And neither did I.

7

Riley

I was on a high from this afternoon when I got home. I felt as if I should give Allie my number. In the moment it felt right, and I had convinced myself that any person who was special to Daisy must be special to me.

Maybe it was a last-ditch effort to feel close to my sister once more. Daisy and I were clearly close while she was alive, but since she died, I don't feel connected to her anymore.

Finding out that she had other friends I had no idea about was also a shell shock to me.

Did I know my sister at all?

Obviously, Daisy was allowed to have her own life apart from mine. Just because we were twins, didn't mean that we necessarily had to share every single aspect of our lives with the other. However… it was still odd.

Now I still toyed with the idea of my sister being murdered. I know that even the happiest of people can also feel the worst of pain, but Daisy didn't seem like one of those people.

I'm trying so desperately to accept her death as a suicide and just move on with my life- but something is holding me back from doing so.

It's this weird gut feeling that I've had ever since she died.

Something isn't right.

I waltzed into the house, in a better mood after my impromptu dip into the lake.

My parents were both lying on the couch sprawled across the other. Right on cue, they looked at me wide eyed, and jaws on the floor.

"Riley... what the hell happened?" My dad eyed my wet clothes suspiciously.

"Lake." I smiled and ran to my room, laughing the entire way.

I could hear my parents chuckling in the other room. It was funny. I knew it was funny.

I'm sure they would have accepted me in any shape or form at this point, as long as I had a smile on my face.

I hopped into my bathroom, and slowly started to peel my wet clothes off of my body.

I started the shower and climbed in, my body erupting in a flurry of goosebumps from the quick transition from cold to hot.

I started to wash the lake water from my hair and let the worries of today wash away with the dirty water.

I was free.

Today had felt like a gigantic step in the right direction for me. I had found a sense of clarity, and finally allowed myself to remove the weight and guilt that had been heavy on my heart and body since Daisy died.

So why did I still feel that gut wrenching feeling?

My now happy thoughts consumed with the worrisome ones- I stepped out of the shower, turning it off, and grabbing a towel.

Don't do this. Don't start overthinking things.

That was like telling a bird not to fly.

Once I got dressed, I started to get an itch to search Daisy's room once more.

The itch didn't go away.

It didn't go away when I cleaned my room once again.

It didn't go away after I ate yet another dinner of hearty lasagna.

And it didn't go away when I turned on Jersey Shore in an attempt to drown out my nagging inner thoughts.

Finally, I succumbed to the pressure and I slowly creeped down the hall into her room. I made sure to close the door.

Why are you sneaking around?

I don't know. Why am I? It's not as if Daisy's room is closed off and forbidden to enter. I just felt as if I was violating her space. Not only that, but if my parents saw me- there would no doubt be a string of questions that not only was I unable to answer... I simply just didn't want to.

Once again, the smell of her room brought tears to my eyes. It's crazy to think that someone's smell can linger like that- desperately clinging to the possessions they once treasured.

Fuck, I miss you so much.

I start rifling through Daisy's clothes. Nothing. Not that I thought I would find something in this damned closet.

Curiosity getting the best of me, I glance up at the shelf hovering over her clothes rack. There are boxes on boxes, and in the corner- a small pink and yellow spotted box.

I grabbed that one and walk over to the bed to sit down. I pulled the top off and glanced at the contents.

Photos.

Daisy had always been big on taking pictures because she felt like, "sometimes they were better at capturing memories than our eyes were able to."

I always thought it was so beautifully put, and Daisy was an artist behind the camera.

There were photos of myself and Cora laughing in front of the lake, my mom and dad snuggling on the couch, pictures from our trip, and more.

I found myself smiling as I flipped through all these wonderful memories that we had made and was eternally grateful to Daisy for keepsaking them so I could cherish them forever.

It amazed me how much you could forget. Maybe Daisy was right. Maybe taking these pictures was a way to never forget a good moment or memory.

I flipped through a few more family photos and stopped on one. It was in the woodsy patch right by the lake, and the photo was of Daisy.

Taken from behind.

8

Cora

Progress. I feel like today was finally a much-needed step in the right direction with Riley. After what felt like forever of her keeping her emotions hidden and bottled up, she finally let me in.

I like to think that it was beneficial to her as well, in the idea that she now feels like she doesn't have to keep all those emotions solely on herself.

This was what I had wanted this entire time, and I felt so grateful that she wanted to finally open up to me.

Allie. That was some new insight to the complex person that Daisy was. I mean, she had this friend who she seemed to confide in about important details of her life, and Riley and I had never met- let alone heard of her.

She was so incredibly sweet and forthcoming, but I did find myself taken aback when Riley so willingly offered up the evidence she found.

While Allie was Daisy's friend, we still knew nothing about her. I didn't get any weird vibes from her, but I don't exactly feel comfortable with sharing all of our personal details with someone we don't know.

Honestly, I am just relieved that Riley opened up at all, that at this point in time I could care less who she opened up to.

Riley had sent a group text to Allie and me this morning asking if we could all meet up at the lake. Allie seemed really excited to go, and I had to admit I was too. I was proud of the progress my friend was making.

Take it one day at a time.

This time, I didn't love the idea of coming home soaking wet again, so I wore my bikini underneath my shorts along with a navy-blue loose-fitting t-shirt.

I was picking Riley up, and we were going to send the location to Allie so she could meet us there.

I said goodbye to my mom, along with disclosing my plans for the day, and I was out the door with a bagel in hand.

I practically devoured the entirety of the cream cheese smeared delicacy before my engine finished warming up.

I started off to Riley's house, sending her a text to let her know that I would be there soon, and to be ready.

She quickly texted back a string of happy emojis, and I felt very spirited and hopeful about the day's events.

It felt good to include Allie. She was someone who was close with Daisy, so she can't be all that bad. In fact, she actually seemed really awesome and I could easily see why Daisy connected with her. *Didn't Daisy connect with everyone?*

Besides the point.

I pulled into the familiar driveway, giving a quick two beep honk to let her... and everyone else in the neighborhood know that I had in fact arrived.

Riley came bouncing out of the house with a shit eating grin plastered all over her face.
"Good morning sunshine!" She announced in a rather singsong voice.
"Good morning to you too. What's sparked this wonderful mood, may I ask?" I looked her up and down, clearly confused.
"Glad you did. I now know that I was right." She smirked at me and began rummaging in her purse.
"Right about what?" Now I was really confused.

Riley handed me a picture of Daisy, taken from behind in a white dress, clearly in the woods. *That's odd.*

Understatement of the year Cora.
"What is this supposed to mean?" I handed the photo back to my friend.

"Daisy was killed. I was right." Her face took a stern note, and I found myself contemplating what to say next.

Oh boy, here we go again.

I unfortunately found myself in a rather uncomfortable silence for the remaining drive, mentally battling over what to say. Did I stay a loyal friend and agree with her? Or did I want to shut this down once and for all?

Daisy was not killed. She killed herself. At this point, Riley had clearly deluded herself so much and now I don't know if the truth would help or hurt her.

So, I said nothing.

Riley didn't make it exactly easy as she didn't offer up any icebreakers to steer the conversation into happier territory.

Neither of us spoke until we pulled into our little parking spot and started collecting our things. Riley started to text Allie, but we were both surprised when Allie was already walking towards us.

"Hey guys!" Allie waved with a big smile on her face, and sandals in hand.

Her ensemble was complete with a gorgeous pink sundress, and a pearl white towel draped over her shoulders.

"How did you know where to find us?" I asked.

"Daisy told me about this place, remember?"

I completely forgot about our chat at the diner yesterday, and Riley must have too because we both started to break out into a nervous and slightly embarrassed laugh.

Don't overthink everything. She's a nice girl.

I found myself feeling good for the first time in a while. I think that I had been so dead set on Riley's recovery, and ensuring that she was okay that I forgot to check in on myself.

I struggled. Daisy's death took a toll on me that I didn't expect, and I found it hard to get up in the morning.

But something that I had kept to myself this entire time was the threats I had been receiving since Daisy's death.

I originally planned on telling Riley, but after she went all in on the "Daisy was murdered" theory, I didn't want to worry her any further.

She was already on edge.

It was two days after Daisy died that I received my first note.

At first, it wasn't threatening at all. More of a slight warning, a small hint that there was more to Daisy's death then met the eye.

It was in a manila envelope, left on my doorstep. Inside was a plain white cardstock paper that read, "Don't believe everything you see. Including D."

I struggled over what to do, with a hint of fear and apprehension mixed in. When I read the "D", I knew the note was referring to Daisy.

Don't believe everything you see?

That only confirmed the tirade that Riley was on, but I really faced an internal battle over what to do and what to say.

Do I worry her further? Or brush this off?

In fact, at the time, I did brush it off. I thought it was some cruel attempt at a joke, and even though everyone seemingly loved Daisy, it didn't mean that people wouldn't try to make light of her death.

The people of this town were really shitty like that.

So, I went on with my life, until the second note came in.

Yet again, this one was encased in a manila envelope. Yet again, it was a white cardstock paper. The only difference was this one had drops of blood all over it.

I was barely able to make out the writing, but once I read it, I knew exactly what it said no doubt in my mind at all.

"The thrill of the chase is much more satisfying than the kill. Run fast."

I considered going to the police, but with no signs of who left it, and clearly no return address stamping nicely at the top- what were they to do?

Nothing.

So, I kept this to myself.

Luckily for me, I had yet to receive any more threatening notes.

So why freak Riley out?

"You coming?"

I was so lost in my thoughts that I didn't see both Riley and Allie strip to their bathing suits and jump into the shimmering lake.

They were laughing, swimming, and both trying to do underwater flips but failing miserably as the water flew up their noses.

The only person I knew who could complete a seamless underwater flip was Daisy, and she looked impossibly graceful while doing so.

I followed suit in removing my outer clothing, and running full speed ahead, pulling my knees up for a full cannonball.

The sound of my body hitting the water, followed by a rush of cold water was absolutely exhilarating.

This.

This was why we loved the lake so much. The time we spent here made us feel better, not to mention it was our place.

I was a little surprised at how easily Allie fit into our group. She was a lot like Daisy, outgoing and really fun.

Just then in the heat of all the laughter and joy, my heart panged with a longing for my friend. I wished more than anything that she could be here.

With the notes I received, coupled with the photos and other obvious evidence that Riley found, I was confused myself as to why I didn't jump in to help her when she started this crusade.

I can attribute that mostly to living in denial.

I hated dealing with scary truths, and as a coping method I decided to avoid, avoid, avoid.

Probably not a healthy way to deal, but I feel like I have finally found clarity.

Daisy was murdered.

9

Allie

For the first time in a while, I feel like I was able to finally breathe again.

I have felt like I was drowning since Daisy died.

Drowning in sorrow, grief, anger, you name it. Some days it was all three.

But today, being around the girl who shares Daisy's face, and a lot of her spirit, coupled with Cora who couldn't be nicer, I feel whole again.

I wiped my hair out of my face and pushed water back at Cora who had splashed me in the eyes as she perfected her cannonball.

I felt grateful more than anything.
Grateful that I'm not alone anymore.

Daisy and I were really close, but considering nobody else knew about me, it had felt weird to show up to her funeral.

Now I wish I did, as I never was able to say a proper goodbye to my friend.

The possibility of being able to discover a newfound friendship with these two gives me a true sense of hope.

Would they be your friend if they knew your secret?

No. Probably not.

The only people who know about my secret are my parents, and they haven't bothered to visit much anyways.

You see, my parents are the type of people who have certain set expectations for their children, and completely write them off if they aren't living up to their "full potential".

My parents have two other children and love them more than life itself.

In their eyes, I'm an unfortunate mistake.

"You hungry Allie?" Riley was drying herself off on the dock, and Cora was pulling herself out of the lake.

Stop feeling sorry for yourself.

"Yeah, I think I am," I said as I comforted my now growling stomach.

I yanked myself up on the dock following Cora closely and started to dry myself.

Riley was all smiles, and so was Cora up until the moment that she wasn't.

She seemed lost in thought, and whatever those thoughts were upsetting her in some way.

Riley noticed it too, and I saw her try and pull Cora to the side for a chat. Cora was having none of it, and waved Riley's advances off.

They both started towards the car, belongings spilling out of their very full hands. I brushed the wet strands away from my eyes, turned and took one last look at the crystal lake, and picked up my stuff.

Stop deluding yourself.

Get. Out. Of. My. Head.

I shook away the negative thoughts that had been very much running the show pretty much my entire life. The doctors claimed depression, and my parents just thought I was damaged goods.

Only problem? I was neither.

We reached the car, and as a result of us all being famished, decided on going to a fast food restaurant.

"I'll meet you guys there." I waved as I headed towards my car.

I started the engine, and like magic, all the negative thoughts drifted away.

Don't screw this up. You have one job.

10

Riley

Our dinner consisted of lots of laughs, gossip, and a casual story or two about Daisy. I was liking Allie more and more with the time I spent with her, and it felt like I was still connected to my sister.

I got this sense of familiarity when I was around her, and that was partly what allowed me to open up so easily.

I know that made Cora really happy, especially since she had come to believe that I was simply incapable of ever moving on.

Have you though?

When your sister dies, I don't really see it as something I will ever move past, but rather accept as my new normal.

I have begun the process of accepting that I will never wake up and see Daisy's bright and happy face in the mornings again.

"Did you hear us Riley?" Cora shoved my arm, munching on a fry, coupled with her and Allie lost in a fit of laughter.

"Ssorry, no. What?" I shook my head, trying to regain focus onto the conversation which I had no apparent idea of the topic.

"DiCaprio or Pitt? Who's hotter?"

They both eyed me warily, each clearly favoring one end of the teeter totter. But for me, the question had only one clear answer.

"DiCaprio, every single time. I mean, have you *seen* Titanic?"

That was enough to spark a new celebrity duel debate between the two, and I took that as an opportunity to hit the bathroom.

I had the bladder of a squirrel, and that was pushing it.

I shoved the stall door open, and pulled the seat cover out in one swift motion. I had barely sat down when I heard someone else enter the bathroom. *Be grateful it's only pee.*

Daisy always made fun of me because I wouldn't be able to go number two in public places, but the thought of having someone hear, or worse... *smell* me is enough to scare me into waiting.

The person out there wasn't going to the bathroom but rummaging around by the sink area making a hell of a lot of noise.

I was just wrapping up when I heard the bathroom door open and close, and I breathed a sigh of relief.

I stepped out and walked over to the sink to wash my hands. I turned on the water, washed, and switched it off to dry my hands. After drying them, I decided that I should fix my now weirdly dried hair from the lake.

I hadn't even glanced at the mirror when I washed my hands, and when I finally did, I felt pure fear eating its way through my chest.

Written in big letters spelled out, "You're next." I didn't know for certain but was pretty sure that it was written in some kind of blood. It was dripping down the length of the mirror.

I backed up slowly, mouth wide and gaping until I felt my back hit the wall. I dropped to my knees and forced myself to take a big breath.

I didn't realize until that moment that I had been holding my breath. I could hear my pulse crashing in my ears, and in that moment… that single moment… I was shaken to my core with the purest fear I had ever felt in my lifetime.

This answered questions I had, and also created new ones.

Daisy was murdered.

It wasn't an accident.

Was I next?

Cora opened the bathroom door, took one look at my current position and immediately changed her mood.

"What's wrong Riley? Why are you on the floor?" She bent down and squeezed my shoulder.

I tried to answer, but I couldn't find the voice to speak. Instead, I managed to point a finger towards the mirror warning.

Cora turned her head sharply and let out a high-pitched scream. This enlisted Allie to come running full speed into the bathroom, followed by an array of waitstaff who looked alarmed.

I saw a worker pick up a phone and start dialing at rapid speed. That was no doubt the police on the other line, and a part of me wanted her to hang up.

I knew the severity of a threat like this, and the only person to write it must have been the killer. *So, the killer was in this restaurant?*

"Do you have cameras?" I looked towards the worker...eyes wide with hope.

"Sorry hon, I wish we did. Don't worry, the police are on their way."

Gee, thanks.

Do I tell them about the stuff I found in Daisy's room?

No, I don't need the police getting involved. Obviously, I am a lot closer than I thought because this threat seems warranted. I must have touched a nerve for the killer. This is good.

But also, really, really bad.

What have you gotten yourself into Riley?

11

Cora

What the hell was going on?

I opened the bathroom door out of sheer curiosity as to why my friend was taking ten minutes in the bathroom.

Seeing her on the floor, crouched up like that, shaking and scared, nearly made my heart stop beating in my chest.

I wasn't sure what had happened, but in that moment, that split second, I just knew something was horribly wrong.

Now Allie and I are sitting here holding Riley as she waits to be interviewed by police. Police officers… go figure. Riley was just telling me about how she thought her sister was murdered, and like a horrible friend- I brushed it off.

You brushed her off.

I did, and now… seeing this, I understand.

Daisy was murdered.

It wasn't an accident. It wasn't a mistake. It was full of intent, and after seeing that message, full of malice.

Now the person responsible for taking Daisy's life was after Riley.

But why?

I had not a single clue how to answer that question.

My head was spinning and hadn't stop throughout the duration of this entire ordeal.

I saw a couple uniformed officers striding towards us, and I recognized them from the station. They were young but seemed very professional. "Riley Carson? Can you explain the events of what occurred this afternoon?" The tall and handsome blonde officer with the hazel eyes questioned. His name tag said Brooks.

I looked to my friend and gave her shoulder an encouraging squeeze. She opened her mouth to speak, but no words came out.

I looked back at both officers who appeared equally puzzled.

"Is there any way we can do this another time? She's in shock," Allie offered to the officers.

"Sure. Just have her come to the station tomorrow."

Officer Brooks handed Riley his hard, and she took it, hand shaking the entire time.

"Riley, it's going to be okay. I'm sure it was just some dumb prank." I tried to be encouraging, but how was I supposed to do that when I didn't believe what I was saying?

You know Daisy was murdered. Trying to sugarcoat things will not help Riley.

Yeah, but telling her that a killer is now after her doesn't really seem like the best friend thing to do either.

Riley turned to me, eerily slow, and threw my arm off of her shoulder roughly, knocking me back in the process.

"Shut up! SHUT. UP. Do you have the slightest clue what it feels like to not only know that your sister, the one who made your life better, was KILLED? Not to mention, now I'm next. So no, it's not a prank, and I would hate to believe that you're stupid enough to believe that."

With that hurtful monologue being put into existence, Riley grabbed her things and stormed out of the restaurant.

I gave her a ride, so I knew she couldn't get far. But knowing Riley, she would only be heading to one place, a place where she felt most connected to her sister... the lake.

"Should we go after her?" Allie looked worried, and I can tell the writing on the mirror really freaked her out.

It's a threat. It should. Why aren't you freaked out?

I know I should be rigid with fear, but I couldn't. I was too worried about being there... being strong for my friend. I didn't have time to be weak and scared.

I knew Riley needed her alone time. She always needed to process things by herself in order to reach logical conclusions. That was the way she had always been.

Despite the insults she had hurled at me only moments ago, I knew my friend was just hurting, and mostly scared.

I shook my head at Allie and approached the small group of officers who were still chatting amongst themselves by the door.

"I'm sorry to bug you, but I am worried about my friend. She headed down to this small patch by the lake, I can show you where it is. Can someone just keep an eye on her?"

The blonde cop from earlier picked an officer to be Riley's temporary protective detail until they get this whole mess sorted.

I went to turn but was stopped by Officer Brooks.

"Can I ask you a quick question?"

"Sure." I looked at him, curious to what knowledge I could be of use for.

"During the events, did you see anyone enter or leave the restaurant?" He pulled out a notepad, ready to jot down any information I had at lightning speed.

I started to stew on his question, recollecting all of the customers in there at the time, and it wasn't until I hit a starting realization that I felt fear spreading through my veins like ice.

"No. I didn't."

The killer was in the restaurant with us.

12

Riley

My heart was beating out of my chest as I broke into a run, and then a full-on sprint. My feet knew where to go in a moment like this, even if my head didn't.

The lake.

It brought me the most peace even now. I ran faster and faster until I stopped abruptly, leaning against a large oak tree for support. I could hear my pulse thumping in my ears, and I started to feel dizzy. *Breathe Riley. Breathe.*

I heard Daisy's voice softly speaking, and I saw a quick glimpse of her red hair.

And then it was all black.

She's running through the forest near the lake. We're playing our age-old favorite game- Hide and Seek. Cora is the one seeking and being as typical as we are... Daisy and I are looking for a place to hide together. We can hear Cora calling our name.
"Daisy. Riley. I'll find you sooner or later."
"Riley!"

I peeled open my eyes to find an officer, accompanied by both Allie and Cora hovering over me looking panicked.

"What happened?" I was confused, and the last memories I had were running full speed ahead towards the lake.

"You must have passed out, come on. I'll take you home." Cora reached for my hand, and the officer stopped her.

"She should really get checked out." He put a hand on my shoulder.

"Really, I'm okay. I was running too fast, and I'm probably dehydrated. I think I just want to go home." I tried with the officer, hoping he would side with me.

"Okay. If you say so. I'll be parked on your house as a safety measure." He turned and walked towards the squad car parked in the distance.

Allie and Cora both took one of my arms with theirs, even though I expressed multiple times that I was fine. What was that about though? Seeing Daisy? Hearing her?

Maybe I was going crazy.

We finally reached the car, and with both of their unnecessary help, I climbed into the passenger seat of Cora's car.

What do I do about the threat?

I had no idea. I was struggling with the idea of telling my parents, knowing full well that they were already hanging on by a thread. The only thing helping me cope with my sister's death was being able to get out of that house.

Being in there with them was sucking the life out of me. Harsh, I know, but true.

If I were to tell them the events that transpired today, I was sure to be on house arrest.

It was probably the safest bet and best route for me to take, but it didn't necessarily mean I wanted to.

This will have to stay a secret, for now.

I need to go through Daisy's room once more and try and find some new evidence. There has to be something there. Now the note that I found makes more sense. Was she in contact with the killer before she knew they were a killer? Did they take that photo of her before she died?

My head was spinning, and I closed my eyes, desperate for some relief. That action alone was enough to grab the attention of Cora who was now becoming painfully curious.

"Are you okay, Riley? We can talk about it if you want." She offered a small smile, surely a desperate attempt to hide the fear she harbored as well.

"No. No talking." Cora knew me better than anyone, and if I started to talk, I would never stop.

Allie was sitting silently in the back, almost afraid to say a word. I didn't blame her. She was close with Daisy, and while Cora and I did like her, we didn't really know her. She didn't really know us. I'm sure she had a million things running through her head, and frankly it was expected.

"Sorry Allie." I turned slightly in my seat and gave a small smile.

"For what Riley?" Now she looked really confused.

"Dragging you into all this. I'm sure you're regretting befriending us right about now." I laughed, but it was lacking humor.

"Not at all. I'm worried for you. Obviously, there is some crazy person out there. Sorry I'm quiet, but today has just made me think." She looked somber.

"About?" Cora entered the conversation.

"Daisy."

The rest of the ride was in silence, and it was due to the fact that we were *all* thinking about Daisy. It didn't take a genius to put together two and two and figure out exactly what the writing on the mirror meant.

Daisy was killed.

I was next.

And while I was terrified beyond belief, I was also angry. Daisy was the kindest soul on this Earth, incapable of hurting a fly.

And yet, she was taken from us.

I knew what I had to do.

13

Allie

What. A. Day.

Cora dropped Riley off first, and then drove me back to my car. It would have been a lot easier for me to just drive home from the diner myself, but it seemed like Riley just needed people in that moment.

I was more then happy to be there for her, because in light of new information, apparently Daisy was killed.

I could have saved her.

I wasn't there for her.

And I would be damned if I wasn't there for Riley when she needed me.

It was clear to me that there was information that they were both holding back, not only from me, but from each other.

I felt mentally exhausted after what felt like the most trying day since Daisy had passed.

It didn't help that I was driving for what felt like forever.

Finding a new place to sleep each night was growing harder and harder. I wanted to go far enough away from town that I wasn't spotted by anyone I knew, but close enough that I had time to shower at the local gym before my shift.

If you had asked me where I envisioned my life, I certainly would have never guessed I would be homeless.

It's partly... well mostly due to my parents. Their clear absence of love and care for me was coupled with a lack of financial responsibility for me as well.

I had been bounced around for years from home to home, and they have yet to ever reach out.

It wasn't as if I expected a handwritten apology. Sure, they decided that I was their only child that wasn't worth the effort, but still. I don't even know my siblings. They haven't tried to make contact with me either, but the difference between them and my parents lies in the fact that they were so little when my parents hauled my ass off for the first and final time.

I could say that I was blessed in the sense that their actions didn't keep me up late at night or haunt my dreams anymore.

No, now I slept peacefully. I was just homeless.

I spotted a flat little bend up ahead and decided to park my car for the night.
Home sweet home.

I shut the ignition off and locked all my doors. I felt grateful for the tint that coated the windows, especially when I slept in my backseat.

I crawled back to my makeshift bed… solely made up of blankets and cheap pillows.

My check from work was enough to put gas in my car, clothes on my back, and food in my stomach. In fact, I put on such a good charade that no one knew of my current living status… let alone my troubled past.

It wasn't necessarily that I was embarrassed. No, because I wasn't in this current situation due to any faults that I made. I was simply dealt a shitty hand in life, and if I were to tell anyone, especially Cora and Riley, they would look at me different.

I knew they wouldn't judge me. They weren't those type of people. But they would pity me, and that was worse than being judged. I don't want anyone to feel sorry for me.

I let my mind wander, replaying the past twenty-four hours, as I drifted off into a peaceful sleep.

14

Riley

"Why the hell didn't you call us?!" My dad had flown into a blind rage after he got a call from the local sheriff reminding us of the squad car they assigned to sit on my house.

Thanks.

He had been droning on and on, complete with lecture after lecture of the dangers of the world, and how something like this was a legitimate threat.

If only you knew.

The police nor my parents knew about the evidence I found in Daisy's room. They did however now have suspicions about the way she died. Was it an accident?

I knew in my heart from the very beginning that Daisy's death was no accident.

My dad was now mumbling as he paced the length of the living room repeatedly.

My mom hadn't stopped crying since they first received the call, and that can all be chalked up to the terrifying truth that the writing on the mirror confirmed.

Daisy was killed.

I was next.

And thanks to the idiot police officers, I was now under strict watch from my parents.

I took my dad's momentary distraction as a means to escape yet another lecture. Truthfully, I don't think I ever would have told them about the events of today had it not been for the call.

I'm not a secrets person. I don't like to keep them or hear them. It gives me far too much anxiety and I overcompensate with talking as a way to not spill it. It's much too stressful.

However, when it's a secret that will keep the people that I loved protected, I'm all for it.

Who would kill Daisy?

This is a question I have been asking myself since she was first discovered and yet I am no closer to the answer then I was back then.

She was a kind person... someone who would give the shirt off her back to a person in need. I can't imagine her ever doing something so heinous that another person felt that she should die for it.

Who does she even know that is capable of such violence?

I needed to find more clues.

I bounded up to Daisy's room and swung the door open. I didn't care if my parents knew at this point, because no one was going to stop me from discovering the truth about my sister, not even some psycho killer.

I closed the door and started to rummage through her stuff. I doubted I would be able to find anything, but if my original suspicions about this killer were right, she knew them.

There had to be some evidence of that person in her room whether it was the card, the photo, or whatever.

I went through her dresser drawers, grabbing clothes and throwing them haphazardly in all directions. My hands found her warm pink sweater gifted to her by my grandma a few Christmases ago. It was quite expensive, and something that she treasured. I pulled it to my nose and breathed in Daisy's scent.

My eyes immediately began to water.
Stay focused.

I put the sweater down nicely on top of the dresser and continued with my rage filled rummaging. Drawer after drawer, I was disappointed to only find clothes instead of clues that I desperately needed.

Maybe there really was nothing more to be found. I started to pick up her clothes, and one of her shirts had a note that slid out underneath and fell onto my foot.

I dropped the shirt, and slowly bent to pick up the note. My heart was beating out of my chest as my palms grew sweaty.
Breathe, Riley. Breathe.

I turned it over, and to my surprise it was a lot lengthier than the previous note I had found.

It read,

"Daisy,

I know that we have grown close, and I'm sorry about our fight yesterday. You have to know I never meant to hurt you. But now, you know too much and I don't trust you. I'm sorry. Forgive me for what I have to do.

-T."

I dropped the paper.

So, this "T" was the person who killed her. They had to be. I now knew for certainty exactly who her killer was. I just had to track them down.

Maybe she told Allie about who "T" was. Allie mentioned that Daisy was going on and on about some boy. Tyler? Thomas? Something starting with a T? I had a gut feeling about "T", and just how volatile they may be.

I finished cleaning up her now messy room and slid the note back into my pocket.

By instinct, my hand reached up to wipe away the tear I had yet to realize was falling down my face. This was a lot to take in, regardless if I want to accept that or not.

"Riley!" My dad bellowed from the living room.
Give me a second!

"Coming!" I opened Daisy's door, stepping out and shutting it softly behind me.

I padded into the living room, mentally bracing myself for another screaming session between the two of us. We rarely fought, and even less so lately because they were scared to upset their only alive daughter.

When it came to my safety, my dad could care less about my feelings. He was being protective. He was being my dad.

Doesn't mean it wasn't annoying as hell.

I strode into the living room, and both my mom and dad were sitting on the loveseat, holding hands. I noted that my mom's crying has ceased, and that meant she had collected herself enough to either scold or yell at me.

This should be fun.

"Sit down Riley." My dad's voice was stern but lacked anger. Maybe this wouldn't be so bad.

I swiftly took a seat, praying that this would be over quickly.

"We have come to the conclusion that it might be better if you stay in the next few weeks."

"Stay in? As in never leave the house?" I couldn't believe what I was hearing. The anger began to bubble up inside.

"Yes. That's the only way we know how to keep you safe. In light of today's events, we have realized a lot. We didn't protect Daisy, but we have a chance to protect you." My mom spoke with a soft, comforting voice.

"No." I was stern, but my voice was shaky, and I knew I was not coming off as strong as I wanted to.

"No?" My dad's voice grew louder.

"Yeah…NO." I stood up suddenly and rushed to my room. I was grabbing my purse, phone and keys as my dad's yelling echoed in the background.

I sprinted down the stairs, past the living room, and out the door before he was able to get another word in. I was tired of hearing people tell me what I should be doing, how I should be feeling.

I was tired.

Sick and tired.

I slowed my sprint down to a jog then gradually to a fast-paced walk. Athletics were never my strong suit.

Almost immediately my phone started blowing up with texts, calls and voicemails from not only both of my parents but Cora as well.

I decided to answer for her.

"Hey Cora, what's up?"

"Riley! Where are you? Your parents are calling me flipping out saying that you ran out of the house all of a sudden. Is everything okay?" She sounded panicked and I suppose that had more to do with my dad's surely angry phone call to her.

I understood their fear, and that was because I felt it as well. I refused to live my life in fear, the same way that I refused to let this psychopath dictate how I live it.

"It's a long story, and I don't feel very chatty right now. Long story short, the cops filled my parents in on this afternoon."

There was a long pause, followed by a soft sigh.

"I'm sorry Riley. Is there anything I can do?"

"Just tell him that I said I'm okay, and to not worry." I tried to come off as stable as I could, when I really felt like I could come apart at any given second.

"Okay. Be careful." The phone call ended, and I slid my phone into my pocket.

I must have been walking for what felt like hours, but the clock on my phone let me know it had only been 45 minutes. I was about to turn around and start cooling down before having to face my parents again when I spotted what looked like Allie's car parked ahead.

The curiosity in me wanted to approach the car and see if she was in there, and the intellectual in me was screaming that it was a bad plan, and that it could be anyone's car.

Curiosity won.

I approached the car slowly, keeping my negative apprehensions alert.

The car was tinted, but I could see the outline of Allie laying down in the back seat.

Did she live in her car?

This automatically felt like it was becoming too personal, and probably wasn't something she felt comfortable sharing with people, so I started to leave.

"Riley?"

I turned around slowly to see Allie sitting up, hair messy, and the back door cracked open.

"How did you find me?" She seemed embarrassed, and my heart ached for her. The last thing I wanted to do was to force her hand on opening up about something she clearly wanted to be hidden.

"Honestly? I wasn't looking. I was trying to get away from my overbearing parents…"

I surveyed her and decided that I had probably overstepped and should make a quick getaway before I inevitably put my foot in my mouth.

"I'm sorry, I'm going to go." I turned away, but she stopped me.

"Don't. It's okay. I guess I should have figured that this would come out sooner or later. I'll make this simple. Come on." She grabbed my hand and led me to take a seat in the passenger side of her car.

"It's quite a long story. My parents never wanted me. They had a few other kids, but for whatever reason that I will probably never understand, they didn't want me. I was damaged goods. So, they shipped me away. I bounced from home to home, growing up without so much of a phone call. Now, I'm homeless. And that's it. It's just the cards I've been dealt Riley. The only reason that I don't advertise it, is because I don't want to be looked at the way you're looking at me right now."

I wiped a stray tear that had fallen, and apologized. The last thing I wanted to do was to make her feel pitied. I felt bad for her. It certainly changed my perspective on my parents.

Sure, I felt like in this moment in time, they were being extremely overbearing and complicated. But I guess in the bigger picture, having parents who cared too much was better than parents who didn't.

I was never good at comforting people, and I didn't feel like Allie even wanted to be comforted in this moment. Her hair fell in her face, and I did the only thing I knew how to do in the moment.

I reached out and squeezed her in a hug. I could feel her body tremble as she started to cry. "Oh, please don't cry Allie. I'm sorry." I squeezed her shoulder.

"It's not that. Daisy is the only person I have ever told about this, besides you. And you know what? She hugged me too."

Of course, she did.

Daisy was amazing. I'm going to find out who murdered my sister, even if it kills me.

15

Cora

My phone was ringing off the hook all night with phone calls from both of Riley's parents. Rather than avoid, I picked up the phone call coming from her dad on the third call.

"Hello?"

"Cora, hi! It's Riley's dad. Have you heard from her this evening?" He sounded panicked, which sparked a sense of worry in my gut.

"No, not since I dropped her off earlier. Is everything okay?"

I didn't get a chance to find out because he hung up swiftly after that.

It was kind of rude, but his daughter just died, and apparently something happened with Riley, so I'll allow him the benefit of the doubt.

Just this once.

I knew he wouldn't call if he wasn't really worried about her, and her being my best friend and all, I figured it would be best to try and call her to see what the hell was going on.

She's had a rough day, and I know it's been eating at her. Riley will stew on something until it practically eats her alive and talking it out isn't really her specialty.

I dialed her number, and she picked up. "Hey Cora, what's up?" She sounded cool as a cucumber, meanwhile my heart felt like it was in my stomach.

"Riley! Where are you? Your parents are calling me flipping out saying that you ran out of the house all of a sudden. Is everything okay?" I strived for the same calmness she was currently possessing but felt like I was failing miserably.

"It's a long story, and I don't feel very chatty right now. Long story short, the cops filled my parents in on this afternoon."

It all made sense. Riley's dad rarely got upset, and almost never at his daughters. Having her safety at risk sounded like something that would throw him into a blind rage and uncontrollable panic. I sighed. "I'm sorry Riley. Is there anything I can do?" I attempted to come off as comforting but knowing Riley- she wouldn't bite.

"Just tell him that I said I'm okay, and to not worry." I tried to come off as stable as I could, when I really felt like I could come apart at any given second.

"Okay. Be careful." I hung up the phone and sent a quick text to Riley's dad.

Here goes nothing.

Cora: Hi. Just spoke to Riley. She didn't say where she is, but that she is fine and to not worry.

No response. After ten minutes passed by, I figured I had done my duty to him in reassuring that his daughter was safe.

Now to worry about my best friend.

What was going through her head?

Actually, probably the death threat she received today.

Poor Riley. She couldn't catch a damn break. I can't even begin to imagine all the emotions she's being going through since the incident this evening.

All that aside, how could she ever think that leaving the house at night with nobody to protect her after what happened would be even remotely safe?

Maybe she knows. Just doesn't care.

Riley was stubborn and headstrong, but she wasn't naïve, and she certainly wasn't the kind of idiot who was careless with their life.

I was getting antsy, and when I got antsy, I started to pace. I hadn't even realized I was doing it until I had circled the windowsill for the eighth consecutive time.

Stop. Sit down. Take a breather.

Riley's okay. She said that she is okay. I know it isn't safe for her to be out there right now, but by the time I were to leave to try and find her, she may already be home.

My mom was always telling me to never worry until I had to. Riley's safety wasn't an immediate risk at this very moment, so stressing myself half to death wasn't necessary.

I texted Riley to be safe, to let me know if she needed a ride, and to please text me when she arrived home.

I sat down on my bed and waited for a response. Fifteen minutes passed by with no response. *What is with this family?*

Screw it.

I jumped off the bed, grabbed my keys and flew down the stairs.

"Be right back." I said to my very clearly sleeping mom.

I started the car, turned on the lights, and peeled out of the driveway without trying to look around at my surroundings.

Oh well.

I was never the person who could just sit back and do nothing. I was a person of action and I knew Riley was more likely than not still out here nursing her ego from whatever fight transpired between her and her parents.

I drove along the streets that bordered our little lake spot, praying that she went somewhere she knows.

Five minutes of ten mile per hour driving, and endless neck craning, I felt like it was fruitless. She wasn't out here.

Finally, my phone lit up with a response from her.

Riley: I'm home now. Hitched a ride from Allie. I will explain tomorrow, love you.

A ride from Allie? Part of me was jealous, but the intelligent, more logical part was just happy she made it home safe.

I parked my car in the driveway of my house and unlocked the front door slowly. Knowing my mom, she had probably moved from the spot she fell asleep on the couch to her bedroom by now.

She rarely checked on me, mostly because from the time she woke up on the couch to the time it took her to lay in bed, she was practically a zombie.

Without all the blood and carnage of course.

My original thoughts were confirmed. The living room was empty, but naturally my mom had forgotten to turn the lights off.

I walked around the room, one by one, shutting every light switch off.

I noticed the picture of Daisy, Riley, and I on the mantle but decided that I wanted it in my room instead. It would make me feel good to be able to look and see the good times, when everyone was happy, alive, and enjoying life.

I grabbed it and noticed this little wire connected to a tiny box on the backside of the photo frame.

I pulled on it, confused as to what it was.
Then it hit me.

Someone bugged my house.

16

Riley

After Allie poured her long story into me, we spent hours sitting there and talking about anything and everything.

I didn't let it show to her, but my heart ached for her and all the trials and tribulations she had to face in this short time here on Earth.

Through the face of all that, she still remained kind, strong, and courageous. I could see why Daisy took to her so easily. It was easy to talk to Allie, because she was one of those people that truly listened.

She asked a lot of questions whenever you told a story. Some people might find that annoying, but I found it quite refreshing. To me, it was the clearest sign that she was taking an interest in what you were speaking about, and the questions were her way of trying to understand it completely.

She offered to drive me home later, and I gladly accepted because my sprint from earlier had me feeling run down.

I really should exercise more.

Daisy was the athletic one. She always was up by six every morning, and out for her two-mile jog. She said it gave her mental clarity and energy to start her day.

A two-mile jog at six am sounded like torture to me, but to each their own.

The drive home was quiet, but not awkward. It was hard to be awkward with each other at this point, especially after the night of soul searching and secret divulging.

I rolled the window down slightly, resting my head on the seat and letting the cool wind caress my face.

I was going to be okay. Daisy would want me to be okay.

She would also want me to find her killer, but not if it was a threat to me.

I don't really care about that tonight though. Tonight, I would focus on the good. The happy. The exciting.

Tomorrow I would worry about my sister's killer.

I said thank you to Allie for the ride, promised her I would call tomorrow, and sent a quick vague text to my best friend with promises that I would explain later.

She had to be worried half to death by now.

Another apology to add to the list, on top of my dad and mom.

Hearing Allie's story really put everything into perspective for me. How was I to get angry with him for doing what a parent does? Especially when someone close to me never had a parent to begin with?

I was blessed, even if that blessing disguised itself as irritation right now.

I opened the door softly, praying that I wouldn't wake up my surely sleeping parents. Oh, who was I kidding? They were sure to be awake and...

Waiting.

My dad was sitting on the armchair looking grim as I slipped into the living room. I didn't see my mom in sight, and that was probably for the better.

I can't even imagine what she went through tonight seeing me leave, especially when visually she was taking Daisy's death the hardest.

Why would you do that to her?

I felt a pit in my stomach.

"Hi dad. Look, I'm sorry." I knew I owed him more than that but found myself struggling to find the words. I turned to leave.

"Sit down." He didn't sound angry but hurt. I listened.

"I don't ask a lot of you Riley. Even less so since your sister died. Today… today let me know that she was *taken* from us. It also let us know that someone is after you. Do you even know the kind of fear and heartache that passes through a parent when they hear that? If you did, you wouldn't have run out of here tonight. We may have been too harsh, but we are just trying to protect you."

I wiped a tear from my face, and he continued. "All I want is for you to be safe. And happy. You have made me a proud father all your life, but tonight Riley, you disappointed me."

My dad got up and headed off to his room without another word. I didn't respond or attempt to defend my actions.

I knew I was wrong. I knew I hurt him and my mom.

But a piece of me didn't feel sorry. I had been trying to take care of everyone and make sure that everyone else was okay ever since Daisy died.

I never made the time to check in on myself and take care of my mental health.

But tonight, I needed a moment for myself to think about everything without the shouting or the parental heaviness. So, I did. And now I could think a hell of a lot clearer.

With both of my parents clearly fast asleep, I headed to my room. I was exhausted mentally and physically.

I opened the door, fumbled the light, and began to undress and put on some pajamas. I brushed my teeth, hair, and grabbed a bottle of water of my nightstand.

Chugging, I sat down and felt something crinkle underneath me.

Frustrated, I moved to the side, and my hands found a picture.

Looking more closely, I see clear as day that it's me. From tonight. It's a picture taken from behind of myself as I was walking down some open road.

I turn it over and find a note.

"Should be more careful. -T"

17

Allie

My phone ringing woke me up early this morning. I groaned, rolling to the side and pulling the pillow over the ears.

Riley and I stayed up later than I usually did last night, and I needed all the sleep I could get. *Maybe it's work calling.*

Shit. I sat up, and grabbed my phone, pressing it to my ear.

"Hello?"

"Well, hello sleepyhead. You sound tired." My heart instantly melted. Definitely not work.

"Hi handsome. Yeah, I am a little rundown. I was talking to Riley last night." I laughed.

"That's good, you're making friends. How are *you* doing though? Need me to bring you anything?" He was so sweet.

"No, I'm fine, thank you. I have work soon."

"Good luck, I love you." He hung up, and I laid down, a lovestruck smile plastered across my goofy face.

He made me giddy.

I checked my phone, about an hour until work. I climbed into the front seat, and started the car, letting it warm up. I was planning to go to the local gym for a quick shower before my shift.

Time to make some money.

I walked into the gym and made a beeline straight for the locker room after flashing my member ID at the front desk.

The great thing about this gym was that I was able to shower and get ready for work, for one small price. It was a great deal, and to someone who had been bounced from home to home, it was pretty nice.

I showered, and blow dried my hair after getting dressed in my work uniform. I would put on my apron later, mostly because it was kind of embarrassing to walk out of here like that.

I wasn't ashamed of my profession, it put food in my belly, and clothes on my back. It just wasn't something I wanted to advertise… much like the homelessness aspect.

The good thing about the guy I was seeing was that he knew. He knew about my being homeless. He knew about my struggles in life, well… what I chose to tell him. He loved me in spite of all that.

I completed my look with a few swipes of mascara and the pull of my hair back into a sleek ponytail.

Collecting my things, I started shoving all my toiletries, along with my dirty clothes into my dark navy-blue duffle bag.

I practically bolted out of the gym, starting to run late. It was always so busy in the locker room, and there were a lot more women getting ready than you would think.

I drove way over the speed limit to work, threw the car into park and was putting on my apron as I entered Amma's front door. She smiled kindly at me as she jokingly tapped her nonexistent watch.

I know, I know.

I put my purse and keys into my locker, grabbed a pen and paper, and clocked in.
Smile, smile, smile.

Waitressing was hard for someone who truly lacked good social skills, but I made it work. After all, I was a master of deception.

Almost immediately, I had my first table. It was a warm older couple who couldn't stop laughing at the other. It was refreshing to wait on an older man without being ogled all evening. He was truly in love with his wife, and apparently, they had been married for thirty-eight years.
When you know, you know, I guess.

Did I know?

They ordered meatloaf, one of our more popular specials. Just as I dropped their dinners off at the table, I was grabbed sharply from behind.
"What the he…" I turned, fully expecting to see some perverted customer, but it was Riley, laughing her ass off.

"Sorry, I just had to. I'm starved. Where is your section?"

Smiling, I pointed to the booth that sit adjacent to the older couple.

"Right there." I scurried off to the back to fetch a cup of hot coffee for Riley. She was an absolute coffee junkie, far different from Daisy, who was a noncaffeinated advocate.

I placed the coffee down in front of her, and she instantly made a joke of leaning over the steaming mug and taking a big, over compensatory breath in.

"Ahhhhhh. Liquid gold. So, how has your day been?"

"I just got here, but so far so good. Cora didn't want to join?" Usually those two were paired at the hip, and absolutely inseparable.

"No. Don't really want to talk about it." Riley turned to the side, and for some reason I didn't understand, I must have hit a nerve.

I get it though.

"That, I can respect. Did you want to eat? The chef makes a mean bacon and egg sandwich." I raised one eyebrow, as I made that inviting proposition.

He really did make the best breakfast sandwiches. Legendary even. Probably part of the reason I gained five pounds since I started here.

"Yes please." She smiled, and I turned away to put in the order without another word.

What the hell was going on with her and Cora? Those two were thick as thieves, so for Riley to not show up with her, that means that they had some sort of falling out.

That sparked my curiosity even more, but as someone who had their fair share of secrets, I would respect Riley's boundaries and that she didn't want to get into it.

I sauntered back around to the older couple's table to bring them their desserts of choice- chocolate pudding.

That I didn't understand.

We have an entire case of homemade pies, and they want package made chocolate pudding. Bleh.

I set their check on the table and thanked the couple once more before offering Riley a coffee refill. Just then, my number popped up and I spotted her sandwich waiting in the window, steam rising off.

I grabbed it and came back around the counter to set it down in front of Riley, who's mouth was now watering.

"Anything else?" I smiled, and a hand snaked around my waist.

"Hey baby." A kiss was planted on my cheek.

I didn't need to turn around. I knew who it was.

Riley's eyes bugged out of her head.

"Officer Brooks?"

18

Riley

I woke up this morning, completely at a loss with the event's of yesterday. Everything had been playing on a constant loop in my mind, from the threat, to my dad's lecture, to Allie's revelation, to the feeling of hearing my dad express his disappointment. *What. A. Shitshow.*

But it was a new day, and I was determined to make some head way on my sister's murderer. I didn't have a clue where to start, but I knew Cora had a knack for stuff like this.

She watched Dateline religiously and could point out a clue from a mile away.

I called her up and she agreed to meet me at the lake.

A walk would clear my mind.
"Dad, I'm meeting Cora at the lake. Is that fine?" I yelled into the kitchen, where I could see him brewing his probably 8th cup of coffee today.

He sauntered out of the kitchen, and pulled me to the side, pressing something into my palm. It was cool, and metallic.

He looked me right in my eye and started to speak.

"Look Riley, I know yesterday was a lot. The last thing I want to do is make you feel like a prisoner in your own home."

He continued,

"I don't want to keep you confined. But I do want you safe. So please, take this." He pulled his hand away, and I was finally able to see what he had given me.

A pocket-knife, really?

"Dad, is this necessary?" I rolled my eyes in absolute exasperation.

"If you want to leave this house, it is." He didn't even look back as he strode back into the kitchen.

I took that as my cue to leave, so I headed to the front door, sliding the knife into my pocket.

Who knows, maybe I'll have to fight off a bear later.

I started my slow walk over to the lake. Something about the fresh air hitting your face that brought such an overwhelming sense of calmness and tranquility.

As I passed the trees on both sides of the road, I was haunted by memories of Daisy and I playing tag while we were young. Our parents would yell at us to keep it away from the road, but Daisy liked to live on the dangerous side.

In fact, she walked a fine line between danger and safety. She was reckless.

Did that get her killed?

I shook the thought away. Regardless of her high level of recklessness, she didn't deserve what happened to her. Not in a million years.

I ran across the open street into the forest clearing that led down to our secret spot. The leaves crunched beneath my feet, and the smell of roughage relaxed my soul.

This was my happy place.

My mind flashed to Daisy.

Our happy place.

I spotted Cora up ahead, her feet hanging off the side of the dock into the sparkling water.
"Hey stranger." I smiled, and Cora turned around, grin stretching from ear to ear.

She pulled her feet out of the water, standing up, and ran to pull me into a tight embrace.

We broke into a fit of laughter, and you almost wouldn't know that we saw one another only yesterday. That's how we always were, whether it was five days or five hours, we were excited to see each other.

We broke our hug and I started pulling off my sneakers then socks, as I dipped both feet into the cool lake water.

This feels good.

Cora sat back down and joined me. For a moment, we both sat there, just basking in the silence.

I glanced over at her, and she looked worried. It was probably about what happened yesterday, but if I wasn't going to let it upset me, then neither should she.

"Spill. It's about yesterday, isn't it?" I pressed Cora, and her face shifted from a somber mood to one with extreme guilt plastered on it.

"I have to tell you something Riley, and I should have told you a while ago, but I thought it was nothing."

Secrets? We didn't keep secrets.

"What is it?" I reached out and squeezed Cora's shoulder. She knew she could tell me anything.

"I got threats. Shortly after Daisy died." She spoke, and then hung her head down, as if afraid to look at me.

Threats?

"So, let me get this straight. You were receiving threats from someone after my sister supposedly "killed" herself, giving you some hint that she wasn't actually suicidal, and continued to shoot down every theory I had about what actually happened to her?" I grew angry. Some friend.

"Riley, I…" I cut her off.

"No, don't. I don't even care that you didn't tell me. But being a hypocrite is something else. You knew she was killed. You knew the person was out there, and yet I had to practically beg and shame you into supporting me. What kind of friend are you?"

I stood up and slid back on my socks over my still wet feet.

I hated the feeling, but I despised being next to a liar and a hypocrite more. I slid my shoes on, not even bothering to fix the laces. I started to storm off, and no surprise here, Cora just sat there like the coward she was.

I can't believe I considered this person a friend. I can't believe Daisy considered her a friend. There was a real threat out there, I knew that now. Problem is, she knew there was a threat long before I did.

And still had the audacity to act like I was crazy for believing that my sister's death was anything more than suicide.

I was in this alone, but in this moment, I didn't want to be alone. I knew where to go.

I started walking down the road, one destination in mind. Amma's Diner.

Allie would offer some outsider insight on this situation, if I chose to tell her.

I was furious with Cora, but I don't know if I was in the mood to bash my best friend with someone that I was still newly friends with.

She confided in you.

And yet, I still felt as if I couldn't fully open up. There's those trust issues coming into play.

The diner came into view, and I could already feel a big weight lifting off of my chest. Allie was hardly judgmental, and most of the time, she didn't even give advice.

Rather, she was an ear to listen. She allowed me to get all my feelings out and allowed me to feel heard but not judged. I really needed that right now.

Her back was turned to me as I walked in, so I ran up behind her quietly and grabbed her side. She tensed up almost immediately and turned around slowly with a shocked expression casing her face. "What the…"

"Sorry, I just had to. I'm starved. Where's your section?"

She pointed me in the direction of one of her tables, and I sat down in the comfy red leather booth. I saw her pouring a coffee cup in the distance, and I knew it was for me. Coffee was the greatest drink, and if I didn't have to drink water to survive, I would exist solely on the substance.

"Ahhhhhh. Liquid gold. So, how has your day been?" I smelled the delectable fragrance that was spilling out of the cup.

"I just got here, but so far so good. Cora didn't want to join?" Allie frowned.

"No. Don't really want to talk about it." I turned away, hoping she would get the hint. I know I came here with intentions of talking, but it felt wrong.

It felt wrong to speak ill of Cora, regardless of how I felt about her at this exact moment.

"That, I can respect. Did you want to eat? The chef makes a mean bacon and egg sandwich." Allie raised an eyebrow, and my stomach instantly grumbled.

"Yes please." I smiled, and Allie walked away to the register.

She made her rounds at her other tables, bringing desserts, and checks, and finally- another refill for me. I didn't really need it. I could feel my hands shaking. I wanted it though, and so I would have it.

I heard a ding and looked up to see the number 7 lit up. Allie had explained to Cora and me one day that each waitress or waiter was assigned a number. When one of their table's orders was ready, the number would be pressed and lit up, so they knew.

I knew Allie was number 7.

And I could see my delectable sandwich sitting up there. Wow, I didn't even realize how hungry I actually was. I grabbed my stomach and could practically feel the drool drip out of my mouth.

She sauntered over to the table, plate in hand, and slid it in front of me.
"Anything else?"

Just then I saw an officer walking up behind Allie. He slid his arm around her and kissed her.
"Hey baby."
What the fuck?
"Officer Brooks?"
She was screwing a cop?

19

Cora

I screwed up. I knew I did. I also knew that Riley was right. To be quite honest, I don't really know why I shut her down when I had the facts all along?

Ever since the very first threat I received… I knew it couldn't be a coincidence. So why, when my best friend in the entire world expressed her concerns about something that I knew in my gut to be true, did I not support her?

Was it due to fear? Was it pride? I honestly couldn't tell you, and today, I couldn't tell her.

She was furious when she stormed out of here earlier, and it didn't help much that I didn't go after her.

Riley needed ample alone time to cool off and properly process things. It was why she ran off after her father confronted her, and it was why she ran off today.

It didn't worry me, but I sure felt horrible about it. I had a few clues about where she may have gone to, as there was only one other person in this town that she could talk to besides me. Allie.

I wouldn't interfere, and I knew better than to try and talk to Riley right now while she was upset, so I went home.

Thankfully, my mother didn't ask too many questions. I sat in my room most of the night, sulking in silence. I felt bad enough and wanted to tell Riley the truth.

I should have known I would be ostracized for it.

I just needed to make it up to her. To show Riley that I really did care about her, and especially about finding Daisy's killer.

I would help her.

I bent down under my bed and pulled out the small box where I kept the notes.

I read them over again for the first time since I received them.

"Don't believe everything you see. Including D."

"The thrill of the chase is much more satisfying than the kill. Run fast."

I got chills down my spine. These notes were comprised by someone truly sadistic.

I knew what I had to do.

I shoved the notes in my pocket, grabbed my keys, and told my mom I would be right back.
"Be safe honey! Take your phone."

I told her I would, and I went outside to my car. I would do the smart thing and turn these notes in to the police.

It took no time at all to get there, and I knew that it made a lot more sense to give the notes to an officer who was involved in Riley's threat at the diner.

I walked up to the front desk and was met with a grim-faced secretary.

"How can I help you?"

"Hi, I have some information. Is Officer Brooks here?" I smiled, hoping it would chip away at her hard exterior.

"No, he just left. I can call him if you would like."

"Yes please." She then motioned for me to take a seat in the waiting area, which I did without hesitation. *This would all be solved today.*

I had yet to see her pick up a phone or make a call, but she said she would help me so I knew she would. Just as I started to lose faith, Officer Brooks strode into the station.

He stopped at the front desk momentarily, and she gestured towards me. He turned, so I started towards him.

"Officer Brooks, hi. I'm not sure if you remember me. I was with Riley Carson at the diner yesterday. You asked me some questions."

"Of course. The desk sergeant said you had some information. Why don't we step into a room and talk?" He opened his arm pointing at a room across from us.

I strode towards it and he opened the door for me. Glancing in the room, I was overcome with a sense of familiarity.

I had never been in a station myself, but I had seen enough crime shows to know that this was an interrogation room.

Was I a suspect?

We both took our seats, and he spoke, "Have you come into any new information since we spoke yesterday?" He raised an eyebrow.

"Not exactly *new* information, no." I reached into my pocket, and took out the notes, handing them to him.

He took them in his hands, examining them closely.

"What are these?"

"Sent to me after Daisy's death. I'm sure that's what the D is referring to."

"Huh. Okay, thanks for bringing these in." He stood and opened the door.

That's it?

"They seem pretty threatening to me. Is there anything we should do about it?" I looked at the officer, who looked like he didn't have a care in the world.

Meanwhile, mine and my best friend's entire world was falling apart.

"Nope. I can assure you that we are doing everything we can to investigate this, and I will take these notes and share them with my fellow investigating officers."

I stood too, not because I felt done or heard, but because he was all but shoving me out of the room.

"Sergeant Adams, will you get this young woman's name and contact information for me please?" He turned to the left, and the pinched face woman from earlier stood up.

"Of course, Officer Brooks." She motioned for me to join her.

I turned back towards the officer, and he extended his hand to mine.

"Been a pleasure." With that being said, he turned and headed off in the other direction.

I scurried over to the desk, in a hurry to give my name and get the hell out of here.

She took down all my information, and I asked her if she had a contact card for the officer I spoke with.

"Sure thing, dear." She reached behind her, grabbing a white card and handed it to me.

I took it from her and strode out of the police station without so much as a thank you for her.

I wasn't feeling very kind today.

I got in my car and started it up.

I grabbed the card and looked at it.

Thomas Brooks, Investigating Officer, followed by his personal cell. Good to know.

I read the first name over once more, and then a third time, and a fourth.

I focused on the first letter of his name, and I felt my chest squeeze.

I took a picture of the card and texted it to Riley.

Pissed at me or not, she would want to know this.

Attached with the image, I sent a message:

Cora: Could this be the T you saw on Daisy's card?

There was a reply within seconds.

Riley: We need to meet. I think I know who killed my sister.

20

Allie

I don't know what happened, but Riley took one look at Thomas and ran out of the restaurant, without so much as a bite of food.

Maybe the thought of you and an officer freaked her out.

It shouldn't. Thomas was a sweetheart. Daisy liked him too. I introduced the two when he and I first started dating, and she told me on multiple occasions that he was, "Perfect for me."

So, what was the problem?

If I wasn't barely an hour into my seven-hour shift, I would have run after her.

"What was that about? Is she doing okay after… yesterday?" Thomas looked concerned, and my heart swelled.

He was incredibly caring, and that was one of the many reasons I fell in love.

"I have no clue."

Thomas's work phone buzzed, and he took the call off to the side near the door.

When he returned, he had a solemn look on his face.

"I came to hang out, but they just called me in to the station. Someone there has information about this whole mess with Riley."

"What, really? Go. I'll call you later." I planted a kiss on his lips, and he bolted out of the door and into the squad car.

Information on Daisy's killer? Was Riley safe? Was she upset with me?

I looked around at the nearly empty restaurant. *Fuck, I hate work.*

I sent Riley a text.

Allie: Are you okay? Do you want me to package up your food and bring it to you later?

Riley: No, thanks though.

Allie: What happened?

Riley: Family stuff.

Weird. I must have done something to offend her. Maybe seeing Thomas brought back everything she went through yesterday. How could I be so careless? I would make it up to her.

But first, I had to work.

21

Cora

Riley and I had planned to meet in an hour, after we both went home and had some dinner first. We both were sure that we were on to something with Daisy's killer.

I wonder if we both had the same person in mind. I think it was Thomas Brooks. He seemed okay enough when the incident at the diner occurred, but the way he brushed off my information had sent a chill up my spine.

This town was small, so when the idea of someone being murdered was brought to the table, it's only safe to assume that the police would be working hard as hell to find out the truth.

So why did it feel like he couldn't wait to get out of the room and brush it under the rug?

We were going to meet at the lake, per usual. My mom spent the entirety of dinner lecturing me on the safety I needed to be executing. By this time, everyone who was anyone had heard of what happened at the diner.

While they didn't know the fine details like Riley and I, they knew enough to be scared.

And they should be. I was.

I knew better than to argue so I simply echoed a barrage of yeah's, as I slowly ate my meatloaf and green beans.

After dinner, I trudged to the bathroom to shower and get dressed in something a little more warm.

I didn't plan on going swimming, so I decided on a pair of jeans, a long sleeve shirt, and a wool sweater.

It wasn't typically hot here during the day but dropped to the 45's in the evenings.

"Okay mom, I'm heading out." I started towards the door, car keys in hand.

"Be safe, Cora. I mean it." She gave me a look, and I smiled.

"Of course. Love you." I opened and shut the door, stepping into the cool night breeze.

Yeah, a sweater was a good idea.

I started up my car, allowing it to warm up before blasting the heater. I slowly reversed and went on my way to the lake. I stopped at the edge of the cul de sac, when my car dropped low on one side.

What the hell?

I pulled over to the side of the road and got out to look. I had not one, but two flat tires.

Fuck me.

I turned on my phone flashlight and inspected them a little more.

Is that a slash?

It felt like ice spread through my veins, and I found myself forced to take a seat on the curb as I came to a startling realization.

Someone slashed my tires.

Officer Brooks?

No doubt.

I would be damned if I let myself be scared into submission by this idiot. I wouldn't let it deter me from speaking to Riley either. He was escalating, going from written threats to physical threats.

I had to warn Riley.

I locked up my car and continued the remaining distance to the lake. It was dark out, but the streetlights provided a sense of comfort.

Plus, the lake was only a two to three-minute walk from my current location.

I texted Riley filling her on the situation, leaving out the fact that the tires were slashed, but that was a conversation best served for in person.

She was apparently already there and waiting. I turned the final corner by the patch of trees and headed down to the moonlit dock.

There Riley was waiting, feet in the water.

Predictable.

"Hey." She turned around, smiling.

"Took you long enough." I started to laugh.

"Hey, these feet are made for driving, not walking or running." I took a seat next to her.

"So, I went to the police station today, and handed in the notes." I looked at Riley, ready to gauge her reaction.

But I couldn't. Her face remained stoic, and I, confused.

So, I continued.

"The officer I spoke to, Officer Brooks, he was acting weird. He kind of brushed it off, and I don't know if I am overreacting or if something really is off. But when I left, I grabbed his card. His first name is Thomas, Riley. I think he's T. I think he killed Daisy."

Riley didn't say a word.

"Riley…"

"But why? Why would he kill my sister?" She started to cry, and I squeezed her hand for comfort.

"I don't know. But we should figure it out."

"We have to warn her." She looked at me, face worried.

"Warn who, Riley?"

"Allie. He's her boyfriend."

Allie was dating the killer?

I stood up, pulling my feet out of the water.

I couldn't process this. This was all one big spider's web, and every time I tried to understand new information, I got caught and tangled in it.

If our suspicions were right, Allie was in a hell of a lot of danger. This guy was on the police force, he had a lot of back up.

What the hell did Daisy get herself into?

How did she get mixed up with someone like this? Was it revenge, or strictly a crime of opportunity? Did he kill Daisy, and then get close to Allie after? My head was spinning.

"Let's go." I grabbed Riley's handed, yanking her up.

She looked determined, as was I. Allie had become a close friend ever since we met at the diner, and I couldn't let anything happen to her.

Especially since neither Riley or myself was able to save Daisy.

I will never forgive myself for that, but I could try and rectify it now.

We both started walking, as I was now carless, the short distance to the diner.

We heard tires screeching behind, and both jumped to the side, turning around.

A light grey van was speeding towards us. My heart squeezed in my chest, and I stood still.

The car continued towards us, and then, right past us.

I let out a big breath I didn't even realize I had been holding in.

But then the car slammed on its brakes, and the driver door flew open.

"Riley…" I grabbed her hand and started to turn around.

I couldn't make out who the driver was, not at this time of night, and not with the hooded jacket they were wearing.

"Riley. We need to go. Now." I pulled her hand hard, and we both turned around, breaking into a full-on sprint.

I could feel my heart beating out of my chest with fear, adrenaline, and anger.

My legs gave out from beneath me, and my face smacked the pavement. I rolled over onto my back as the killer hovered over me. Knife in hand, they plunged it into my side as I felt a sharp pain spread throughout my abdomen.

I started to lose consciousness but was trying to look around for Riley. Did she make it away?

I was beginning to fade but heard her high-pitched scream ringing in my ears.

No. Don't.

I tried to sit up but felt like I had no control over my body. The screaming continued, and I felt absolutely helpless.

You need to get up Cora.

I used every last ounce of strength in my body to pull myself upright, propping up on my elbows.

I looked around just in time to see Riley being shoved into the back of the van, before the driver climbed in, and hit the gas.

No.

22

Riley

I remember screaming. Crying. Kicking. Fighting.

It was useless because this person was twice my size, and apparently twice as determined.

I was now bound, gagged, and chained to a makeshift pole in the back of this dirty van which smelled horribly of petrol.

The person, no, my abductor…

My abductor. The word feels foreign in my head, but I know in my heart it is the most accurate depiction of such.

Am I going to die?

No. You're going to fight like hell, because it's not your time, and this person sure as hell has no say in the end of your life.

Daisy would have wanted you to fight.

I looked around the back of the van. Either this was planned, or this person had the cleanest car. There wasn't a single thing I could use to my advantage, much less to get me the hell out of here.

I glanced at the pole which looked new and looked like it was put in by an idiot. My dad was a mechanic, and the bolts on this thing would have given him a hard attack.

I had hand cuffs keeping me on the pole, but if I could just pull hard enough, maybe I would be able to pull the pole out of the bolts.

Come on, you can do this Riley. You have to.

There was a metal lattice looking divider between me and the front seats. It wasn't fully open, and the driver had cranked the volume up to what I can only suspect to be max.

Asshole.

So, I pulled.

And pulled.

And pulled.

Ow!

The pole had snapped loose of one of the bolts, causing it to shoot out to the side, and nick my wrist.

Great, now I was injured.

I pulled my wrist across the back of my shirt, drying the blood, and continued the tedious rhythm.

Where the hell where we going?

I had no clue, we felt like we had been driving forever. I didn't want to find out while I was still locked to this damn pole, so I continued to yank as hard as I could.

It snapped, and the noise was so loud, I thought the driver would stop, but he didn't.

Thank god.

The pole was still attached to the top of the van but now that I was free on the bottom, I lifted the edge up and slid the cuffs out.

I slowly crawled towards the door, which had no fucking handle on the inside.

Oh god, oh god.

I'm going to have to wait until he opens it. It's not a fair fight by any means, but I had a lot of fight in me, and I had people to live for.

My back when I was restrained laid opposite the door, so I inched myself with my back to the pole, just like before, but this time simply hid my hands behind my back.

I fixed the pole into place so he wouldn't notice by grabbing in. I felt around and grabbed a bolt just to be safe. Not that a bolt would cause much damage.

Shit!

The driver slammed on the breaks causing my head to smack right into the pole. I felt him shift the gears and the car was at a full complete stop.

We're here, wherever here is.

Brace yourself, Riley.

The bolt was long, but unlike a nail, it wasn't sharp… however with the right amount of force I was sure it could do some serious damage.

The back doors flew open, and I did my best to look contrite and defeated.

The hood was now off, but the ski mask was on, and I was much too frazzled to even begin trying to identify the features. Besides, they didn't look familiar.

"Don't try anything funny." The voice was gruff, and a sense of familiarity stung through my veins, but still I came up with nothing.

He began to climb in the van and approach me.

My heart was beating out of my chest, palms sweaty, and I felt like I was seconds away from blacking out.

Pure fear.

I had never felt it before in my life, and yet, I felt like in this moment the fear would be enough to kill me before my abductor had a chance to.

Now.

I lunged forward, shoving them back. Obviously catching them off guard, they fell backwards, and nearly out the back of the car. Their back was now to me and rather than trying to escape, I did what I felt I should.

I took my still cuffed hands and wrapped them around their throat. Being behind them, I put my feet on their back and leaning backwards as hard and as sharply as I possibly could.

I heard them take a large intake of air, and I felt adrenaline pumping through my veins.

They began to make choking noises, and finally, went limp.

I took my hands off and then climbed out of the van. Curiosity was blooming in my stomach, and I reached for the mask before deciding that getting the hell out of there was the better option.

I stuck my hand in my abductor's pocket in an effort to find the keys.

Bingo. I grabbed them and went to close the back door of the van. Their foot became caught, and as I went to move it, I felt a sharp pain through my leg. I looked down and saw the pocket-knife sticking out.

No, this isn't happening.

I knew better than to pull it out, so I tried closing the door, but my abductor was already up on their feet ready for a fight.

As if I wasn't already at a disadvantage before, now I felt hopeless. I turned to run but it was reduced to more of a jog due mostly to the knife protruding from my leg.

My sneakers began to get squeaky from the amount of blood that was dripping down my leg and pooling in them.

I'm not going to get away.

My abductor grabbed me from behind, and lifted, as if it was the easiest thing in the world to do.

They walked swiftly down the road, continuing to carry me.

We left the van in this patch of greenery, and I became confused.

Where were we going?

I saw a house come into view, and my abductor put me down.

"Walk." I felt something press against the back of my skull, and I knew exactly what it was.

I complied, the fear of death so vivid on my mind. The house was yellow but brown due to decaying wood, with a bright green roof, and a bunch of miscellaneous crap dirtying up the front yard.

This place is abandoned. I looked around and didn't see houses at all.

Nobody was going to find me.

I continued walking straight, the barrel of the gun not leaving my head once. My hands were sweaty, and I could begin to feel tears blossoming in my eyes.

My mind kept flashing to the people I love. Trying to remember them, or preparing to die, I don't know which.

My mom, who would be absolutely broken when she heard I was taken. Daisy's death destroyed her, and if I died, she would never recover.

My dad, who gave me warning after warning. He was right. I'm so sorry.

Cora, who had to see me taken in front of her eyes and unable to do a single thing.

And Allie, my newest confidant, and Daisy's good friend.

None of them would be okay.

I was sure Cora had already made it to the police station. I couldn't rely on that especially when it looked like we were miles out of town. We had been driving for forever after all.

Up the creaky steps of this old home we went. The front door was hanging off it's hinges, but they still used a key to open it up.

What am I going to do?

We stepped into the home, and I was shocked. The outside was nothing compared to the inside. It was decorated with paintings, carpeting, beautifully unchipped wall paint, and brand-new furniture. Someone lived here.

What a lovely place to die Riley.

I'm not going to die, and if I am, I sure as hell am not going down without a fight. I owe it to myself, my friends, family, and most of all- Daisy.

Did she fight?

Stop. You need to focus. We headed towards some stairs that let upstairs. Each step I took, I mentally braved myself. I knew I couldn't try anything, not with a gun to the back of my head.

That was a sure death sentence.

But the intellect in me knew that this person had to want something from me. Obviously, they wanted me dead. But why not just kill me and leave me in my car like Daisy?

Why go through the trouble of kidnapping me?

Maybe they wanted to torture me.

Dark thought Riley.

It's kind of hard to not have dark thoughts at this point in time right now. I'm in a dark situation faced with impossible choices: fight, lose, and die or do nothing and die anyways.

There was sure as hell no way that I was getting out of this on their accord. I had to fight, but I knew that already. So, I suppose it wasn't much a choice at all. I would fight.

I expected the upstairs to be this horrible, paint peeling off the walls, musty attic situation but much like the downstairs it was beautifully decorated.

I had to be in their home. But why?

So many questions, but no time to ask, or courage to ask.

"In there." The gun pushed my head to left and I took a swift turn into a bright yellow room.

The room was tiny, complete with a bed that looked disheveled. There was nothing else in the room but the single bed.

"Sit." I nearly fell forward after a sharp blow between the shoulder blades.

I sat immediately, not even trying to sit on the bed. I had no clue what would happen to me if I sat on the bed, and to be quite honest- I didn't like the ideas flowing through my head right now.

My adrenaline was through the roof. By now, I had determined that this was a man. The voice, the build, I was sure. Determining who exactly he was, was an entirely different story.

What man would want both you and Daisy dead?

We were young enough that I couldn't imagine pissing anyone off this much that they would want me dead, but who knows.

He pulled a key out of his jeans and opened the cuff on my left wrist. The voice in my head told me to try and fight in that moment, but the gun on his holster told me otherwise.

Not the right time. You will die.

So, I sat there docile and waiting, in my attempt to be the perfect little captive.

I was smart enough to know when to bide my time, and when to attack. I had to be.

My life was on the line.

The free cuff was attached to the metal post.

I mentally breathed a sigh of relief.

It would prove difficult, but I had already wrangled my way out of one metal pole. I'm sure I could do it again. Getting all the way downstairs and out of the house, miles back to my town, would be the harder bit.

I looked around and zoned in on the window above the bed. It was small, dark wood, and looked like it was falling apart. This guy took his time planning this. There was no doubt a barrage of nails keeping that window from ever opening.

He sat down opposite me, sliding down the wall.

"You were a lot harder than I originally thought. Daisy didn't put up nearly as much as a fight. Funny too, because she was the fiery one." He laughed, but it was lacking humor.

I felt a pit form in my stomach. Pure fear, disgust, anger... maybe all three.

Sick bastard.

He wanted a reaction out of me, that was why he said it. I would bring him no satisfaction. I kept my face straight, eyes looking ahead directly into his. "Nothing to say Riley? Oh, come on, I'm sure you have a million thoughts going through that bright beautiful head of yours." Another laugh.

Don't say a word.

Nothing. I sat there in silence, giving this monster full range to pick me apart and break me down. I could recover mentally but trying to fight now would only satisfy him. No. I wouldn't. "Alright then." He reached for his chin, hand grasping the edge of the mask as he started to pull upwards.

And then it was off.

Dear God.

Officer Brooks.

"Officer Brooks?" I tried to hide my shock, but I must not have done a good job, because once again, he broke into laughter.

"Wow. She speaks." He rubbed his stubble and cocked an eyebrow.

Smug bastard.

"I don't understand…" I felt tears start to well up in my eyes, but I shook them away.

No weakness, Riley.

The police were supposed to protect us. He was there in the restaurant helping me that day. What the hell was going on? He was dating Allie for god's sake!

Allie.

Someone has to warn her.

"I'm sure you don't. By now, I'm sure you have realized that Daisy was a much more private person than you ever thought. I was her confidante. We fell in love." He smiled warmly, and for a split second I was able to forget he was a cold-blooded killer.

Just a split second.

"Do you usually kill people you love?" I spat, voice dripping with disdain and disgust.

So much for docile captive, Riley.

Oh, to hell with docile.

"Ah. Well you see, Daisy found out some information. Information that I couldn't let her live knowing. So, I did what had to be done."

I closed my eyes, anger now evolving into full on rage.

"And me?"

What information did I know that warranted my death?

"You… you are just too damn stubborn. You should have stopped when they ruled it a suicide. You were getting too close to the truth, and now you have become a problem for me. Even so much as sending your little friend to the station with the notes." He grew angry, as if I was truly the person in the wrong here.

So, he was psycho and delusional.

"Cora? You wrote those notes… why? She had nothing to do with it." Nothing was making sense.

"But you see, it did. It can be so dull here in this town. Sometimes, you have to make trouble, so you have something to fix." He smiled wickedly.

I turned away. I couldn't look at him and I sure as hell couldn't stomach to hear anymore details about his plan.

Daisy… what did you find out?

And why didn't you come to me?

"You're going to stay here, because well, you have no choice. I, on the other hand, am going to get some food. Kidnapping has me starved." He waved and left the room, closing and from what I heard, locking the door.

And then it was just me.

Left alone to process the information that was wracking my brain.

Daisy…Cora…Officer Brooks… Allie, it was all too much.

I couldn't protect Daisy, and now knowing everything, I had to tell Allie. But I was stuck here, and Cora didn't know my kidnapper's identity. I knew she had ideas about Officer Brooks, and to be quite honest, so did I. I wanted to meet, so she could tell me I was crazy and wrong. I guess she wasn't.

Unless she was dead.

No, don't think like that.

Someone had to have found her.

I'm sure she's okay, with my parents, and at the police station now.

What if he has friends? Other officers in on it? Once again, I drew a damning conclusion: I was screwed.

When all the adrenaline slowed down and stopped, I began to feel the pain again.

Why didn't he pull the knife out? Was this his plan? Take me here, spill his guts and let me die?

Just then he came back up the stairs and opened the door, holding medical supplies. "You know, I hadn't planned on stabbing you, but you really gave me no choice. I can't let you die, because I have other plans for you Riley."

He stepped towards me, setting the supplies down on the floor. He took out a few zip-ties out of his pocket, connecting my free wrist not only to the bed post, but to the cuffs.

"Just in case you feel violent." He winked, and I don't think I have ever wanted to kill someone more in my life.

He sat back on the floor, grabbing gauze, stitches, and some type of liquid.

He yanked the knife out without warning and before I had time to react, pushed the gauze down on my now profusely bleeding wound.

He peeled the gauze back an inch or two and eyed it.

"Surface wound. You're fine. Not deep." He was muttering and focused on my leg.

Trying to keep me alive for what? What did he have planned?

He spread some cream into the wound and started to lace up the stitch needle.

The wound began to numb up. Not fully, but a little. He started stitching the wound, and the sharp pains of the needle tearing through my flesh spread up and down my entire body.

I was on fire, and he was laughing. Enjoying this.

He was done so damn fast you would have thought he was a sadistic doctor, rather than a sadistic cop.

He covered the wound after putting some liquid on top. He left two Advil and a bottle of water next to me, before using the scissors he brought to cut the zip-ties.

"Thomas!" I recognized Allie's voice.

Fear struck across his face, and he gathered all the supplies before leaving, slamming the door hard in his wake.

I could hear him bounding down the stairs, and a very loud conversation between the two.

My heart was beating out of my chest with worry for my friend who was talking with a guy who had a gun holstered to his hip.

What do I do?

I started to shout. I yelled so loud, that I heard my voice crack.

"Help me!" I screamed at the top of my lungs.

I heard a chorus of screaming from downstairs, followed by heavy footsteps ascending the staircase.

The door slammed open, and Allie was standing there wide-eyed, with tear-brimmed eyes. She covered her gaping mouth with her hand, and slowly turned to her crazy boyfriend.

"What have you done Thomas?"

He begun to laugh and took a hand on each of her shoulders as he leaned down and whispered in her ear. I couldn't make the words out, but she looked horrified.

She shook her head at him, and fury ignited his face.

He hit her over the head with the handle of his now freed gun. She dropped to the floor in a heap, and he took the opportunity to secure both of her hands to the same bed frame.

"She was a lousy girlfriend anyhow."

With a final snicker, he looked over at both of us and slammed the door shut.

23

Cora

The pain was excruciating. I knew better than to pull it out. Between the shooting pains in my head from the concrete, and the sharp burning in my side, I somehow managed to pull my phone out of my pocket.

911. It was painfully slow, but I was able to dial those three live saving numbers.

I hit the speaker button.

"911, what's your emergency?" A chipper voice answered the call.

"Been stabbed. Need help."

"Okay, where are you located?" Now the voice sounded more immediate, more focused.

"Uh, Carrington and Brose. In the middle of the road. Hurts." I gasped as I felt the knife poke inside.

I could barely hear the words that came next, because I felt weak. I dropped the phone, and the sound of it hitting the concrete was the last conscious memory I had, before the sirens became louder and louder.

"Cora!"

Mom.

"Is she going to be okay? What happened? That's my baby!"

Mom, I'm okay. Don't worry.

"Ma'am, we were able to repair the stab wound, but the damage from her hitting her head on the pavement was extensive. Due to the swelling in her brain, we have to keep her in a medically induced coma. At least until it can go down." A male voice spoke to my mother, one I did not recognize.

I was in a coma? No. I had to help Riley.

"Thank you, doctor." My mother began to sob, and every fiber of my being ached to reach out and touch her, to console her.

I'm so sorry.

"Erika…" I recognized Riley's dad's voice.

"Oh! Thank you for coming. Have they found Riley?" My mom sounded hopeful, when there was no hope to have.

But they didn't know that.

"No. Someone did this. They hurt Cora and they took Riley. I have been calling the station every hour and they still have no new information! It's bullshit!" Now Riley's dad was shouting.

       I understood it. To know that something has happened, something bad has happened to your child and to be unable to do anything is horrendous. I was there.

I was there as Riley was being taken away, and I was too useless. Too useless to do a damn thing, and now I was unable to tell everyone what happened.

It had to be Officer Brooks. It all made sense. I wasn't able to see the kidnapper's face, but the height and build looked incredibly similar.

Then again, it was dark, and it could have probably been anyone.

My mother and Riley's father communicated in hushed tones, almost as if they knew I could hear every word they were saying.

Where was Riley's mom?

My heart broke for her, knowing that this would absolutely break her.

The minute the swelling went down, the minute I was taken out of my coma, I would find her.

I had to.

"How is Cora doing?" I heard footsteps approaching.

And then my mother was the first to speak. "They are keeping her in a medically induced coma. There was too much swelling in the brain. Have you found Riley?" Once again, my mother sounded hopeful, and I felt that much guiltier for not being able to save her.

"Unfortunately, no. But, I can assure you that we are doing everything in our power. Could you please let me know when she wakes up? She may have remembered something useful."

Oh god.

I know that voice.

I would never forget that voice.

Officer Brooks.

Slimy bastard.

I knew it.

My pulse started to raise, and I could hear an elevated beeping noise on the machine that began to climb rapidly, and loudly.

"I'll get a doctor!" I heard my mom shout, which was followed by Riley's dad's, "I'll get a nurse."

No. Don't leave me here.

"You know I'm here, don't you?" I could feel his hot breath against my ear, and I wanted to scream, kick, shout, something, but it was fruitless.

He didn't say another word but laughed a cold laugh into my ear. I felt him move away, and a chorus of people rushing into the room after.

"She is fine. I'll check the monitor once more, but it happens. She likely was stressed out, but please, if you see anything else abnormal do not hesitate to call us." The doctor was addressing my mother, who sobbingly replied, "Okay."

"I should get going. I have a mountain of paperwork at the station, and I need to confer with other officers about the case with Riley." His slimy voice still felt hot and present in my ear, even though I knew he was across the room.

I hate him.

I have never hated anyone more.

And yet, I didn't understand him.

I couldn't fully comprehend why anyone would ever want to hurt Daisy, let alone Riley. Both sisters, attacked within a month or so apart? Something was really wrong.

When I recovered, would he come after me next?

No. I was going after him.

I had no idea of how long it would take for the swelling in my brain to go down, but for Riley's sake and my own, I hoped it was soon.

So, it really was him. It was Officer Brooks.

Fuck, Allie was in danger.

What are you supposed to do?

I'm *supposed* to save my friends, but in reality, I can't. I can't even save myself right now.

I had never felt more pathetic or weak in my entire life. My head was spinning with possibilities on the motive behind all of this.

Maybe they were dating. Allie did say that Daisy had mentioned a man that she was talking to and very much happy with.

Maybe they were together, Daisy broke it off, and Officer Brooks, or Thomas, got angry.

That was definitely a possibility, but it failed to explain why he would go after Riley.

When I turned the notes into the police station, Officer Brooks was cold, distant, and showed no interest in them.

Maybe because he wrote them.

But why?

Nothing was making sense and absolutely none of this added up.

I had more time on my hands than ever, and with the ability to speak ripped away from me, I was forced to drown in my thoughts.

My thoughts were beginning to suffocate me, and the thought of being unable to move, to speak, and laying in a hospital bed vulnerable while my best friend was being held captive and my other friend was dating the kidnapper... scratch that- murderer. The thought was too much to bear.

I heard my heart monitor began to race again. *Stop it Cora. Stop before you give your mother a heart attack.*

I slowed my breathing, and instead tried to focus on the positives.

Riley was still alive. I knew in my heart she had to be.

At this time of day, Allie was probably at her shift... safe and away from that scumbag.

My mom, I could feel her hand on mine, and I knew she was safely in my room. She wasn't out there where Thomas could get to her.

Focus on the positive, and it would all be okay.

Yeah right.

24

Allie

I peeled my eyes open and the first person I saw was Riley. She was crying and chained to a bed frame. I looked around.

The same bed frame I was attached to.

I examined my hands which were secured using zip-ties.

Thomas.

Oh my god. What have I gotten myself into? "Riley…" I was at a loss for words. I had done this. I had brought this psycho into our lives.

"He killed Daisy. He killed her." She started to bawl, and I felt my heart drop into my stomach.

Killed Daisy? No, he couldn't have. He never even knew Daisy, not personally anyways.

He only became familiarized with her investigation, even going so far as to oversee everything. He was passionate about that case…

For a reason.

I covered my mouth. I was in complete and utter disbelief. How could I be so idiotic?

I followed suit and began to yank violently on the zip ties which were now digging sharply into my wrists. Why me? Was it all a lie?

Was this the plan the whole time?

I have to do something. If there was ever a tiny ounce of love between us, then I was the only one who held the smallest glimmer of hope in getting Thomas to change his mind about whatever sick plan he concocted.

Killed Daisy… why? There was no logical explanation, not to mention reason, that he would take her life. To then go and threaten her sister, and later kidnap her… well that didn't sound like Thomas at all.

Because he's not the Thomas you thought you knew.

He's a monster.

A cold-blooded killer.

I didn't want to cry. The satisfaction that it would surely bring to him was reason enough for me to never cry again. I wouldn't show weakness. He lived for it. He needed it.

I would die before I became some victim. "Riley…I'm so sorry. I will fix this. I promise." I tried to console her with my words, but when I didn't believe them myself, how could I?

She didn't respond, but rather continued crying.

You can't do this Riley. Be brave.

The door slammed open, and standing in the large doorframe was an angry, pinch-faced Thomas looking absolutely murderous.

His hands were clenched at his sides, both balled into fists.

I surveyed the man I had spent my time with for quite some time now, and I didn't recognize him. Not only did I see clearly just how demented and twisted he was, but his physical appearance had done a 360 as well.

His usually neat hair was disheveled, and stringy, as if he hadn't showered for a few days. His eyes were bloodshot and wide, and his skin sallow and pasty.

Who are you?

"Stop making so much goddamn noise!" He punched the wall and Riley jumped back a few inches, her tears drying up instantly.

He turned and exited the room, not even bothering to pause to close the door on his way out.

I looked down at my hands once more, now red and raw from the constant rubbing and pulling. I didn't care. I knew I couldn't stop trying.

I remember seeing a post on Facebook years ago showing that if you were in a situation where your hands were zip-tied, and you were able to maneuver one of your shoelaces over them, you would somehow be able to break it.

I thanked God or whoever was up there a million times over that I decided to wear Converse. I reached to my feet and started to untie my shoelace.

I had to act quick, especially if he decided to come back in with another fit of rage brewing, and a lot of anger to take out.

I got the shoe untied, and slowly but surely maneuvered one of the laces over the top of the zip-tie in between both of my hands. I then lifted my feet into the air and extended them to where the shoelace was tight against my zip-tie.

I began to shift my feet back and forth, right, and left, in a frantic motion.

The noise was soft, and for that I was eternally grateful.

I turned to Riley who had still not yet cried since Thomas's wall punch, and she was watching me intently, hope blooming within her no doubt.

I could do this.

I would do this.

So close. So damn…

Close.

I heard a snip and just like that my lace dropped to the floor. I couldn't bear to look because I could very faintly see the scissors hovering between my hands.

Thomas.

"You see, I knew you had brains. Not very smart considering I already have you hostage, I'm pissed off, and in case you forgot you haven't been the best girlfriend lately." He laughed, but it was lacking humor.

I haven't been the best girlfriend? This is coming from the guy who killed a woman, hid evidence, threatened the woman's sister, kidnapped her, and now me? Yikes.

I felt the anger erupt with the power of a million active volcanoes, but still, I couldn't express it.

The thought of giving him any satisfaction off of my reactions to the words he said, and his actions against me was not going to happen. Not at all.

So, I simply stared. I stared right into his cold, emotionless eyes and tried my best to look strong, and unbreakable.

But I was so sure that I looked weak. Fragile.

He smiled, and it wasn't one of those sweet smiles I had grown to love, but rather one that made my skin crawl.

He then turned his attention to Riley. "Why do you think you're here?" He sat down against the wall opposite her and waited for her to answer him.

What the hell is this?

"Maybe because you kidnapped me." Riley's voice was strong when she spoke, and not at all weak or fragile like mine had surely been.

I was proud.

"Kidnapped you... but why?" He continued to stare, as if any second it would all magically click for Riley. "No clue. Why don't you tell me, T?"

T... that sounded so familiar.

Possibly the T from the note Riley showed me when we first met.

My heart stopped, and my palms grew sweaty.

My head was spinning, as thought after thought, and realization after realization swept in uninvited and unannounced.

I looked back up at Thomas, who had yet to respond to Riley.

Instead, his face was white as a ghost, and he stared straight ahead, lips forming into a grim line. "Do you need me to repeat myself?" Riley was now grinning victoriously, and while part of me was proud, the other half knew Thomas was a hothead. *Don't get yourself hurt Riley. Please.*

Still no response.

Could it be possible that Thomas truly thought that Riley didn't know about any of it? About the evidence Riley found... that she was looking?

But he had to, because he wrote that note in the diner.

How the hell did he manage to pull that off?

It was like someone found the on switch on Thomas and switched it.

He pulled himself up, sitting up straighter. He rubbed his eyes and looked into Riley's glossy eyes.

"T huh… you went snooping." He smiled and continued.

"I'm sure you think you know everything… about your sister anyways. But what if I were to tell you that Daisy's death had nothing to do with her, and everything to with your parents?" He grinned from ear to ear wickedly.

"Get comfortable Riley, it's story time."

25

Riley

"Get comfortable Riley, it's story time."

I did nothing but gape at Officer Brooks' revelation. My parents were involved in Daisy's death? Or they caused it? Neither seemed likely and I was interested to know why.

"See here's a little story that will make your heart melt. One day, a man and woman had just gotten married, and they immediately wanted children."

I listened intently, and he continued.

"So, they try, and try, and try. Finally, they take a test, and congratulations, they are pregnant! So, like the responsible parents that they are, they make a doctor's appointment."

"Well, imagine their surprise when they go in and the doctor finds twins! They wanted one baby, but when they found out they were having two, they couldn't have been more excited. Still following Riley?" He regarded me carefully, and I nodded, so he went on.

"Well they began to tell everyone the good news. They didn't know the gender, so they bought a bunch of neutral clothes, and started decorating a nursery complete with two cribs."

"About four months into the pregnancy, at what was supposed to be a regular checkup, they get some news. They aren't having twins, but instead, triplets. The doctor has no idea why he hadn't seen it earlier, but like before, the parents are elated."

He smiled eerily at me.

"So, they spread the news again, going out to buy a third set of every outfit they had already purchased. They picked out more diapers, more of everything. They add a third crib to the room, and decide on a few names…"

"…everything seems perfect. They find out that they are having three girls. They already had the names picked out, and the mother had already felt like she was carrying girls."

"So now Riley, they decorate the nursery pink. They add flowers and prepare for the oncoming birth of their three beautiful girls."

Officer Brooks stopped talking and started to rub his hands together nervously.

"The day comes, and the mother goes into labor. The father is nervous as can be so obviously excited for his children to come. The birth was seamless, and there were no complications."

"The complications came later in life, at least for one of their children. You see, children need a lot of love and attention. They just do, and I think parents desperately want to obviously give that to their children…"

"…but the problem with having three children is that there will undoubtedly be some days where one child or more receives less attention than the others."

"One of this couple's daughters felt like this everyday of her young life. She was often neglected and pushed to the side. She was made to feel a mistake and told many times as a toddler that she should have never been conceived."

Officer Brooks rubbed his face now, and I could tell this story was personal.

"So naturally, this child started to act out. She started to do bad things as a desperate last-ditch effort to finally, finally win the attention from her parents that she so desperately needed…"

"… and she got attention all right. The bad kind. The parent's decided that she was too much for them to handle, and they didn't want her to be their problem anymore. So, they shipped her off. First to a school that was states away. Then, when trouble had raised there, they shipped her off to a boarding school. At this point, she must have been ten or so. As you can imagine, they had troubles there as well. So, then the last place this child went to was a mental institution for young adults."

I sat there, chained up, and yet rather than feeling sorry for myself, I instead felt sorry for this little girl. It sounded like she never had a single chance in life, and that she was mistreated horrible. I looked over at Allie who shared the same shocked expression.

She turned to me with tears in her eyes, and then buried her face in her shoulder to dry them up. *How does this relate to Officer Brooks, and Daisy?* "Tell me Riley, how does that story make you feel?" Officer Brooks looked me dead in the eye.

"Horrible. It sounds like a horrible way for a child to be brought up. Is this story about your sister?" I feigned interest, as this was obviously something important to him.

"No... she was yours."

"I don't understand." I cocked an eyebrow. Daisy was my sister. We were twins. My parents never had any other children besides us, and they weren't the monsters this guy was describing anyhow.

"Of course, you don't. You were too young. But your parents did have triplets. They did send their daughter away. Being as young as you were, you don't even remember her. All you remember is Daisy." He was now crouching in front of me, stroking my face, and I hated it.

I hated all of this. The mind games, the bullshit stories, not knowing how Cora is, how my family is, and watching Allie go through hell.

I spat in his face, and he coiled back, face full of rage.

He pulled his hand back, and lunged forward, palm connecting with my cheek.

He had a hell of a swing, and it knocked me full force onto my back, the cuffs yanking at my wrists.

He stood over me, scowling. I braced my body for another blow, but it never came. He reached down, grabbing my arms and pulling me upright.

He turned and rejoined his spot against the wall.

"This is the truth Riley. Your family deceived you. Daisy found out the truth, and that's why she had to die." He shrugged his shoulders, and I couldn't fathom how anyone could be so casual about murder. *I'm dead.*

"So, you're telling me all this now because… you want to kill me?"

"Aw Riley, I don't want to. But I have to. Not yet though. I have plenty more to share, and if you didn't already know, we have all the time in the world." He stood up and headed towards the door.

Before he left, he looked over his shoulder at Allie and rolled his eyes.

"You done playing victim yet?"

I looked at her, expecting her to cower or cry, but instead she laughed. Really laughed.

She winked at Officer Brooks, and he walked towards her smiling. He took scissors out of his pocket and cut her free.

She stood up, took his hand in hers and began walking towards the door without a single glance back at me.

"Allie!"

She stopped, turned, and smiled.

"Please, call me Taylor."

26

Cora

I was still here. Lying. Waiting.

I was desperate to wake up, to open my eyes, to tell the truth about what had happened.

The fact of the matter was that Officer Brooks either killed or had something to do with Daisy's death. He took Riley. I knew that it was a matter of time before she was dead too.

All around me the conversations ran wild, and yet I was silent. Meanwhile, my head was overflowing with thoughts I was desperate to get out.

From the small tidbits of conversation that I had picked up on lately, it seemed like my brain's swelling was reducing just perfectly. They would continue to keep me in my medically induced coma for a while longer, but that everything was looking up.

Yeah, and what about Riley?

I had no plan. I needed to tell someone, anyone, the real truth about Officer Brooks.

But he was an officer of the law. What, or even who could I tell that would have any chance of going head to head with someone like him, and win?

I still needed to try.

I knew that they wouldn't wake me up until I was fully better, so I tried to relax my mind.

Sometimes it felt like it was working, but other times the whole effort felt absolutely fruitless.
"How is she doing?"
Riley's dad.

My heart squeezed in my chest. I can't even begin to imagine the hell he was going through. I almost hoped there was no news. No news is good news, at this point in time at least.
"Oh, hey. Doctors say she is doing better. She's on the road to recovery. Any news on Riley?" My mother's voice sounded clear, and a lot stronger than it was when I first arrived.
"No. But I heard that Allie girl they were hanging out with hasn't shown up for her shift. I know they were friends." He let out a big sigh, and I was mentally screaming for them to put the pieces together.

I couldn't really blame them, not when it took me going into a medically induced coma to put the pieces back together. I could hear a lot, but sometimes I wish I didn't.

Good news is that Thomas, or Officer Brooks, has yet to come back.

Bad news is that means he is either with Riley, or at the police station putting on the act of his life, and no doubt steering the investigation further and further away from the truth.

God, I need to wake up.

I can't lie here useless, not when I knew something everything else didn't.

I knew who had Riley.

My mom and Riley's dad were quietly talking amongst themselves, almost as if they knew I could hear and were purposefully trying to keep something hidden.

I struggled to hear but was sadly unsuccessful.

Instead, I let my mind whir some more, quickly finding myself overcome with thoughts of Riley and just how scared she must be right now.

The fact that Riley's dad said that Allie missed work threw me for a loop. I knew she was dating him, which had me assuming she would be safe. Maybe something went wrong, something unexpected and now she was in trouble too.

Point was, I would not be able to help either or bring peace of mind to Riley's dad until I got better.

Now how in the hell was I supposed to do that?

27

~~Allie~~ Taylor

The look on Riley's face sent chills up my spine.

In the best way, of course.

I have to admit, I was a much better actress than I could have ever dreamed, and the story that Thomas told Riley was perfect.

I couldn't have told it any better myself. The sad part was that it was all true.

I was the girl in the story.

My parents had always treated me like not only the black sheep of the family, the odd one out, but the child that they never wanted.

Growing up, I had no idea what I could have done to deserve such hatred and contempt from the people who gave me life, especially when my sisters were being treated differently.

So that was the truth. Riley and Daisy were my biological sisters. We were triplets.

The thing is, I really did like them. Both of them, in fact. Daisy was bubbly and possessed an absolutely infectious personality. She lit up the room, and I never felt judged or less than when we spoke.

Riley was just as amazing. She was kind, and so compassionate it would make your head spin.

So, what's the problem, right?

The problem right now was that Riley knew the truth. She was already getting much too close for comfort, and I told Thomas that it would be better to take care of the problem now.

Daisy was hard.

Getting her to take those pills was like pulling teeth. She always did have such a spitfire personality. Having Thomas hold a gun to her head while she took them made the whole situation run that much smoother.

Killing my sister was much more work than I ever anticipated.

I never wanted Daisy dead. In fact, I had hoped she would keep my little secret just that- a secret.

But she was much too good.

She thought that I must have been exaggerating about our parents. She said that the parents she knew and loved could never treat anyone like that, let alone one of their children.

Daisy had not even an inkling of the pain I went through at the hands of our parents.

Then again, she was the golden child, and even Riley herself knew it.

"How good did that feel?" Thomas turned to look at me, a wicked gleam sharp in his eye.

"You have no idea," I leaned over and kissed him on his cheek.

I hadn't shown up for work clearly, but I needed to if I wanted to keep up appearances.

The captive bit was my idea. Things were getting a tad bit dull around here.

I hopped in the shower, the water as hot as it would possibly go, and then quickly got dressed for work. I phoned into my boss with a horrible sob story about how I was out looking for Riley all night.

She bought it like the useless sap she was. "All is clear with the boss. I have to head into work now." I stepped into the kitchen where Thomas was eating a sandwich.

"Gotcha. I will keep an idea on our prisoner. Hey, what did you want to do with her? We never got that far in plans?"

I didn't know what I wanted to do about Riley. Once she started digging, I knew that I wanted her to know the full truth and not some chopped up story that our parents would surely feed her.

But I hadn't gone as far as to think of the after. After the kidnapping. After the truth was revealed.

Not. A. Damn. Clue.

"Hello? Earth to Taylor." Thomas waved his hands in front of my face, in an annoying attempt to snap me out of my thoughts I was clearly lost in.

"Sorry. I don't know. I need to think about it."

With that hasty goodbye, I turned and headed out of the house.

Thomas took the blame with everything with Riley, although I was sure she was now beginning to piece everything together after my name reveal.

I was T. I was the person that Daisy was spending time with, and I made the mistake of divulging everything to her.

That was a mistake from the moment I opened my mouth. I should have known she wouldn't have immediately taken my side.

The favorite child always wanted to appease mommy and daddy, and when Daisy wanted to get their side of the story as well, I knew my intuitions were wrong about her.

As far as they knew, Taylor was still locked up in a mental institution where they felt happily content to leave her there for the rest of their lives.

They could care less about me, and I, them.

When I broke out, my first thoughts went to them. I wanted revenge, and I wanted it immediately. I never once thought of the two sisters, and what I would do to them.

They were kids, same as me, and I never held them culpable for our parent's actions. I was sane enough to know that none of it was their fault, but sadly shitty parenting.

I climbed into my car, consumed by thoughts.

What was my game plan here?

I had been absent at work, but I had the story covered with my boss.

Even in our secluded hideout, I was not unaware of the buzz that had overcome this town since Riley was taken last night. I know Thomas told me that he hurt Cora, and so I can safely assume she's at the hospital.

As a matter of fact, I can fully assume that. I remember him mentioning that he decided to pay her a visit. I called him an idiot.

To be honest, the idea of being prisoner was very spur of the moment, and very, very fun.

It was like a sweet sister bonding moment. Until I had to cut it short.

Riley was an awesome person. I knew killing her when it came time would be just as hard as with Daisy. However, her knowing who I was, and that I was free, made it unsafe to me for her to be alive.

She was a liability, and I didn't like loose ends.

I know how it must look.

I'm sure I look like a monster. What kind of person would kill one of her sisters, kidnap, and have plans to kill the other?

I wasn't born this way. In fact, I remember as a child being excited about all life had to offer. But slowly, over the years, my so-called parents chipped away at that excitement for life.

They chipped, and chipped until I was left with nothing. Soulless.

They made me into the monster that I am.

So, to thank them, I'm going to take everything away from them. I'm going to be the person responsible for leaving them with nothing.

Because it is exactly what they did to me.

I was nothing if a firm believer in eye for an eye.

Make that two eyes.

I parked my car and noticed a police car camped outside the restaurant. One quick once over of the vehicle and I could clearly see that there was nobody in there.

I was silently praying that the officer inside was there for a quick bite to eat, and not an interrogation.

I walked inside the yellow framed door, and sure enough, the officer was standing up towards the back talking to my boss.

Once I stepped inside, they both ceased talking and turned towards me. The officer, who I now recognized as one of one of Thomas's friends, started towards me.

Better dust off those newfound acting skills of yours.
"Miss Decker?" He pulled a notepad from his pocket.
"Yes, Allie, hi." I reached out to shake his hand, which was uncharacteristically sweaty.
"I already spoke to your boss about you missing last night. Clearly it was a misunderstanding and you are in okay condition. I wanted to know more about the night that Riley went missing. Did you hear or see anything unusual?"

"I wasn't with them. I did see Riley earlier that day, and she was upset with Cora. I wasn't sure why but didn't want to pry. She left pretty abruptly, and I haven't seen her since..." I gave my best attempt at a sad gaze.

I continued,

"...and I have felt so terrible. I mean, what if I had pried harder? What if I ran after her? Would she still be okay?"

I felt a tear roll down my cheek.

Nice touch!

Okay, maybe I am a much better actress than I ever thought before. Clearly my act was incredibly believable because the officer reached out and squeezed my shoulder.

"Hey, this is not your fault, and there was nothing you could have done differently. I have the information and will let you know if we find anything."

He turned to leave, and I decided last minute to add some final touches to my performance that would really sell it.

"And Cora? Is she okay?"

"She will be fine. But she is still in a medically induced coma at St. Jent's hospital. I hear they are taking visitors," and with that, he turned and walked out of the restaurant.

I hadn't even noticed that my boss had crossed the rest of the restaurant and was now standing beside me.

"Are you okay to work today Allie? I know she was your friend, both of them." She also squeezed my shoulder, and I was beginning to get tired of all the touching and my personal space being invaded today.

I casually stepped to the side, carefully and successfully I might add, removing her hand from my shoulder.

"Yep. I need to work."

I stepped around her pitiful gaze and made a beeline for the locker room.

I couldn't deal with all this pity today. I was fine. Truly, I was. Life could really not be going any better for me right now.

The only problem was that I had to put on this mask for the entire world to see right now. I had to play the worried and grieving friend.

"Hey Al, you okay?" I heard Carrie, who was the other waitress come in behind me.

I rolled my eyes long and hard, before slowly turning around.

"I'm fine, just trying to keep busy until there's news. Thanks."

She continued towards me and enveloped me in a suffocating hug.

What is with these people today?!

I hugged her back, against all of my better judgement.

"It's going to be okay Allie, really. I have a good feeling that Cora will pull through, and that Riley will make it back home. Safe and sound."

I wanted to barf in my mouth and was grateful when she left the locker room swiftly after that touching sentiment.

Being a waitress and dealing with rude and difficult people on a day to day basis is one thing, but the people in this town were practically suffocating.

Maybe I could consider myself lucky that my parents decided to haul my ass out of here.

Maybe if they didn't, I would have grown up to be one of those "talk about your feelings" kind of girl just like my sisters, Daisy and Riley.

I finished wrapping the final knot on my apron and headed out to start the shift from hell.

The mood change from this morning to now was drastic and could all be chalked up to the overly friendly welcome wagon that rolled in this morning, followed by the busload of concerns.

I really had all these people fooled,

…and I loved it.

"Hi, what can I get you guys to drink today?" I had walked up to a table with two young girls who looked nice enough, but what did I know?

Looks could be deceiving.

"Two cokes. No ice."

Neither of which looked up when placing that order, and also lacking a please as well.

I see they skipped the lesson on manners.

With working in a customer service job, I have discovered something new. It does not matter if you are old or young, ignorance is everywhere, and that goes to include rude people.

I grabbed both of their Cokes, lacking ice for whatever reason that I will probably never understand, and headed back to their table to take their order.

I set the Cokes down softly and was pleased to see that they had set their menus down as well. "What can I get you to eat?"

I smiled kindly as I wrote down their massively complicated orders.

Seriously though, how many tweaks could you add for a fucking hamburger?

I was going to lose my damn mind.

I grabbed their menus and turned to put in the order.

The rest of the day went as follows: nice customers, good tip, rude customers, bad tip, questions and concerns about my "friends", unsolicited advice, and the list goes on and on.

I was about twenty minutes from the end of my shift, and I could feel it looming.

I had been texting Thomas for the better part of the day. I guess he decided to call in on a sick day, so he could stay at the house and keep an eye on Riley.

According to him, she was a little spitfire, and kept him on his toes.

That's my sister.

I pushed the warm and fuzzy thoughts out of my head in order to get my last table. It was what looked like a middle-aged couple, and very much in love.

I stepped towards their table when I heard my boss calling my name.

"Allie, come here a second."

I looked at my table apologetically.

"Give me one second." I turned away, shoving my notepad back into my apron, and started towards my boss.

"What is it Amma?"

"Cora is awake."

28

Riley

My head was spinning, and my mind was running at the speed of Olympic sprinters in a race. I couldn't comprehend what had happened, but at the same time, I felt like everything was falling into place.

Allie, no scratch that, Taylor, was in on this. She had been lying to not only Cora and I, but to Daisy. She wasn't who we thought she was, and from what I could gather, this was all a part of some elaborate scheme.

I had to get out of here. I had to expose them for the snakes that they were.

Thomas, or Officer Brooks had gone on and on about some sob story about triplets, and how one of the siblings was treated poorly by her parents. That sibling was sent from home to home, and later to a mental institution where she broke out.

Am I to infer that the story is true? That this girl I have gotten to know and love for the past few weeks shares my DNA? She was in on this. She had something to do with Daisy's death. Whether she and Officer Brooks conspired together, or it was an individual effort, I was sure of this.

Taylor was bad news. My parents were good people. We volunteered at soup kitchens. Daisy and I grew up never needing a thing, and unconditional love was given, never having to be asked for.

No. I was sure she was some desperate attention-seeker, who had spun these lies into a web that she felt she could push onto me. I'm not an idiot, and I am sure as hell not going to sit in here, waiting for the crazy people to kill me.

I was worried about Cora, and about my parents. They had to be losing their minds trying to figure out where I was. I was sure it was only a few days since I had been taken, but I couldn't be sure.

What I was sure of however, was that I needed to get out.
Today.

I was in handcuffs. There was no way to get out of them without the key, or with a bobby pin. And I seemed to be fresh out of both.

I wasn't nearly naïve enough to believe that I could sweettalk either of these two into letting me go. Unless, I made Taylor to believe that I was one hundred percent behind her and her bullshit story.

Even so, she has an agenda, and unfortunately, I think me dying may be a part of that plan.

But it wasn't apart of mine. The bed was metal, and it had already seemed fragile enough. With just the right amount of force, I was sure I could get out of here.

Earlier, I was able to hear Thomas moving around freely downstairs. It helped, as it provided a way to gauge where he was in the house, and act accordingly.

It had been silent for at least an hour, and there were a million answers for that. He could be sleeping, and my yanking on a metal bed post would surely wake him. Or, he went out for a while, only to return to find me halfway through my escape efforts.

All the possibilities flying through my head ended badly for me, and I kept trying until I came to an unfortunate conclusion.

I just needed to try.

The more time I sat here wondering if he would catch me, was more time that I was allowing myself to be caught. I needed to fight, and I needed to fight now.

I started by leaning all the way towards the bed post, and then suddenly a sharp jerk backwards sent the bed swaying slightly.

I repeated this motion, again, and again, and I was hoping I was able to make some progress.

It did seem that the only dent I was making was in my back, which was now killing me.

Stop being such a damn baby.

I continued on with the torturous rhythm. Push, pull, push, pull. Finally, I heard a loud snap, followed by myself falling to the side.

I felt fear pulsing through my heart, fully aware of the volume of the noise that had just been made. If he was in fact still in this house, he would have heard me, and I needed to work fast.

I slid my cuffed wrists down the length of the broken pole. I was still handcuffed, but at least now I was free from the bed frame which once held me captive.

I scrambled out of the door, quickly, but also carefully trying to recollect my steps from earlier, and remember the pathway that Thomas led me down. I rounded the staircase, descending the stairs until I reached the bottom.

I stopped for a moment and looked around. It was quiet, as if there was nobody in this house or around it for miles on end.

I saw Thomas's car through the window. He was still here. I found the kitchen, grabbed a knife, after practically walking on my tiptoes, and went out the back door. I saw him hunched over, headphones in, working on something by the shed.

His back was to me, and as if all my adrenaline kicked in, I started running. The field looked like it went on for miles, and even though I had no idea if this was the right way, I didn't care.

I needed to get the hell out and away from this house and Thomas, regardless if I got lost or not.

I ran and ran, and it wasn't thirty seconds before I heard Thomas's familiar shrieking behind me. I continued the sprints but turned my head for a split second.

Sure enough, Thomas was heading in my direction at a full sprint, face red and angry.

I hadn't noticed the pistol loaded on his hip earlier, and I had to force myself to push the fear out of my heart.

There was no place for fear right now.

Only survival.

Soon, I found myself entered into a wide patch of forestry, and the brush became thick and wide.

I had trouble keeping the same pace especially with all of the branches and bushes in my way.

I could hear Thomas quickly getting closer and closer. I looked around and saw not a single patch that would allow me a good place to hide.

So, I looked up.

I was a notorious tree climber as a kid, as I had always loved the outdoors. That was partly why I enjoyed our lake spot so much. It was home.

Enough reminiscing. Climb.

I took the knife I was wielding in my hand and stuck it in my belt. I put one hand in front of the other and followed suit with my feet. The tree had to be at least forty feet tall, and I was nearly to the top when I heard Thomas right below me.

"Riley…c'mon. You can't seriously think you'll get away, can you?" He followed that with whistling that sent a chill down my spine.

He walked around in circles before leaning against a tree opposite me.

Don't look up. Don't look up.

My foot slipped and I hit a small branch, snapping it right off the tree.

It dropped all the way down, and I watched it almost in slow motion as it landed five feet in front of Thomas.

His head whipped up, and a wicked gleam spread on his face.

"Gotcha."

29

Cora

I figured as much we were probably on day two...or three... of being in the hospital, but as you know it can be quite hard to keep track of time.

The tidbits I had been hearing were positive, which in turn made me feel positive. I heard an update on Allie from Riley's dad.

He clearly wasn't speaking to me. In fact, he was talking to my mother and I like always, overheard the entire thing.

She showed up at work. I guess she had been looking for Riley the night she didn't show, and I completely understood.

If I wasn't stuck in this bed, that was exactly what I would be doing. I would start by looking in her boyfriend's direction. I knew with certainty that he was the one to take Riley, and I would nail his ass to the wall the minute they woke me up.

Which apparently would be today.

I heard the doctor come in a little while ago, and my mother screamed with joy. I knew it was good news, and I don't know if it was because she knew I could hear, or simply hoped, but she leaned down into my ear and whispered,
"They're going to wake you up baby."

I practically screamed for joy, and while I couldn't very well do that, I did it mentally and it wasn't nearly as satisfying.

You win some, you lose some.

I mulled over the idea of going straight to the cops when I woke up. I could tell them everything I knew about Officer Brooks.

I didn't see his face that night, but if I lied, then they would have all the proof they needed to go after him. Lying may be wrong, but last I checked- so is kidnapping and murder.

I knew the loyalty in that police department ran deep, and I needed to have solid evidence to back up my claims, or I feared they may not be thoroughly investigated.

I didn't understand the entire medical process that went into waking someone up from a coma, but I heard the nurse, or doctor, I wasn't really sure if we're being honest, at my bedside all day fiddling with the damn monitors.

I could slowly feel my consciousness coming more into focus. I could hear just a tad bit louder, and the brightness of the ceiling lights was peeking through my eyes.

Then all at once, it was as if a huge weight lifted on the entirety of my body, leaving me feeling weightless.

I tried opening my eyes, and I must have been making progress, because my mom started yelling. "C'mon, Cora! Open your eyes!"

So, I did.

The brightness of the room became overwhelming and slightly painful to look at.

I tried to find my voice, but it was a low volume at best.

"Mom...lights...off. Please."

She turned around immediately and feverishly scrambled to the light switch as if it were a hose, and I was on fire.

My heart swelled. My mom. I can't even begin to imagine the absolute hell she went through.

She grabbed a cup of water and held it to my incredibly dry lips. I was so thirsty.

I grabbed the edge of the cup and threw it back like it was nothing. The cool water felt like butter going down my throat, and I was grateful beyond measure for my mom and the comfort she provided in those moments.

My comfort was further provided when I saw Allie glide through the doors.

"Allie...I'm glad you made it." I attempted a smile.

"Please! I'm glad you're okay. You are okay, aren't you?" She hugged my mom, and then took a seat on the edge of my bed, grabbing my hand.

God, I need to find Riley.

It didn't make sense how I could feel so comforted, and have such a full heart in this moment, but still feel so empty.

I had to find Riley.

And as much as it would suck, I needed to tell Allie the truth about the man she was dating.

"Mom, can you see if they have some Jell-O down there?" I feigned a super sweet smile, and it seemed to work like a charm.

"Sure honey, I'll be right back." She patted my leg and walked out of the door.

I looked at Allie, who now had a very confused expression cased all over her face.

"You hate Jell-O. What's going on?"

"I have to talk to you about Officer Brooks." I had no idea how I would do this, but I knew I had to protect my friend.

She deserved to know the truth first, before she heard it from anyone else, especially after I called the police over here.

"I don't understand." She pulled back an inch like I had offended her.

"He took Riley. He was behind everything, including the note at the restaurant. I am so incredibly sorry. I didn't want to be right about this, but I am. I don't want you to put yourself in danger, so I wanted to tell you the truth."

I closed my mouth and braced for it. What I was bracing for exactly… I had no clue. I was expecting sadness, anger, maybe confusion, but not what I got.

She… laughed. Laughed right in my face. "What's funny?" I looked at her dead in the eye, but she continued cackling.

"You. Thinking you got it all figured out. I hate to break it to you, but just like your friend Riley, you know a small piece of the story. See, I thought I would come here, and find you confused but you seem like you want to stir up some trouble. We can't have that."

She got up and left, without a goodbye, and without an explanation.

What the hell does that even mean? Is Allie in on this whole thing or just delusional? Does she think that I made this up, or am trying to frame Thomas?

It didn't matter, because I was sure as hell not getting any answers out of her.

My mom came into the room carrying not one, but three lime Jell-O's.

Oh joy.

I didn't know what to do about Allie, but her abrupt exit left me wanting answers. I texted her.

Cora: Look, I'm sorry if I upset you. I just wanted to tell you before I went to the police.

My message came in thirty seconds later.

Allie: Talk to the cops, and Riley is dead.

I dropped my phone.
Not stupid, not delusional.
Allie is in on it.

30

Taylor

These people were giving me a migraine. So righteous. They pretend to care about one another, when really, it's a load of bull.

It was honestly quite a risky move to show up at the hospital like I did, but I had to see Cora for myself. I guess Thomas didn't do a very good job, and now she's a loose end.

I enjoyed having her as a friend, but if I have learned anything in my short span on this Earth, it's that nothing lasts forever. Nor, should it.

I half expected to see my father at the hospital. From the stories I heard from both Daisy and Riley, he was not only a doting father on them, but a surrogate one for Cora as well.

I don't know if that made me more angry or sad. Probably both.

Seems like he can be daddy of the year to all but me.

I never expected much of him, and after all he and my so-called mother have put me through, I never will. I was finally regaining some sense of control in my dismal life, and things were beginning to look up.

I held all the power right now. I had power over whether Riley lived or died, and Cora… well, Cora could be easily dealt with as well.

I had been toying with the idea of Cora's fate ever since I heard she had not only been hospitalized but put into a medically induced coma.

Did she get to live? Die? At this point, I felt she may have already known a bit too much. That factored into my decision to visit the hospital today. I wanted to see for myself where Cora's head was at, and gauge just how much she really knew.
Or thought she knew.

When she immediately pulled me into a conversation about my oh, so horrible boyfriend, I knew she knew too much. She was digging deeper and deeper into history she had no business in. She already had her sights set on Thomas, and it was only a matter of time before she realized that I was not only a loving girlfriend, but the puppeteer behind it all.

I sent a text off to Thomas a few minutes ago, requesting the status report of our lovely little captive, my dear sister.

Nothing yet, but Thomas was never one to fawn over technology. I'm sure he has his device charging, or better yet, on silent.

Nevertheless, Cora knew to stay silent. My work there was done…for now. Now, all I had to do was go home to my loving boyfriend, and bonus- I could squeeze in some family time. That was one of the perks of having your sister at your disposable twenty-four-seven.

I sent one more text to Thomas letting him know that I was on my way home.

I climbed into my car and started the engine. As it was warming up, I continued to check my phone. Why was Thomas AWOL?

And why was I overreacting? Like I said, he was never big on technology.

I threw my phone into my backseat as a way to distract myself from hopelessly refreshing my messages. I was a mess. I needed to regain my clear head, so I could properly focus on the endless tasks at hand.

The drive was quick, and that could be attributed to the fact that I was going fifteen miles over the speed limit.

A girl's gotta do what a girl's gotta do.

I parked my car, and forced myself to walk, not run, to the front door.

It was quiet, but that was to be expected. I stuck my key into the lock but felt no resistance. Unlocked… weird. Thomas made it a point to never leave the door unlocked but that may actually be my fault.

I walked in.

"Thomas? I'm here. I don't think you saw your phone."

I dropped my purse and keys by the front door on top of a tabletop.

Nothing.

"Thomas?"

I started to search the ground floor for him and found nothing. I looked in the kitchen and found a half-eaten sandwich.

What the fuck is going on?

I suddenly got a gut wrenching feeling that something was horribly wrong, and I sprinted up the stairs faster than any Olympian ever could have.

Just what I thought.

The door to the room we kept Riley in was wide open, and upon further inspection, she was nowhere in there. I stepped inside and looked around. It was very clear to me how she made her big escape. The dismantled iron wrought bed frame gave it away.

The only solace I found in this moment, was brought to me by the idea that the reason Thomas was gone was because he was out collecting her, and that the idiot hadn't lost her for God's sake.

I ran down the stairs, and out the back door. I would hate to think that they made it as far as the woods, but I never knew when it came to Thomas.

I slowed my pace down to a fast walk and continued on my way.

Why did I ever shack up with a dumb cop anyhow?

Validation, daddy issues… quite frankly the list could go on and on.

I heard screaming and did a quick transition back into a sprint. It wasn't long before the screaming grew louder, and louder. It was crystal clear that this was a girl's scream, without a doubt.

Thomas soon came into view, with a gun on his hip, and he was looking up.
"Thomas!"

His head shot towards me, and he began to take large strides towards me.
"I'm so sorry, she got out. But don't worry, I got her now." He rubbed my arms, an obvious attempt to console me.
"Where?"
"Right there." He motioned upwards to an empty tree.
"So, she's Tarzan now? No really, where is she?"

His head snapped up at the empty tree, then around, and back at me- eyes wide with alarm.
You have got to be kidding me.

We heard branches snapping and I looked to the side just in time to catch a glimpse of red hair.
"Over there!"

Thomas ran off in the direction I motioned towards. I decided to head straight in case she tried to cut across and confuse us.
"Thomas… don't shoot!"
"Okay!" His voice was slightly broken, as if he was incredibly far away in such a short period of time.
Those police training camps did pay off.

I still had on my work pants and shoes, and quite frankly I wasn't in the mood for a rendezvous through the woods.

I didn't want Thomas to shoot Riley. She would be of great use to me in the near future. With Cora now informed of where she stood, and where her place was, I needed to get Riley to fall in line.

We shared the same DNA, and I don't know why, even after meeting Daisy, that I thought she wouldn't also share the same fire within her that both Daisy and I possessed.

Nevertheless, while this fire was admired, it wasn't appreciated or needed. We had a task at hand, and Riley was the key to accomplishing everything I had been planning for years.

It wasn't until today as I was sitting in the hospital bed with Cora, listening to her drone on and on about what an awful monster Thomas is- that I finally chose how this all would end.

I had my own plan, one that would better suit me and my future than any of the previously concocted ones.

The only obstacle I faced in this moment was finding Riley… and keeping the damn cops off of our trail.

Interesting to me that my own father couldn't have been more unbothered with news of my escape from the psychiatric facility, if they even told him, and here he was day and night searching for his "golden child".

Anything brought down onto Riley at this point was all her own doing. She was too nosy for her own good, much like Daisy.

Soon enough, she would meet the same fate. "I got her!" I heard Thomas yell in triumph, and I stood in silence basking in the small yet monumental victory.

That could have ended very differently.

I continued my slow walk towards the two, when they slowly came into my eye view. Riley was laying flat against the dirt, Thomas kneeled down with his knee digging into her back as he held her hands together.

Luckily for us, he was a cop, and always had a spare pair of handcuffs on him. He hooked her hands together, pulling her up, and then shoved her towards me.

The shove sent her stumbling, but she was able to find her footing as I grabbed the back of the handcuffs leading her back to the house.

"You're becoming a lot more trouble than I think you're worth, sis." I made sure to say the last word with contempt dripping from my voice.

"Nice to see you again. Tell me, was your hair always so disgusting? Is the blonde hair the reason our villainous parents didn't want you? Or was it simply the shining personality they couldn't handle?"

Part of me felt like I had been slapped, part of me felt like I could kill her in that moment, and that last bit- the tiniest one of all, was impressed.

"The hair? A wig." I grabbed a hold of the top seam and yanked the blonde wig off of my head.

She was right, the wig was nasty. I had to buy it from a cheap hair place, but it was the best I could do on short notice, and short funds.

My sister wasn't the only one shocked when I pulled off the wig, exposing my similar luscious red locks underneath.

Thomas gave an appreciative glance, and Riley let out an audible gasp.
"Triplets... did you really think we wouldn't have the same hair?"

We reached the back door, and I opened it wide before shoving Riley through it. This time, she actually fell to her knees after stumbling, and I had to stifle a laugh.

Naturally, I wasn't this cruel. But to be fair, it had been a rather trying day, and I wasn't in the mood to deal with anything crazy. Riley escaping fit into the lines of crazy, and I felt myself growing more and more irate.

Not only with her, but with Thomas.

I escorted Riley all the way back up the stairs and fastened her yet again to the now fixed bed frame. I had Thomas reinforce it before I re-attached her, and she had little to no hope of being able to maneuver herself out of it again.

I locked the door behind me, a measure we had not taken earlier- but one that was absolutely necessary at this point.

I headed into the kitchen to fix myself something to eat, starved after the wide range of festivities I faced today.

Thomas came into the kitchen behind me, sliding his hand across my waist and planting a kiss on my cheek.

Dumbass.

I pulled away, anger clear on my face. "What?" He stepped back and eyed me up and down. "You seriously let her almost escape Thomas. We wouldn't have been able to explain that away. Why weren't you more careful?" I practically shouted, fully aware that Riley could probably hear.

"How am I supposed to know that she would break through the bedframe? Get real Taylor." He now seemed irritated with me, which would have been hilarious if it wasn't so damn infuriating.

Knowing I wouldn't be able to reason some sense into him regarding the subject, I decided to drop it and focus on the chicken I was about to burn.

"Cora didn't accept your warning. So, I made sure she heard me loud and clear." I turned and gave a half smile to Thomas who was still sulking from my earlier outburst.

"What do you mean?" He looked confused, an emotion that wasn't foreign to him.

"Don't worry about it… you hungry?" I offered him a plate of the charred chicken, and he graciously accepted.

Dinner was eaten in silence that night, and Thomas did the dishes following as it was our deal we made when we moved in here.

The place was definitely a fixer upper, but we had managed to start making it look better already- on the ground level at least.

It was kind of hard to do home renovations when you were killing family members, working part-time, and kidnapping other family members.

Truly, I found it exhausting to be me. Fortunately, if everything went to plan, I would soon not have a care in the world.

It was just such a shame that Thomas had to take the fall, but we all have to make sacrifices.

Right?

I know, I sound awful. Thomas has been there for me in more ways than one, and a lot of the time, I feel like he is the only person I can count on in this world.

But if today shows anything, it's that I can't. The only person I can count on is myself, and clearly when I leave my fate to other people, I can soon find myself in some very deep water.

So, from now on, I will be handling all my business myself. I would see to it that Thomas be given as light a workload as possible, ensuring that there are no more slip ups to come in the future.

"Taylor, I'm going to bed. You coming?"

"I'm not tired. I'll meet you in there later," I stood up and planted a sweet kiss on his lips.

I needed to think.

He retreated into the newly remodeled bedroom, and I took a seat on the couch watching as the fireplace lit with flames of orange and yellow embers.

I became lost in thought, consumed with the history of the past few months.

From escaping, to planning to meet Daisy, and to the whirlwind I found myself in now- it was a lot.

However, I knew my common working goal would prove to be worth all the obstacles and challenges I faced and overcame on the way there.

As much as I did care for Thomas, I knew that it was only a matter of time before they either found Riley or began to look in this direction.

If the latter happened, I had no plans to be caught in that sure crossfire. I did talk to Cora today, and I know that bought us some silence, but not for long.

Her and Riley aren't friends because they share similar taste in shoes. They are both stubborn to a fault, and fearlessly courageous. That sounded good and all, but in this moment in time it was the one personality trait I wished would go away.

No. This would all go up in flames soon enough, and I had no plans to kill Riley yet. There was still so much to be done.

Someone needed to be the scapegoat for all of this, and if it had to be Thomas, then so be it.

I hadn't worked this hard, planned this much, and come this far to let a summer romance derail all of that. He may have slightly more impact in my life then a summer romance but having the childhood I did- I have always found it easy to let go of people.

Thomas was going to take the fall for this.

I just had to make a plan.

31

Riley

I failed.

The words rang through my head on a repetitive loop for the remainder of the day. I, however, knew the truth.

Of course, I couldn't escape. I had never been in those woods before, let alone try to navigate through them. This escape was planned, and it proved most useful.

While I wasn't able to get as far as I would have wanted, I got deep enough in that I am sure I knew which way to take when I got out again. However, I also knew of a few good hiding spots that I scoped out.

Taylor, Allie, whatever her name was, and Officer Brooks may have thought that today meant they won- that they were in control, but it couldn't be further from the truth.

I could hear them arguing from my chained place in the room, and it gave me an overwhelming sense of satisfaction. My sister, if she really was that, wasn't exactly as smart as she thought she was.

She was an idiot, and this plan to take me felt very much like the opposite of that. It felt rushed, and far from planned. She would make a mistake eventually, and either I would be discovered, or I will have already escaped on my own by then.

Her boyfriend is not the brightest crayon in the box either. It was his idle and inattentive behavior that allowed me my first escape, and there wouldn't be a third. I would get out of here, mark my words.

While there was enough commotion going on in this house to last my brain a lifetime of thought, I couldn't help but allow my mind to be with Cora all day.

The unknown was killing me. I was sure that either Taylor or her boyfriend knew some type of news concerning Cora and whether she was okay or not. In fact, I had no doubt that they kept themselves very well informed on matters of the outside world especially at this very sensitive point in time.

I wouldn't dare ask them about Cora, as the level of satisfaction it would bring both of them was far too discouraging. No. Instead, I allowed my idled mind to wander, ravaging with thoughts of the worst possible scenarios.

It feels like a lifetime since this all occurred, and while I couldn't be sure, I think it had only been a couple of days. Minutes felt like hours in this place, and so my stay here felt like months.

I knew in my heart that it rang true for my parents as well, and it hurt my heart immensely to imagine the personal form of hell they were going through right now- especially my mother who took Daisy's death hard.

Unfortunately, I could do nothing to calm down my loved ones, and the best thing for them and myself right now was to strategize a way out of here. I knew better than to assume that I could get out of here using the same tactic as before. The bed frame was not only fixed, but I assumed they were smart enough to reinforce it.

Can't hurt to try.

Sure enough, a slight tug of the cuffs revealed what I already knew.

I heard footsteps ascending the staircase, and I played a fun little game of who's going to fuck with me today?

The door swung open.

Taylor.

She strode in, carrying a plate of bacon, eggs, and French toast.

The smell alone practically had my nose caving in on itself, and I could feel myself salivating. "Want some?" She offered a strip of bacon to me, and I knew it was a test.

I shrugged my shoulders, trying to attempt to look as unbothered as possible, but it was really hard.

"Hm. More for me then." She took a seat at the very same wall spot where her boyfriend revealed her "life history" to me not to long ago.

She continued to eat the remainder of the plate painfully slow, in a chorus of silence.

What point she was trying to prove… I didn't really know. It probably had almost everything to do with her wanting desperately to prove she still had all the power.

Yeah, that was most likely it.

Once she finished her meal, she popped each one of her fingers in her mouth, sucking and then followed it with a, "Mmm-mm!"

"You really should have had some Riley… I am such a good cook." She gave me a sinister smile, and I wished more than anything that I wasn't handcuffed.

"Tell me again how we are related. How am I supposed to believe you're not some psycho who created this false story?"

"You don't believe me? Fine." She stood up abruptly, leaving the room and taking the tray of emptiness with her.

Now I was alone and starving. The truth is, I had toyed with the idea of her being some weirdo who met my sister, became infatuated with her and our family, and concocted this off-the-wall story about being the triplet, and whatever else bullshit she spewed.

I couldn't even bring myself to consider that her story might be true.

Why would I be here, and not my parents who are apparently the devil incarnates?

She strode back in, smile plastered all over her face, breaking me from my chain of thought.

She tossed a photograph into my lap.

I looked at it, and it was my parents, much younger and grinning from ear to ear. My dad had two babies in his arms, and my mother… had one.

Three babies.

"Believe me now?"

"This doesn't prove you're my sister." I tried to get her to give me hard proof, even though I knew it in my heart.

She bent down, pulling keys from her pocket and began to unlock me.

What the hell?

"I'm letting you go. I know you're smart enough to keep your mouth shut. But there is one condition, you owe me." She stood back as I tried to pull myself up.

"Owe you what?"

She pressed a burner phone into my palm.

"I'll let you know."

32

Cora

I was home- in my bed. However, I didn't feel any safer. My run in with Allie yesterday threw me for a loop. It only gave me that many more questions. I felt in my gut that there may be tons more to this story, but I sure as hell was not going to get answers from Allie.

My mom shouted downstairs.
"What is it mom?"

I heard her footsteps thundering up the steps before she threw open my bedroom door, letting it slam against the wall.
"Riley is SAFE. Thank you, God!" She threw her hands up and ran towards me before enveloping me in a huge hug.
Riley's safe? Oh my god.

I felt as if the weight that had been heavy on my body was finally relieved. I felt weightless, ecstatic and immensely relieved. My best friend was okay. I was okay.

We would all be okay.

But what happened with Allie? Did she ever even have Riley, or just covering for her boyfriend?

I needed to see Riley.

"Where is she?!" I practically screamed at my mom, who had still not wiped the gigantic grin off her face.

We both loved Riley.

"She's with her mom and dad at the hospital being examined. Apparently, she was spotted walking down some road, alone, and without any identification. But I already spoke to her father, and we can visit when she's home."

My mom turned and left my room. I couldn't sit still and could feel myself practically twitching. I was antsy, and it could all be chalked up to the crazy amount of questions and ideas floating around in my head.

I was so glad that Riley was safe, and now I just needed to figure out if she would remain safe, or if Allie and her boyfriend were still threats. If they were, if I had so much of an inkling that they were still up to something, I would take both of them out.

I had always been a pretty good schemer growing up, and no one could orchestrate a take-down better than me, especially if my best friend had been hurt by somebody.

Allie needs to watch her back.

I decided that I needed to at least attempt to dress in appropriate clothes, since there would be a reunion today. I stood up slowly, just like the doctor instructed, and walked even slower to my bathroom.

I switched on the shower and climbed in under the still cold stream. I felt the temperature slowly rise, and I began washing my face.

I don't know what it was about hospitals that made me insanely itchy and skeeved out. Truth be told, while they did hold a lot of sick and dying people, they were incredibly sanitized. However, I felt dirty.

Once I felt clean enough, I stepped out and sat on the toilet seat while I dried myself. I pulled on my plush rose robe and walked into my closet to pick out some clothes.

I was feeling slightly lazy, so I settled on my favorite pair of leggings, complete with an oversized navy sweater. I brushed my hair back and pulled out my blow dryer. Today was one of those rare days I felt grateful for having thin hair.

It took me all of five minutes to dry my hair. I didn't have it in me to style it, so I simply threw it into an updo. I pulled on my black combat boots and a white scarf to complete the look.

I stood in front of my mirror to survey the look.

Yeah, you look perfect. Mentally stable and all.

I pushed the negative thoughts off to be worried about at another time.

"Cora! She's home!"

"Coming!" I grabbed my things, took one last look at my room, and headed downstairs.

I was a bundle of nerves the entire car ride over to Riley's house. My palms were sweating, and I tried to compose my thoughts.

What would I say? What would I ask first?

Did I want to know?

I had no time at all to figure it out, because just then my mother pulled into an all too familiar driveway. Riley's dad was standing by the front door, waiting for us with a big cheesy grin plastered all over his face.

Here goes nothing.

"So glad you guys could come. If I'm being honest, I feel like Riley could really use the company right now. She hasn't said two words to her mother and me since she has been home." Her dad shook his head sadly and guided my mother and I through the large front door.

The mood in the house was tense, awkward, and a million other adjectives I was having trouble choosing. Riley was sitting in the armchair facing the television. The tv was showing one of her favorite programs, but the mute button must have been on.

Nevertheless, she seemed content in her little bubble, not talking to anybody. She didn't even turn her head when we walked in.

Riley's dad pulled my mom and Riley's mom into the kitchen, probably for what I'm assuming is some plan of intervention.

Riley was probably in shock, and knowing her, I knew full well that sometimes she didn't feel fully comfortable opening up to her parents, especially now.

I walked over to the couch that sat opposite the chair. I put my arm on Riley's leg. She flinched and looked at me wide eyed.

"Cora!" She grabbed me and embraced me in the best hug I have ever had in my entire life.

I'm so glad you're okay.

"Are you okay Riley?" I guess I decided that that would be the first question I asked. Okay. Let's go with it.

"Yeah, I'm fine. Are you? I remember you getting hit." She looked sad and turned her head to the side.

I took a beat to survey my best friend. She seemed okay, or at least that was the face she tried to put on for the rest of the world but by now I knew better.

The girl I was staring at was a shell of the Riley I knew and loved. She had been through something, and for whatever reason did not seem comfortable sharing it with anyone, especially me and we were best friends.

"I'm fine. They put me in a medically induced coma and weened me out of it when the swelling in my brain went down. What about you though?"

A small tear rolled down her cheek. She squeezed my hand hard.

"I'm so sorry Cora. I never wanted anything to happen to you. I'm okay. I don't really remember much of what happened."

"It was Allie and her boyfriend, Riley. They both visited while I was in the hospital." I looked at my friend, who apparently seemed startled by this revelation.

A phone beeped, and she pulled a cellphone out of her back pocket- one I didn't recognize.

"It wasn't them. Why would you say that? I know Allie, and I didn't see her- not once. I didn't see Officer Brooks either. It was a woman, and she was masked the entire time." She shook her head at me.

"But I heard them. He threatened me." I was surprised at her ignorance in this situation. I was never one for tall tales, and she knew that.

"Well you went through some trauma. I doubt you were really able to remember things correctly." She stood up abruptly and turned to walk away.

"New phone, Riley?" I pointed to the cell phone, clenched tightly in her hand.

"Hmm. Thanks for coming. Glad you are feeling better." She turned and walked out of the room, leaving me confused and angry in her wake.

Just then, my mom emerged from the kitchen followed by Riley's mom, and then her dad.

"Hey, where's Riley?" My mom walked towards me, looking around for my friend.

"Tired. She went to her room. Can we go Mom? I am a little hungry."

"Sure thing, hon."

My mom and I both said our goodbyes to all but Riley who was camped out in her room.

She went through something, and I couldn't figure out what is was especially since she swore adamantly that it wasn't Allie or her boyfriend.

Whatever happened to my best friend had changed her, and not for the better. I still had so many questions, and the sight of my best friend only brought more confusion into the already scattered mix.

What happened to my friend… and how could I bring her back?

The car ride home was a long period of silence, and I think my mother understood I wasn't in any mood to talk. She respected that, and that was something that I loved about her. She knew and respected boundaries, and it allowed for us to have a much better relationship.

Plus, I was sure without a doubt that Riley's parents filled her in on Riley's progress and how detached she really was.

What was up with that phone? It reminded me slightly of the phones your parents got you at 12 years old with the prepaid minutes. That was the phone you got before you hit the stage of actually having a phone.

And why was she so secretive about it? When did she have time to get a new phone?

God, I felt like my head was practically about to burst.

"Hey, I know you don't feel like talking right now, but I am here for you. Always." My mom had parked the car in our driveway, touching my shoulder and gently pulling me out of my head fog.

I didn't really want to talk, so I simply nodded my head letting my mother knew I understood. The sentiment was genuine, and while appreciated, I needed time to process and sort everything.

I went straight to my room and grabbed my old notebook out from a drawer. I flipped it to a blank page and grabbed a pen.

I wrote Thomas's name. I put an arrow and added Allie's name. On the arrow, I put dating. With another arrow stemming from Thomas's name, I put "threatened in hospital". Okay, so he knew something. Either he was in on it or helped the person who was. That is a sure-fire thing, but him being simply an accomplice could explain why Riley claims she didn't see him.

I looked over at the other name. Allie. She texted me that day saying that if I mentioned anything, Riley was dead.

Again, Riley claims that she never saw her either. Riley also was let go. So maybe, Allie knows what happened as well. Maybe she's just an accomplice.

I still couldn't even begin to understand why Allie would be a part of anything like this.

Cause she's an asshole?

I haven't known her long by any means, but I never got the feeling that she was anything other than a sweet girl.

Goes to show how good of a judge of character you are.

Ugh.

Moving on from Allie for now, I wrote Riley's name.

An arrow- "weird behavior". Was that really a notable trait, or simply a biproduct of all she has been through?

Is she merely trying to piece together the events of what happened in her own way, or trying to cover up something?

This was all one gigantic cluster fuck, and one that my best friend would provide no use on.

I had to look into Allie. She was the one link in the entire thing that I was sure played some sort of major role. She flipped the switch too quickly at the hospital, and I wasn't even interrogating her.

She has got something to hide, and I sure as hell am going to figure out what it is.

I grabbed my keys and headed out the door without another word to my mother.

I jumped into my car, not even allowing the engine one minute to warm up before I peeled out of the driveway.

I needed to get away from the house, away from everything. I couldn't stand to sit there one more minute. It was not very loud there, but I knew just a place that had an overwhelming sense of tranquility and peace.

The lake.

Maybe it would allow me some insight into this situation.

The police weren't even doing that much. From what my mom had told me, Riley didn't remember that much, and wasn't saying much so it is being put on the back burner for now.

Some officers even feel that she may have ran away all on her own.

Real bright, those ones.

How would that little theory even begin to explain myself? I didn't hurt myself, and it sure wasn't my best friend.

After seeing just how crooked Officer Brooks was, I had little to no faith in our lovely police department.

I arrived at the lake and decided to send a text to my mother who was already blowing up my phone.

Cora: I'm sorry. Needed air. At the lake.

Mom: Okay, I love you. Be safe.

I knew my cell phone signal was bound to cut out any minute, so I had to assure her I was safe first. She tends to be a worry wart, and after my exit... well, let's just say I wouldn't blame her.

As I walked through the woods, and felt the familiar snaps of twigs beneath my feet, I felt that sense of calm I was hoping for slowly start to creep its way in.

The lake was sparkling in the sun, as it was almost about to set. Another hour or so, tops.

I stopped dead in my tracks when I spotted somebody sitting on my dock with their feet hanging into the water.

I would know that red hair anywhere.

Riley.

I started again towards the lake, seeing this as a wonderful opportunity to talk to my friend without the pressures of anyone else around. It was clear to me earlier that whatever it is she is going through… she is struggling, and I want to help.

She was standing up and drying her feet with a towel.

Oh, she was leaving.

What the hell?

Allie. That's not Riley.

Jesus. They could pass for…sisters.

I stopped, leaning against a tree and trying to reign in my breathing. They looked too similar for it to be a coincidence.

Allie reached down to put the towel into a duffel bag and removed a blonde wig.

Holy shit.

My heart started to race, and I reached into my back pocket scrambling to get my phone out in time.

I opened the camera, looked up, but it was too late. She had the wig on, the duffle bag slung over her shoulder, and was slowly walking up the dock to where I was at.

I sprinted to the left, taking cover behind a slightly large tree trunk. She was only ten feet away max, but I couldn't risk her seeing me. I stayed where I was, praying with everything in me.

As if the universe was listening, she walked by, completely unaware.

What is going on?

I came to the lake so I could find some sense of clarity, and by all means, it seems like I found some indeed.

Allie looked like a carbon copy of Riley and Daisy. I had never noticed the similar facial features before, but her bright blonde hair didn't do her face much justice.

Pieces of the puzzle were starting to come together. If they were related, it could explain Allie's role in all of this. It maybe explains why her boyfriend would take Riley, and why Riley was distancing herself from everyone.

She was probably reeling from the news.

Oh god, I needed to find my friend.

I tried to take a step backwards slowly, making sure to stomp right on a thick fallen branch. The snap was deafening, and Allie made sure to turn around.

She looked around for a split second before hyper focusing on the area I was hiding out in. It wasn't a minute later that she was continuing on full speed ahead right towards me.

I had to get out of here.

The bushes were thick enough to hide the pathway to the water, but the other side was right out in the open. I got on all fours and crawled as fast as I could. I ditched my keys and phone in the last bush, knowing full well I couldn't get them wet.

Before I knew it, I was right at the edge of the lake, and had to do the only thing I knew how.

I slipped into the lake as quietly as I could.

Still underwater, I swam further and further towards the dead center. I figured I had a better chance of getting away from her the more distance I put between us.

When I finally felt like my lungs were on fire, I slowly raised my head and body above the water. Allie was no longer in the area but gone.

I figured she probably decided to head back to her car, and I breathed an audible sigh of relief.

Now I was wet, had more questions than before, and a revelation that I wasn't even sure if Riley knew about.

Was I even right? Was this possible? Was it logical?

I pulled myself up and onto the dock. With absolutely nothing to dry myself off with, I simply started shaking like a wet dog.

The act itself made me laugh, and it was one that made my stomach hurt from laughing too hard. I sauntered over to the bush to retrieve my phone and car keys.

My walk back to my car allowed me some head space to properly piece all the scattered events into a timeline.

Fact: Riley had been weird since she returned.

Fact: Officer Brooks threatened me.

Fact: So did Allie.

Fact: I was lost.

Maybe this was the key to why Riley had been acting so different since she had been found. She discovered something that she clearly didn't feel comfortable sharing with myself or anybody, and after seeing what I saw- I couldn't exactly blame her.

I started to compose a text to Riley. I was never a fan of the long text messages that seemed to drone on and on. No, this was something that would be better suited for a proper face to face conversation.

Cora: Riles, could we talk? Miss you.

No answer. She was probably resting. Hell, I would be.

You wouldn't be in this mess to begin with.

No, I wouldn't, because I'm not the girl who gets taken- but rather the one who gets a medically induced coma.

I just wanted to be there for Riley- that was it.

If only she would let you.

Wouldn't that be a dream?

I kept checking my phone constantly throughout the duration of my slow-paced walk. I tried to tell myself that it was no big deal, but seeing Allie, or whatever her name was, blew my fucking mind.

I had to tell someone, or the very least talk to Riley about it, and soon because I felt like my head was going to explode.

"Well, well, well... couldn't stay away?" Click.

Familiar voice, followed by an unfamiliar sound.

Allie.

I turned to my right to find Allie leaned up against an old tree, gun in hand.

Funnily enough it wasn't pointed at me.

Rather, it was hanging loosely in her hand, idly pointed at the ground.

She doesn't want to hurt you. Play it cool.

That was kind of hard to do when she was swinging around a loaded weapon like it was nothing. "Allie... what's going on?" I tried my best to make my voice sound incredibly confident, but the look that passed over Allie's smug face made me think I fell short.

"C'mon, you can't think that I didn't see you. Crawling? Standing up and running full speed into the water would have been less obvious." She chuckled and slid into a sitting position on the floor.

She motioned with the gun for me to do the same, and soon enough we were both sitting on the forest floor staring at each other.

"Who are you?" I asked the question that laid the most heavily on my mind.

To my surprise, Allie didn't even flinch. She was expecting that question, although I don't know how she wouldn't have especially given her appearance. She was a carbon copy of my best friends that I knew and love, only without the kind exterior… clearly.

"I think you know." She motioned over her body from head to toe as if it was an obvious answer.

It didn't take a Brainiac to piece together who Allie was. I just wanted to know the full story, because it made zero sense.

All my life, I knew twins- Daisy and Riley. They were my best friends, and there was never anyone else.

If this girl- Allie, really was their sister, then where in the hell had she been?

"Well you could be Riley and Daisy's sister. Are you?"

"In the flesh, darling." She cocked a sly smile and stared out at the sparkling lake.

"I don't understand."

"Well, and why would you? To be honest, its quite a long and dull story about a girl who was abused by her parents and treated like garbage while they put their other two children on pedestals." She scoffed at my ignorance.

That story didn't add up. I know Riley's parents. I have all my life. The people I know weren't capable of what Allie was saying. I knew it in my heart, and I knew it in my bones.

"You're full of shit." I moved to stand up.

I wasn't going to give in to these lies. I wanted to find my friend and get the real truth, not this spider web of lies constructed by Allie and her lunatic boyfriend no doubt.

"Sit… down. Remember when I told you to stay out of it? To drop it? You seem to have a knack for sticking your nose in where it doesn't belong. This is a family matter, and last I checked… you weren't family." She finally rose the gun and had it pointed right at me.

Stay. Calm.

I sat back down, frozen, unable to move or speak coherently. Instead, I waited, watching, and patiently wanting Allie to speak. To explain. To tell the TRUTH.

"So, tell me… the whole story."

33

Riley

It hurt pushing away my best friend, who for days I prayed to see again.

But it had to be done.

It was nothing that Taylor instructed me to do, but something I felt in my heart would be the better path in the end.

I loved Cora with every fiber in my being, and in my heart and soul, she was as much my sister as Daisy was and she always will be.

But I'm worried about what Taylor will want me to do. My freedom came with a price, and I may not know what exactly that it is, but I know it's not good... and I don't want my best friend anywhere near it.

I had a slight upper hand.

I could go to the cops right now and blow this whole plan up. I could tell my parents, have Taylor thrown back into the loony bin and life would resume as usual.

That's what a normal, sane person would do.

But I didn't feel normal or sane right now.

In fact, I felt angry, livid even.

My kidnapping had revealed an influx of new information that has apparently been kept from me my whole life. My parents had done horrible, unspeakable things to their own daughter.

They were things that I feared I may never forgive them for.

I felt sorry for Taylor, and all that she had endured at the hands of the two people who gave her life.

But Daisy… she didn't deserve what happened to her.

Daisy was a big ball of energy, light, and all that was good and right with the world.

Taylor made me believe that she took Daisy's life from her due to the fact that Daisy found out who she was.

But I knew who she was, and I was still alive. I was free, if I could even be considered free.

I was metaphorically chained to a cell phone that would undoubtedly have very real consequences should I choose to not obey.

Daisy and I both knew Taylors secret. We both knew who she was.

So why was only one of us alive?

That's what I needed to find out. What did I have that was so useful to my illegitimate sister that she would allow me a pass she didn't also offer to Daisy?

I had something she needed, and once I figured out what that was, I had all the power I needed to stop her once and for all.

So yeah, I was angry. But I was also smart, and I knew when and how to bide my time.

Whether Cora knew it at this moment in time or not, everything I was currently doing was to benefit and most of all- protect her.

Seeing my parents after hearing the stories that Taylor told me churned my stomach. I mean, these were the people who raised me, and despite our rare differences, gave me a wonderful life.

How could they be all those things, and also the horror-show parents they were to Taylor?

The motives behind everything they did were unclear. Taylor says they never gave her a chance. She had to have done something pretty terrible for them to disown her the way they did.

Or maybe she didn't. Maybe my parents are just as vile and disgusting as she made them out to be.

But none of that mattered now, as the only thing I needed to be focused on was keeping my best friend safe, and not upsetting Taylor or her equally psychotic boyfriend.

My phone had yet to ring, minus the check in text earlier, and the waiting game coupled with my parent's incessant hovering had me feeling like I wanted to run away.

I felt like I was suffocating, on the outside and on the inside. The favor that my sister would call in scared me to death. I knew now the lengths she was willing to go to achieve whatever she wanted, and that included murdering people.

She clearly drew no lines when it came to family, and that's how Daisy apparently met her tragic end.

After all that searching, and endless nights laying awake telling myself that it simply wasn't possible that Daisy could have killed herself... I was right.

I don't know if I necessarily wanted to be, nor did I expect to find the truth that lay waiting for me.

This was one, big, gigantic clusterfuck. I felt like I would drown trying to survive this. But I had to. For Daisy. For Cora. For myself.

I sat up. There was a knock on my bedroom door. Well, there was a short list of possibilities, but I'm going to bank on my father. My mom was hovering, but she wasn't one for much chit chat these days. She seemed to be processing everything, and luckily for me that meant sitting in blissful silence.

I knew my dad was the parent who had taken all of this the hardest. We had struggled at our relationship lately, but he felt all the same emotions that my mother did, but he didn't get to just simply fall apart like she did.

No, he had to be the strong one, therefore, he was put through the emotional ringer.

"Riley? Can I come in, sweetheart?" My dad's voice rang through the hallway.

Bingo.

"Sure."

He opened the door softly, complete with a somber look on his face. He shut the door and sauntered over to my bed, taking a seat on the edge. "Do you want to talk about it? You have been quiet since you returned home… and more than usual so that is definitely saying something." He chuckled, probably as an attempt to lighten the mood.

I couldn't see any bright side to anything right now. It was all panic, what ifs, and maybes. I didn't know what tomorrow would bring, especially as I was now a human puppet with my sister pulling all the strings.

"I'm good. I just need to process everything. I don't see you getting on Mom, and she doesn't say two words the entire day." I said the sentence with a little extra contempt dripping from my voice.

I didn't want to be cruel to him, but I didn't really know what to think of him or my mother right now, and I really needed a little bit of time and mostly space to figure that out for myself.

Everyone was so hell bent on hovering over me, making sure Riley was okay. Quite frankly, I was sick and tired of being a pawn. I was tired of being a victim. I was dead set on finding my sisters killer, and I did just that.

It may not have been what I expected or even wanted, but it was the truth and I now knew the full extent of it.

"Okay, well I'll just leave it to you then." My dad rose from the bed and headed towards the door, opening it.

Before he left, he turned with one final glance, and spoke.

"I love you. I hope you know that. And I will give you all the time you need... but I am here for you. Always." He turned, closing the door behind him.

I knew he meant well. But, right now... I just didn't know what to think.

Sister or not, I only knew one my entire life and that was Daisy. She was murdered in cold blood by someone who we share DNA with. I may not have been able to protect her before, but I could now.

I just needed a plan, and a solid one at that. Quickly.

No time at all. My phone rang.

My heart froze in my chest. The familiar sensation of true fear shot through all my limbs leaving me with a feeling of paralysis.

I answered.

"Hi dear sister. Are you ready to hear what I have planned for you?"

No.

"Yes."

She began to tell me the full details of her plan, and I felt myself shrink smaller and smaller.

God no.

34

Taylor

They were right. The lake was such a tranquil spot. I needed a little bit of calm in my life right now. You can plan something for years and years, but no one, not even one as meticulous as myself can predict the amount of mayhem that will ensue.

Of course, all the mayhem is in my head. I feel like the puppet master desperately yanking on the strings praying that everything looks good on the outer surface. I'm breaking a huge mental sweat, and I don't look cute with a shiny face.

While I did care deeply for Thomas, he was falling flat in the boyfriend department.

Well actually… he excelled there. He was kind, caring, and overwhelmingly empathetic when I hit another roadblock.

It was the devious partner department where he was lacking, and I struggled with what exactly to do with that. I loved him… at least I thought I did.

However, when you grow up with no love from your parents- the people who should love you the most I might add… you have a hard time grasping what love is or should be.

So, did I love Thomas? Or did he just fill a void in my life? I guess I needed to figure it out- and quickly. It was getting to the part of the plan that I had been most excited about.

If anything, and I mean anything even went slightly wrong at this stage, it was game over for me. My family would never pay for treating me the way they did, and I would be stuck right back in that personal hell hole they called an institution.

I let my feet dangle back and forth in the cool water. I let the worries of the day slowly roll out of my mind as I set my sights on the shining lake.

I hear a twig snap behind me.

I had accompanied my sister and her follower enough times to know that it was close to dead out here. It was an undiscovered spot with not much wildlife- and had a scarcity of people.

There was someone here.

I breathed a sigh of anger as I pulled my feet from the water. Whoever was here saw my real hair, as I wanted just one single fleeting moment to not have to be restricted with some hot wig.

I didn't want to have to kill anyone today, but gee, here we are.

I wasn't dense or wistful enough to believe in consequences. It was either Cora or Riley, and I was pushing for the former.

Spend enough time with anyone and their true colors will start to pop out.

Riley was an overachiever. She was a goody two shoes who up until Daisy died- did whatever Mommy and Daddy said. I knew she was a nervous wreck over the anticipation of a call to her little cell phone and was probably at home.

Cora was the nosy one, and that was a problem. Clearly, she didn't value her life as much as she valued her career as an amateur detective.

She's also upset my relaxation day, and that made me angry.

I stood up and gave a casual glance around my surroundings. No sign of her, but I trusted she would make her appearance sooner or later- or not.

She had seen the hair, and while she was annoying as hell- I knew in my heart she wasn't dumb. She was probably having the time of her life crouched in some bush trying to piece everything together.

I would hate for curiosity to kill the cat before the cat was able to have the chance to hear the entire story… the truthful story.

If you were ever to ask my sorry excuse for parent's version of the story- it would most likely go one of two ways.
Both lies, of course.

The first version would probably teeter along the lines of a full out lie- that they only had two daughters and I was crazy.

The second- a little more "woe is me", would be that I was the horrible daughter… that I made their lives hell and would've hurt my siblings had I not been stopped.

Yawn.

I wonder if it ever gets hard playing the victim. My mother is oh so good at it.

I was continuing through the woods, and I heard the slight splash of water.

Not as bright as we though, Cora.

Showtime.

I was sure as hell that Cora decided to hide out somewhere until I was out of sight. So, that was precisely what I was to do. I ducked behind a rather large tree… and waited.

To be fair, it did take a lot longer than I expected, but that Cora is always surprising me with her tenacity.

After an eternity of standing in wait, I heard a soft and very "drippy" pitter patter of footsteps crunching leaves in their wake.

One small peek out from behind the tree confirmed the best possible scenario- her back was turned to me completely and blissfully unaware of what lie for her.

I was smart enough to hide a gun in these woods at an earlier time. I knew about the lake long before either of these two told me. I mean, I had been stalking my "family" for quite some time.

Now who sounds crazy?

I watched her round the corner, back to me, and I cocked the gun.

She stopped dead in her tracks, and I could feel the palpitating fear that was running through her heart.

"Allie… what's going on?" I could tell she was trying to appear as brave, but the quavering voice made that a little hard.

I did a mental eye roll.
"C'mon, you can't think that I didn't see you. Crawling? Standing up and running full speed into the water would have been less obvious." I laughed and I slid down until I was sitting.

I motioned for Cora to sit down opposite me, and she quickly obeyed.
"Who are you?" She eyed me up and down.
Surely you can't be that dense, Cora.
"I think you know." I motioned from head to toe, noting the obvious- I looked exactly like her two best friends. It didn't take a genius.
"Well you could be Riley and Daisy's sister. Are you?"
Duh.
"In the flesh, darling." I smiled and gazed at the still lake water.
"I don't understand." Cora was clearly desperate for the truth, which meant her best friend wasn't as forthcoming as she may have wanted to believe.
Another mental eye roll.

"Well, and why would you? To be honest, it's quite a long and dull story about a girl who was abused by her parents and treated like garbage while they put their other two children on pedestals." I scoffed.

Cora flinched backwards as if I had slapped her. She didn't believe me. Why would she? I have no doubt my parents treated her better than they ever did me. They had a soft spot for everyone.

"You're full of shit." Cora started to stand up, which only pissed me off that much more.

"Sit... down. Remember when I told you to stay out of it? To drop it? You seem to have a knack for sticking your nose in where it doesn't belong. This is a family matter, and last I checked... you weren't family." Once again, I rose the gun and had it pointed directly at Cora.

Now, don't do anything you're going to regret Taylor.

Cora sat back down immediately, finally seeming to realize that I wasn't in the mood for games. If she wanted the truth, she would need to sit her ass down, and listen.

She stared at me for a minute in silence before speaking.

"So, tell me... the whole story."

My pleasure.

And so, I went on and on about the horrors I was put through as a child at the hands of those who gave me life. I could see the range of emotions plastered on Cora's face as I continued to speak.

They went from disbelief, to anger, to sadness, and maybe even pity?

Useless emotion, that one. I didn't need her pity and I sure as hell didn't want it. All I wanted was the truth to finally be known. I was tired of everyone seeing my parents as these wonderful people and putting them up on the highest of pedestals.

It made me sick, it really did.

They took years away from me. My childhood should have been spent playing with my sisters and enjoying my life. Instead, I was told I was a waste of space so many times that there was even a brief period where I started to believe it myself.

Everything that was bad about me was due to them, and they would pay for it. I knew exactly how they would too but putting my cards on the table this early in the game was a recipe for disaster.

Say something Cora.

Poor girl sat in silence, no doubt struggling with the wave of emotions that were surely passing through her. My interest was peaked. Despite what she was portraying on her face, she could have a much different outlook on this.

She could side with them for one.

I didn't get the feeling that she would. She was much too righteous for that.

"I'm… so sorry. I never knew that."

Yawn. That's what everyone says.

"Of course not. None of you did. But you do now." I laughed.

"What are you doing here? You're planning something." She became defensive, and I could sense it in her voice.

"Whatever I have planned is none of your business, nor should you try and make it yours. I know you're not that stupid but given the fact that you heeded my warning earlier- we can never be too sure. You have the truth. Now its time for you to play your role."

She straightened her posture nervously.

"And what role would that be?"

"The same as your best friend Riley. You're going to help me."

35

Cora

I felt like I was losing my mind. I didn't know what to believe, but everything that Allie, or Taylor said was way too elaborate to be fake.

This is what Riley had been hiding from me.

Now everything was beginning to make sense. If I had to keep something this huge a secret from her, I would explode. Her not talking to me must be her way of trying to keep the secret in.

Although I never do appreciate having a gun pointed at me, being able to finally hear the truth about everything that was going on made me feel grateful I stumbled upon her in the woods.

Allie, no Taylor… god this was confusing. *Taylor* was both Riley and Daisy's sister. Triplets. I don't think either of them knew that growing up. How their parents could hide an entire sibling from them their entire lives baffled me. I would have never had a clue.

They were always the warmest people growing up, and even now before Daisy's death. While I was in a coma, I could hear Riley's dad visiting. The memories are a little fuzzy, so I don't exactly recall how often he was there- but he was.

They were good people. How could they do something like this?

Never mind the secret that she had to keep, but how could Riley stay under the same roof as these people especially with everything she found out about them. I imagine she's probably hurt, scared, angry, and every other emotion you could possibly have in a situation like this.

She must be going through hell.

I wanted to be there for my best friend, and now that I knew what she was hiding… I could be.

Everything wasn't exactly all hearts and roses though. I was now to "help" Taylor.

What exactly that entailed… I had no idea.

She gave me a phone that looked eerily similar to the one I saw glued to Riley's hand. I didn't really believe in coincidences, but I was sure that it was probably what Taylor used to secretly stay in contact with Riley.

I did get a chance to ask Taylor about the whole kidnapping situation, and she explained that it was all her, and she only did it to be able to talk to her sister face to face and be able to explain the truth.

I told her that it was incredibly unnecessary, which she did acknowledge and agree with- but stated that in the moment, it was what she felt was right and she wanted to allow her sister time alone and away from everyone to process.

Still crazy.

What didn't make sense to me was why her boyfriend was threatening me. She said that while the plan was all hers, that her boyfriend was the one who did the physical deed of taking Riley. I was never supposed to be collateral damage, but he panicked.

While I still had a million questions, I simply wanted to talk to my best friend first.

My phone buzzed. I pulled it out of my pocket. Nothing.

Not that phone.

Shit. Something already?

I pulled the burner phone out of my other pocket, and sure enough there was a text message from Taylor.

I felt a knot in my stomach, and slowly swallowed. Here goes nothing. I opened the message.

Taylor: Ready for your first task?

Not really. I replied.

Cora: Yes.

Taylor: That's what I like to hear.

Cora: What is it?

Taylor: You're going to kill Riley.

What?

No, no, no.

I nearly dropped the phone, and my heart was thumping nearly out of my chest.

Kill Riley?

Now I knew she was insane.

Cora: No. You're crazy.

There was no response, not that I expected one. Whatever. She could lash out for all I cared. I wouldn't hurt Riley, and I certainly wouldn't kill her.

She was fucking insane. I had to see my friend, now.

I pulled out my real phone and sent a text to Riley.

Cora: I'm coming over now.

I slid the phone back into my pocket. I grabbed the burner one, and sure enough there was another text.

Taylor: Sure, you will. You just don't know it yet.

Rot in hell, bitch. I took hold of her stupid burner phone and chucked it as hard and as far as I could into another direction. I wouldn't be controlled by some fucking lunatic.

I was a few feet from my car, and I scrambled in. I locked all the doors before I even stuck the key in the ignition. I guess you could say I was a little bit on edge.

I barely let the car warm up before I peeled out of my spot and was hauling ass towards Riley's house. I planned to tell her everything.

However, I struggled with what we would do. Surely, we could not simply go to the police, as Taylor's loving boyfriend was a part of that, and no doubt had some pretty good friends who worked there as well.

No, the police were dirty. We needed to figure this out for ourselves and find some way to get this crazy bitch out of our lives.

I must have broken at least ten traffic laws on the way over here.

I pulled into the driveway of Riley's house, not even bothering to check my phone for a response from her. We had much bigger fish to fry than the secret she had been harboring.

I had no clue of the lengths that Taylor was willing to go to, and I feared that if I didn't come through- she would find someone else who would.

Riley was in real immediate danger, and I had to warn her before it was too late.

I threw the car into park and ran up the steps. I banged my fist on the door like a judge would with a gavel on the stand.

I was panicking, and I knew that if they looked out the peephole at me this moment- it would be incredibly obvious.

Take. A. Breath.

The door swung open, and Riley's mom was standing there with a smile pasted on her face. It looked alien on her after all this time. But she seemed to be doing better and that was good.

"Cora… what a nice surprise. Come in dear. Riley is upstairs holed up in that room of hers." She motioned for me to step in, but I was already running past her, there living room becoming a blur.

I bounded up the steps one by one, well- more like two by two.

I skipped the niceties and opted not to knock on Riley's door.

Instead, I swung it open with such force that it slammed back against the wall.

She sat up sharply from her bed, anger clear on her face.

"I told you not to come." She rolled her eyes and laid back down.

"Don't care. I didn't check my messages. Look, I know everything- Taylor, who she is, all of it. But something happened today, and its really bad."

"What do you mean you know all of it? And what happened?" Riley sat back up on her bed and I could tell I had peaked her attention.

"I wanted to go to the lake. I needed to clear my head, and I saw her there. I saw her there with her hair that looks exactly like yours. I tried to hide but she saw me and threatened me with a gun. Then she told me everything, but that I would be useful, so she gave me a phone similar to the phone I have seen you holding lately."

I don't think I paused to take a breath during the entirety of that sentence delivery. I stared at Riley, open mouthed and completely out of breath and she stared at me with an odd look on her face.

"I'm sorry Cora. I never wanted you mixed up in all of this. That's why I tried to distance myself but knowing you I knew you wouldn't let me. We're too close." She smiled and grabbed my hand.

"Of course not. But look, Riley, that's not the worst of it all." I looked away, not even being able to stomach the words that would come stumbling out of my mouth next.

She dropped my hand.

"Cora, what is it?"

I looked back and her, steadying myself, and repeating exactly what her sister commanded me to do earlier.

Her face was pure shock, and I thought she might have passed out had she not been sitting already.

"She...what?! Kill me?!" She stood suddenly, and the shock turned to rage as she began to pace the length of her room.

I couldn't really decipher what she was thinking, so instead I sat there silently saying nothing as I allowed her to process and deal.

I started to become worried as the pacing continued on for several minutes. She had turned from anger into pure rage within a matter of seconds. I could tell that underneath that façade of anger was a bucket of hurt. They may not be close, but that was her sister and I know that it hurt like hell.

"Riley... come sit." I motioned for her to sit next to me on the bed, but she was having none of it.

"No. I won't let her do this, not again." She grabbed her bag, swinging open the door, and heading down the steps in one fell swoop.

"Riley, wait!" I tried to run after her, but by the time I reached the bottom of the steps, I was met with her parent's confused faces and a glimmer of Riley flying out the front door.

Riley's mom was on the couch working on paperwork, and her dad walked out of the kitchen drying his hands on a towel.

"Cora, what's going on?" Her dad asked as he walked over to his wife, worry clear on his face.

"Sale at Macy's. She can't wait to get there. Be right back!" I ran out of the already open front door before I owed them any more explanations that I couldn't come up with.

She was gone.

I got in my car, knowing full well she couldn't get far. Where was she even going?

And then it hit me.

She was going somewhere that wasn't too far for her to get to on foot, and she had one person in mind that she was furious with.

She was going to the restaurant. To confront her sister.

Oh god, this was going to be bad.

I decided to just head towards the restaurant, but I was calling Riley over and over again. The same result transpired each time- no answer.

Like before, I got there in record time. *They really should take my license away.*

I pulled into the familiar parking lot, and sure enough there was Taylor's car.

I went inside the restaurant, not even bothering to lock my vehicle up. I had bigger things to deal with in this moment than petty thieves.

Taylor was standing at the counter refilling an older woman's coffee cup, and Riley was sitting docile at a table.

I went over to Riley and sat across from her. "Whatever you're thinking of doing, stop. She's not wroth it. We will find another way."

Taylor must have walked up behind me, because she spoke next.

"Yeah sis, I would listen to your friend. I am always one step ahead, and any retaliation may cause me to lash out as well. Just ask mom and dad- my tantrums are legendary." She winked and walked away to help a table that just sat down.

Crazy bitch.

I looked at my best friend, who was just staring blankly at the table.

"Riley…"

All of a sudden, her eyes shut, and she fell face first, head hitting the table.

I shook her and she rolled onto the floor completely passed out.

The customers in the restaurant started to scream and panic, just like me.

What the hell was happening?

I looked up and saw Taylor walking towards us.

"Oh no, she doesn't look good. Maybe you should call an ambulance," and with that she took the glass of water from our table that was in front of Riley and she walked away.

She drugged her.

I pulled out my phone and called 911 immediately, unsure if whatever Taylor gave Riley was intended to make her pass out or kill her. I wouldn't put either past this psychotic bitch.

Before I finished the call, I heard the loud sirens coming towards us. Someone in here must have already called.

The paramedics rushed in and started to load Riley who was already coming to, onto a gurney and started to take her vitals as well.

"If I wanted her dead, she would be dead. Don't fuck with me Cora."

I didn't bother turning around or reacting. That would give her far too much satisfaction.

I decided instead to focus on my friend, and helping her out of whatever situation Taylor put her in.

I ran outside along with the paramedics and a sedated Riley. They heaved her into the ambulance, with one of the EMT's running towards the front. I climbed in the back and delivered one last look at the restaurant before the doors were shut.

Taylor looked smug, triumphant even. Clearly family meant very little to her, even those who had not hurt her or even knew of her. She would stop at nothing to fulfill this dire agenda to make them all pay.

And I would stop at nothing to put a wrench in those plans.

I turned towards my friend and grabbed her hand for comfort as the doors shut.

I dialed my mom's number, wanting to give her an idea of what was going on- leaving out all the parts about the homicidal third sister of course.

Part of me wanted comfort from my mom, to hear the words "It will be okay"… but the other part wanted someone else to be the one to break it to Riley's parents that their daughter was in trouble once again. Once again, they had a child that was not okay.

I knew Riley would be fine- for now. I knew Taylor was lethal, but her outburst right now reeked of a warning shot rather than an end all be all. She was letting both of us know who was in charge and trying to push me towards her request once more.

Riley's breathing was shallow, or so the paramedic told me. My mom remained calm on the phone, assured me that everything would be okay just like I knew it would, and then she promised to call Riley's dad.

We arrived at the hospital, and I felt a weight lift off of my shoulders. I could rest easy knowing that for the time being, nothing could hurt Riley, and that she would be safe as the doctors helped to eliminate whatever Taylor gave her.

Of course, it didn't help that we knew nothing of what she did give her, but I had faith in the doctors… and hope.

Hope was all I was holding onto right now. Without it I would fall apart.

What a mess.

I used my time in the waiting room as a way to devise a plan. Taylor was not someone that we could easily get rid of. As much as it made my stomach churn, I knew in my heart she was also someone who would only disappear truly if it was permanent.

Something as permanent as death.

I didn't relish in the idea of taking anybody's life, even one as dangerous and awful as Taylor was. But the alternative was much more horrific.

How many more chances would we allow her to end our lives? How many more times would we allow fear to be a guiding factor in our lives? I couldn't let her control me or my best friend anymore.

She had to be stopped.

We needed to set a trap.

I knew of an old farmhouse off of the freeway that had long been vacant. Once you got off the freeway, and made an immediate right down a dirt road, it was a few miles up.

It was perfectly secluded, with nobody around for miles and miles.

Thinking about the actual act, and how we would accomplish that was much too heavy for me to dwell on right now, especially as I noticed my mother walk in the door.

You have a location. Relax.

I couldn't really relax though. Riley was ill. My mother was worried. I was a nervous wreck. Most of all, I had made too smooth of a transition from innocent to murderous that it worried even me.

"Hi sweetheart. Any news?" My mom sat down in the chair next to me and took my hand in hers.

"Not that I have heard yet." I wanted to be strong, to hold it together, but I started to cry.

Once the first tear fell, the rest quickly and soon followed and not before long, I was a big ball of tears and emotion.

My mom enveloped me in her arms in a tight squeeze. She probably chalked my temporary burst of emotion as my worrying about my best friend.

I guess that was partly true. I was worried. I was also sad, scared, nervous, and most of all- angry.

I was so angry that it consumed me. I didn't ever think of myself as being someone that be consumed by this much rage.

Every ounce of my body- from fingertips to toes, was dripping with pure and heightened hatred for Taylor.

She was evil and had hurt the people I love countless times and in countless ways.

"Shhhh, it will be okay Cora. Your friend will be okay." My mom tried to soothe me, and it was working.

"I'm okay mom. Thank you." I wiped my final tears from my face and sat up straight.

I could do this.

The doctor walked out and looked around. "Is she okay?" I walked up to him, nervously wringing my hands.

"Are you family?" He eyed me suspiciously.

"We are." I turned and Riley's mom and dad were walking in and towards us.

"Okay good. Well, she had roofies in her system. That was why she was so incoherent. It was an incredibly high dose, and you can consider yourselves lucky she got here when she did. You can see her now." The doctor grabbed ahold of Riley's dad shoulder and led him and her mother towards the double doors.

I sat back down, and my mother smiled at me. "Did you hear that? She's going to be fine."

Ugh.

"I need some air, Mom." I got up abruptly and headed towards the front door.

I felt like I was going to be sick.

I rounded the corner once outside and started heaving violently into a rose bush.

Whoops.

"Not feeling well? I didn't drug you." The line was delivered with equal amounts of contempt and humor.

Taylor.

"What do you want?" I was pissed.

"Hmmm... a million dollars, a house in the Hamptons, and for you to follow through on my request."

"It's not going to happen Taylor. You're insane. I would never hurt my best friend." I shoved her away from me. I couldn't stand to look at her face.

"That's a shame. It seems as if I am going to have to start hurting all the people you love. You know... as an incentive." With that, she turned and strutted away.

I'm going to kill her.

36

Riley

I woke up attached to an IV, in a hospital bed, and with a very hazy memory.

I tried to piece together the events that happened prior to me getting here, but all I was drawing was a bunch of blanks.

When I opened my eyes, they felt like they weighed in at one hundred pounds each. I felt exhausted, drowsy even, and incredibly thirsty.

I searched the bed for my phone. It was under my ass coincidentally, and the first thing I did was text Cora. I knew enough to know I was with her earlier.

Why wasn't she here?

"Riley honey, you're awake." My mother came to my bedside and grabbed my hand just as I pushed send on my message to Cora.

"What happened?"

"You were drugged sweetie. You may feel a little hazy for now, but I promise you'll be okay. Doctor said we can take you home." My dad spoke.

"Where's Cora?"

"She is in the waiting room with her mother. We can have her meet you at the house if you like, but you're on strict bed rest for the remainder of the day young lady." My dad's voice was stern, but I could feel the worry in it.

"Okay." I allowed them and a nurse to help me into a wheelchair, which I insisted several times that I did not need, but I guess it was hospital policy.

Drugged? By who? Cora? There was no way.

The last thing I remember was anger. I remember being so angry I felt like I had flames licking at every point of my body. Who was I angry with? I had no idea. I was tired. I wanted rest, and to see my friend. I knew if we were together, then she would be able to fill in the blanks I had.

She would have to.

To no surprise, the drive home was suspiciously quiet. That was my parent's go to when they felt uncomfortable or worried- a void of silence.

It made them feel better, not talking, but it forced my mind to run rampant, and my thoughts were not kind right now.

I had a world of possibilities running through my head, and only one person that would be able to settle my mind.

Thankfully for me, she was already at my house when we pulled in.

My parents each took one of my arms as they led me into the open front door being held by Cora. Again, I insisted that I could walk on my own as I was perfectly fine, but they were having none of it, so I simply left it at that.

There was no use in arguing with them anyways.

Cora helped me up to the remainder of the stairs leading to my room and we both sat on my bed. I waited a few minutes as my mother fussed over me and ran downstairs and back up bringing me juice. I needed liquids she said. I obliged out of the sheer fact that I was so thirsty. My throat felt like I had eaten a handful of hot sand.

Once she finally gave up and went downstairs, closing the door, I turned to my best friend to grill her.

"What the hell happened Cora?"

"What's the last thing you remember Riley?"

Anger. I was so mad.

"Being with you, I guess. Nothing after that."

And so, she began to piece together the events of this afternoon. She went from explaining the task that Taylor gave her, which coincidentally made me mad all over again, to going to the diner, and to Taylor slipping a drug in my drink.

By the time she finished her story and looked up at me, I knew the fire blazing in my eyes was obvious. I was so mad that I felt like I was running out of words to describe the fury. Because that's exactly what it was- fury.

Cora clearly didn't know the whole story.

She didn't know that Taylor killed Daisy. If she knew that, and then adding the fact that now Taylor wanted me dead, she would meet my level of disdain for my sister.

I hated even calling her my sister. She wasn't family. Regardless of how bad mommy and daddy treated her, she used those circumstances to become even worse than them. She was a murderer, and there was no excuse in hell that would justify her horrid actions.

None.

"Well, we need to do something." I put my face in my hands. My frustration was obvious and warranted.

"I agree. I think we should set a trap." Cora sounded very sure of herself, and that brought me a slight sense of comfort.

"A trap? Like catch her in the act of doing some bad, like, I don't know, trying to kill me?" I was confused.

"No. We need to set a trap to lure her somewhere. Then, we need to kill her."

What scared me the most about my friend's statement wasn't the act itself, but the fact that I didn't flinch or deter at all. I was oddly okay with it, which wasn't like me or in my character at all.

What was happening to me?

You're standing up for yourself. For your family. For Cora. For Daisy.

I was finally becoming the person Daisy had pushed me my whole life to be. I was the survivor. I would not be a victim, not to anyone, and certainly not to Taylor.

"Fine. How do you propose we do this?"

Cora grabbed my hand and gave it a light squeeze. She began to throw herself into a very detailed explanation of plan which seemingly sounded like it took years to plan. Knowing that it was only a short amount of time made me feel slightly uneasy and unwaveringly unconfident to say the least.

I gave her some thoughtful input on areas which seemed grey to me, and within the hour we can constructed a plan to kill my only living sister.

I expected some gut-wrenching feeling waiting at the end, but alas- it never came. Unfortunately, there was a time conflict when it came to the plan. We had to make sure the plan was solid, and it needed to be enacted as soon as possible.

Taylor was a fucking ticking time bomb, set to go off at any moment and obliterate everything and anything good in my life with her.

She was a miserable person, who wanted to take her pain out on me, and Daisy. In hindsight, I do believe that it made sense. In her twisted mind, Daisy and I practically stole her life.

We got everything she ever wanted, received all the love she never did, and got the chance to experience life the way it should.

A part of me would always sympathize with her, because no child was deserving of that type of mistreatment.

But what she took from that trauma was not strength. It wasn't compassion- but vengeance- and she had to be stopped.

It would be two days from now. The day after Christmas. It sounded a lot more morbid than it was.

Everyone was on holiday, and most were set to go back the day after thankfully. I know the usual method was giving everyone a proper holiday break ranging anywhere from one to two weeks, but now it was only a few days.

Horrible for everyone else naturally, but wondrously perfect for me and Cora.

The only issue that Cora and I disagreed on was the execution.

How would we do it?

I was angry- that went without saying. However, I was still me. I don't think I could drive a dagger through someone's heart. I don't think I could torture anybody.

It had to be something quick. Immediate. Easy. Painless.

Put her out of her misery quickly, and then soon we would be put out of ours. She would be buried far down in a pre-dug hole, never to be seen or heard from again.

A gun would be the way to go. Since my parents were finally letting up on the reins a little, I was tasked with picking one up today.

We knew someone growing up who was kind of an outcast, but great with fake IDS. I didn't need one necessarily- I could legally buy a gun.

The thing was… I didn't want anything traced back to me should her body ever be found.

This plan had to go off without a hitch, and an essential part of ensuring that was getting a weapon that couldn't be tied back to either of us. There were a few gun stores in town, but I decided to go to one that was a little bit further out of the way. This was another one of our precautions.

Cora was on distraction duty today, or needless to say- surveillance duty.

She was staking out the diner, making sure that my treacherous bitch of a sister stayed where she was supposed to. Part of her job entailed her letting me know if Taylor should decide to make a surprise exit anytime before her shift ended.

While it seemed like everything was starting to fall in place, and like the plan was set in motion, there was a certain loose end that I couldn't stop worrying about.

Her cop boyfriend.

What in the hell would we do with him? I mulled over this for days, sure that we could probably work around him without ever needing to get him involved or hurt.

Truthfully, I should shoot him and drop him in the hole alongside with her so that they can be happy for the rest of eternity together, unable to make anyone else as miserable as they have made me.

I also know that he probably joined the police force originally with good intentions. He only recently met my sister, and she was a bombshell- clearly. I knew she could sweet talk any guy into doing practically anything. Daisy was the same way.

He seemed innocent in all this- someone who is simply along for the ride.

I wouldn't allow anyone else to be hurt as a consequence of Taylor.

While I'm all for getting your daily recommended dose of exercise, this store was a little too far for my liking in terms of a nice walk.

I had Cora drop me off closely to the store, and I decided to walk the rest of the way. It couldn't have been more than half a mile from where she dropped me off, and besides- she had to get to the diner.

Taylor's shift started any minute.

How did I know that? Well, unlike some other redheads in this town... I was actually a good sister. In this point in time, there was only one sister I wanted to be loyal to and that was Daisy.

Everything I do from this point on is for her, the memory of her, and to keep all my loved ones who are alive- alive.

I couldn't stand to lose one more person. I already felt like a piece of me died right alongside with Daisy, and if I lost Cora, or worse- my parents, well I might have to let the ground swallow me up whole.

The store came into sight, and that pit in my stomach that I was so proud of myself for not getting had finally worked its way in.

I knew it was nerves, but there was no place for nerves today. Today, I was strictly here on business. I needed to pull off my best cool girl act and not act like a jittery mess who was days away from killing someone.

Should be a piece of cake.

I opened the front door and a cheery little jingle went off. I looked around at all the guns hanging on the walls. I had not a single clue the type of any of these, but there were some that looked small enough to fit into my pocket. There were also a lot of gigantic ones that made me shiver.

Be. Cool.

There was a big red and white sign hanging on the adjacent wall that read, "All first gun purchases must be accompanied by a range lesson. No exceptions."

Great.

I couldn't deny the annoyance I felt but knew that it was probably for the better. I needed to learn how to shoot first before I did something as permanent and insane as killing Taylor.

"Hi there. Sorry about the wait, I'm the only one working today." It was an older man who strode into the shop from the back, decked out in a red flannel shirt and the oldest blue jeans I had ever seen.

"No worries. I need to buy a gun. First time buyer." I pointed at the sign, to which he laughed.

"Yeah, sorry. Those are the rules, but I know in the long run you'll thank me when you can safely handle a firearm. Mind if I ask why you need one? You look awfully young." He didn't pry, but instead seemed genuinely curious.

"I have a stalker. I just need to be able to protect myself."

Well, that's not completely a lie.

I chuckled to myself softly.

"Well, its always a fine idea to be able to defend yourself. Let's get you to fill out this paperwork, and then we will head on back to the range. But uh, first things first. I need to see some form of identification."

This was it. This was the moment. I had my acting skills all built up, and now we needed to see if Loser Reggie from back home was really worth all the hype everyone gave him.

I produced the fake card and handed it over with as much cool as I could possibly muster up.

He glanced over it for no more than a minute, then smiled, and handed it back.

"All in order Samantha, now just fill out the paperwork."

Samantha?

I looked at the ID he handed me back, and read the name that Reggie produced for me- Samantha James.

I hadn't even bothered to look at it beforehand, but it made perfect sense. Of course, he would give me a different name. That was the whole point.

I finished out the tedious stack of paperwork that seemed to ask the same question five different times in five different ways.

When it was finally completed, I rang the snazzy little bronze bell that sat next to the register. The older man reemerged from the back and had me come with him.

I don't know what I expected the range to be, but I figured it would be indoors, you know- with those little paper headshot things.

No way Jose. This shit looked like it came straight out of Rob Zombie's firefly family backyard.

It was outdoors- for one. Second, it had a bunch of odd-looking targets scattered all over the dusty land. It ranged from cans, to bottles, to an old table.

"First, I'll show you how to load a basic handgun. Here, hold this, and this is where you'll load the cartridge, got it?" He handed me a small handgun and I felt my hands tremble ever so slightly.

Pull it the fuck together Riley.

"Okay, like this?" I loaded the gun, and proudly showed it to the old man.

"Perfect. Now you always want to make sure that you turn the safety off beforehand." He then showed me how to do that as well, which I observed and then mimicked his exact movements.

"Now aim and keep your eyes on your target. Don't waver. Focus."

My first shot went completely over the top of the table. To be fair, it was a pretty low to the ground table, and it was my first time!

You're going have to be a tad bit more accurate then that if you're going to take Taylor down.

While kind of snarky, my inner thoughts were right. I needed to focus.

The second shot was also a bust, but lower than the first shot. Progress. I'll take that.

The third shot right through the right leg of the table, and I practically jumped for joy.

Okay in the spirit of full disclosure, I actually did jump for joy.

The instructor laughed and decided to quit hovering and allow me to practice. He had a store to run, after all.

I moved from the table to the cans. One by one, I knocked each one off their post with ease, and pleasure.

Who knew this could be so thrilling?

Adrenaline was surging through my veins, moving faster with each loud bang that rang in my ears. It was absolutely exhilarating. I ran out of bullets, and not seeing any other ones in sight, decided to head back inside.

He was leaned against the counter with a big smile on his face.

"I see you got the hang of that pretty quickly. That stalker doesn't stand a chance against you."

I handed over the empty pistol, and he smiled as he dipped it under the counter and onto a display shelf.

"I'll take that one, or a similar one."

He turned around and reached in between some bottom shelving and retrieved a gun that looked almost identical to the one I had been firing.

"Consider this her sibling. They are almost the same, but slightly better range."

He rang me up, and I will say that I would have paid that price tenfold if it meant getting this monster out of mine and my family's lives for good.

I thanked the nice man, who I now know as Ray, and headed to my meet up spot.

It would be a few more hours until Cora was set to pick me up and having a gun at my side wasn't enough to make me feel safe about casually walking on the side of the road.

Been there, done that. I don't exactly feel like rehashing another kidnapping quite so soon.

I dipped into a little coffee shop, knowing that I could ease my worries and anxiety with a nice cup of hot green tea.

"One green tea please, hold the sugar." The barista took my name and my money while I took a seat.

I purposefully brought a large bag so nothing would be obvious, but that didn't stop be from feeling like everyone here in this coffee shop knew about the handgun I was toting and my plans for it.

I really was starting to fly off the handle, and that was a complication that needed to be nipped in the bud.

I pulled out my phone.

Riley: Got the package. How's everything?

       Cora: All good here. Normal.

Riley: Good, see you soon.

"Riley!"

I looked up and there was a friendly barista holding a cup with my name spelled very oddly on it. "Thank you." I took the piping hot cup into my hands and sauntered over to a table in the far back.

I wanted to be able to stare at everyone without them all having a clear-cut view of me.

You can imagine my surprise when Officer Brooks sauntered in.

I was definitely out of eye view, but the pit in my stomach was telling me otherwise. Just to be on the safe side, I ran off to the ladies' room and hid in a stall.

I must have been in there for thirty minutes because by the time I finally emerged, I had finished my entire cup of tea, and I had gotten a large.

I lingered by the back, desperate to get a look around the coffee shop before I stepped any further.

I didn't see him at all, but I wanted to be sure. I sat down at my previous table, which thankfully was unoccupied, and glanced around. He was nowhere to be seen.

I breathed an audible sigh of relief and closed my eyes. If my deranged sister didn't kill me first, then my anxiety would.

Cora sent a text saying that she saw Taylor get in her car and leave. She was on her way to pick me up.

I ordered another tea while I waited, along with a blueberry muffin as coincidentally I was starving.

It was odd to me that Taylor had yet to make any moves or requests in the past few days. The roofie in my water at the restaurant was a warning, and sooner or later she would try again- only this time with something much more lethal. I was sure of it.

She had yet to send a follow up text to mine or Cora's burner phones. I knew that her boyfriend was back at the station, seamlessly blending as a functional member of society when really, he was a big puppet with my sister as the puppet master.

I remember him vaguely before all of this mess. He seemed like a nice person, a decent cop, and someone who was very much interested in not only keeping our town safe- but making it better.

How he got roped into being with someone as cold and calculated as Taylor was beyond me.

The news and shock of this whole situation had a good while to sit and sink in. But there were times where I caught myself sitting there, shocked.

The girl who I befriended along with Cora, who was close with my deceased sister, was in fact my estranged sister. While she looked like a carbon copy of myself and Daisy, Taylor couldn't have been more different.

This girl had some very elaborate plan that she must have worked on for years in that institution my parents stuck her in.

I felt bad for her. I did. But now, I wonder if she was always this crazy and that's the reason my parents did what they did. Maybe its not the way she tells it. Maybe she didn't get mistreated and then turned cold from circumstance, but rather was always a sociopath.

Yeah, that had to be it. It was really the only explanation that I could handle right now. I remember thinking that it was odd that she let me go.

She killed Daisy for knowing her secret, or so she says, but now both Cora and I are walking around free knowing it as well.

Originally, I assumed that she had some other plan for me, and that was why she let me go. Is Cora a part of that plan? Or is she lying about the reason she killed Daisy?

My head felt like it was going to explode, and it didn't necessarily help knowing that the only person who could answer my endless amount of questions was the person who was slightly murderous and shared the same DNA.

"Do you need anything?"

The kind café worker broke me from my thoughts.

"No, thank you." I smiled and she walked away, going to help other customers.

I hadn't noticed, but it was dark outside. I needed to send my parents a text letting them know I was okay before they started to panic.

Riley: Hey, I should be home in an hour or two. What's for dinner?

Dad: Spaghetti, your favorite. How was your best friend day?

Riley: Just what I needed. See u soon. XO.

I smiled at my phone, partly due to the dinner. I did love spaghetti, but my dad was such a thoughtful person and even thought we have been constantly disagreeing lately- he still went out of his way to do something that he knew I'd love.

I never really told him enough, but I loved him so much. He did so much for me, and I always appreciated and was proud of the fact that unlike a lot of the executive guys who go to school, he worked his way up through the company he was at. He did it through hard work and dedication. He was the smartest person I knew.

You should tell him that in person.

Well, I was sure he already knew. The sound of my Christmas ringtone started to play throughout the café. I answered the phone.

"Hey girl. I'm outside."

I dumped my second empty teacup in the trash and took the remnants of the blueberry muffin into my mouth before adding the muffin liner to the trash as well.

I stepped outside and was slapped with the cold breeze. Yeah, I probably should have worn a jacket, but it was seventy-five and sunny this morning.

Its winter, dipshit. Always bring a jacket.

I climbed into Cora's car, and found myself feeling grateful that the heater was blasting.

"How was your day on stakeout duty?" I laughed as I pulled my seatbelt on.

"Dull. Yours?" She pulled away from the parking lot.
"Slightly less dull." I reached into my bag and pulled the gun out ever so slightly and flashed it to Cora.

She stared at it mindlessly for a second before tearing her eyes away to focus on driving.
"Wow. I know we have been talking about it for days, but that made it all feel so… real. Not that she doesn't deserve it, of course."

I knew exactly how she felt. But she wasn't there at the range. The feeling of the gun going off in my hands, the noise of the firing, it was euphoric. I know that the feeling would be different when it was someone on the other end of the barrel, taking away a human life.

And it couldn't be happening to a nicer person.

Not.
"I get it, I do. If it makes you feel better, you don't have to do this with me Cora. I can handle my sister on my own." I put my hand on top of hers.
"No, I can't let you near her all by yourself. It's just, a lot to deal with, you know? I'll be fine. I would rather have the piece of mind knowing you and I, and everyone we love is safe."

We pulled in front of my house, and the beautiful decorations lit up the front porch. I loved the holidays, but more than that I loved the sense of unity and love that seemed to be overflowing in the air.

It was always Daisy's favorite holiday-Christmas. It makes me both sad and angry that she won't be able to experience it this year. Last year was her very last Christmas on this Earth, and we had no idea. That's even more heartbreaking and does lots to fuel my hate fire for Taylor even more.

"And... we're here. Want me to come in?"

I debated but figured it would probably be best to spend some time with my family. I was tired of fighting with them, especially when I knew everything that they were doing was simply to keep me safe.

"Not tonight. I need family time. Talk tomorrow?" I smiled at my friend, and I knew she understood.

She simply nodded and pressed the unlock button on her driver's door. I stepped out, bracing myself for the harsh weather and ran inside.

I turned and delivered one final look and wave to Cora before I entered my house. The smell of spaghetti floated throughout the entire front entrance, and it was nothing short of heavenly.

"Riley, that you?" My dad yelled from the kitchen.

"Yep!"

"Well, go wash your hands and join us dear," my mother's voice rang through the living room as she walked by carrying a small stack of placemats.

I walked by her into the downstairs bathroom. I set my purse down and began to wash my hands and then I remembered the handgun that was still very much in my purse.

I dried my hands and yelled to my parents as I ascended the staircase lading up to my room.
"Give me one second! I want to throw on something a little more comfy!" I slipped into my bedroom, closing the door shut behind me.
Where on Earth would I hide this?

Then, it hit me. My parents were never much for snooping, but I had very little places to hide it. The one room in this entire house that they never went into was Daisy's room.

I quietly opened the door and slipped across the hall into hers.

I took a large piece of duct tape from her art desk, switched the safety on, and taped the gun perfectly underneath her bed frame.

I wiped a little bead of sweat off my forehead and went into my room to change- quickly.

In record time, I was in my favorite pair of Christmas pajamas that I had for years.

Daisy picked them out for us at the local mall.

I ran downstairs, and I spotted both of my parents already sitting at the dinner table.

Both my mom and dad were smiling, and it was a sight that I hadn't seen in a while. My mom seemed to be on her path to healing, as was I.

I took my seat, which was always right across from my dad.
"Let's eat." My dad smiled and began to heap spoonfuls of my favorite dish onto my plate.

37

Taylor

I grew quite tired of this "cat and mouse" game I was playing with Cora and Riley.

I wish I could say it was a fair fight, but quite frankly- it wasn't.

The harsh truth was that I was smarter, faster, and way more devious than both of those two put together. They couldn't beat me on my worst day, and yet I had an unshakable feeling that they would try.

That was fine and dandy. I wanted to give them a fair shot to take me down- I wasn't evil of course. They wouldn't be able to- and then I would be met with immeasurable satisfaction watching them fail.

I worked today, and I noticed Cora's car parked outside all day. That was my first clue that these girls were utter idiots. I mean, if you're going to do a stakeout, at least make sure you're hidden properly.

I was actually able to catch a glance of Cora inside her car, with big sunglasses as a way to hide her face I'm sure. She fails to realize that we were once "friends", and I have been inside her car.

I didn't see Riley, and I wondered about it all day. If Cora is on Taylor duty, then where is my dear sister?

Probably scheming up some way to take me down. At least they made it exciting. It would be that much more fun when I killed both of them.

I had originally planned to keep my sister alive for a little longer, as a part of my plan. But she grew annoying and became more trouble than she was essentially worth. The plan was still in place, but everything needed to be moved along a tad bit faster.

Cora was never meant to die, but like my sister, she has become a liability as well as a nuisance. I was tired of both of them.

Unfortunately, so would my lovely boyfriend. I needed all three of them gone and out of the way if I wanted to achieve my goal. They were all loose ends, and I hated those more than anything.

A small part of me wanted to call Cora out for her spying on me, but I also wanted to see just how much she and Riley could accomplish if they thought I wasn't onto them. I broke out of a mental institution… I wasn't exactly senile.

They underestimated me, and it would be the oversight that ended them.

My boss had been really on my case lately about arriving on time, and I had half a mind to add her ass to my hit list as well but opted against it as she did sign my checks.

I wondered how my lovely parents were doing, but I knew I would see them both soon enough.

In fact, they were a vital part of this entire plan. I mean, I couldn't very well break out of a mental institution, kill both my sisters, their friend, my boyfriend, and not have them in mind as well.

They were the ones who did this to me, who made me this way. They owe me everything I ever lost growing up.

There were days that I sat in my locked cell, with nothing more than a toilet and bed in my room wanting to just have their love. That was all I wanted growing up. I just wanted my parents there, and to know that they cared for me.

But day after day, year after year of not ever seeing them hardened me. It helped me to make a swift transition from vulnerable child to strong adult. Not only did I not want or need their affection, but I wanted them to suffer. I felt nothing for these people, and I wanted to slowly take away everything they ever cared about just to have them see how I was made to feel growing up.

Cold? Probably. Deserved? Absolutely.

Table after table I felt the energy drain from me. It was incredibly exhausting to have to put on a smile and answer people's trivial questions all day when there were far more pressing matters that needed my immediate attention.

Thomas had been camped out at the abandoned house getting everything ready. He insisted that I stay with him, so I didn't need to be in the van, but I liked it.

It gave me a sense of freedom and independence. Plus, I didn't jump at the thought of having him over my shoulder watching my every move.

It was also one thing that I had paid for all by myself with no help from anyone. By now you know that was a common occurrence, doing things on my own. Everything I have now, the car, the job- it's all due to my own ambitions and hard work.

That's why everything had to be planned in vast detail. If I were to get messy in any part of this, I would be caught- I would lose everything that I built for myself. Part of the plan was always to have someone on the inside, someone who stood as backup should I make a mistake. That person turned out to be Thomas, a sweet cop who would do anything to help me.

He was perfect, just what I needed. But once he stops being of use to me, I can get rid of him.

Riley thinks she knows everything, but she only knows what I chose to tell her. I didn't kill Daisy because she knew too much.

I had always planned to kill Daisy. She was collateral damage. They all are. But... I did expose all my secrets to my sister before I forced her to cram pills down her throat.

She fought me every step of the way, and when that didn't work, she tried to play the doting sister card and sympathized for me. I hated being pitied. She had no chance really, but her efforts were admirable.

Between my two sisters, I did care for Riley more. But that doesn't matter, and she knows that now. She probably thinks I hate her, and that's why I'm doing this, why I am trying to get her best friend to do my dirty work.

I really wish Cora would pull through, as it would make my life a hell of a lot easier if she did. But I always had a backup plan if she didn't.

I don't hate Riley, at all. In fact, I rarely feel anything these days. Anger is about it. I don't feel loneliness, or love, or anything of the mushy gushy feelings that everyone seems to strive for.

That probably would make a lot more sense if you had seen how many times they implemented "shock therapy" as a part of my recovery routine.

The lead doctor at the facility was a total nutcase, and really should have been locked up in a room of his own had he not convinced everyone he was a brilliant doctor.

He was a quack.

Thankfully the lovely days of electroshock therapy are long behind me, another thing I did for myself.

"Excuse me? We're ready to order."

I turned my head and snapped out of my thoughts to see a young couple waiting patiently with their menus closed and stacked.

I plastered a smile on my face and waltzed over, joyously taking their order.

And so, my shift went the same, order after order, smile after smile, and measly tip after measly tip.

The day finally ended, and as I was getting ready to go, I got pulled aside by my boss.

"You're doing a really great job, you know that?" She smiled at me.

That was a really big compliment, considering the fact that I was simultaneously planning at least three murders while I was tending to customers.

"Really? Thank you so much!" I replicated her same beaming smile, and she squeezed my shoulder before heading out of the locker room.

I grabbed my things, sent off a quick text to my boyfriend letting him know I was too tired to go over, but that I would see him tomorrow and headed outside.

Once I peeled away from the parking lot, I caught a glimpse in my rearview mirror of Cora's car leaving in the opposite direction.

She knew my car, and I wasn't sure about her exact levels of stupidity so didn't even want to risk her recognizing it following her.

Curiosity would not get the cat today, I guess.

Instead I went to the local gym, grabbed my nighttime pajamas, and headed inside for a quick workout before showering all the worries of the day away.

Working out and sweating it out on the treadmill brought me some clarity, and now that everything in the plan was reaching the "crucial" phase, I needed to be on top of my A game.

After all, it was just me alone in all of this.

I hopped in the shower after sweating out what felt like all of my water in my body.
This feels amazing.

Living in a van was cool and all, but a hot shower was absolutely unbeatable.

It wasn't until I dressed myself, combed out my hair, brushed my teeth and got comfortable and cozy in my bed that I realized I had put a tracker on Cora's car back when I had weaseled my way into their life.

I had to calm the mini victory party that I was holding for myself in my head in that moment.

It only gave me addresses of stopped points.

I opened the coordinating app on my phone and searched all the last addresses of the stopped points today. There were a handful. I recognized one address as Riley's house, one as Cora's, the diner of course, and an unknown address.

I selected and copied the address on the screen and pasted it into Google.

The Blue Rifle.

A gun store?

Oh, I underestimated my sister big time. What was she planning to do? Kill me? As if!

My sister had the guts of a carrot. She couldn't do anything she set her mind too, let alone take someone's life.

I'm sure she felt better knowing that Cora had her back. They were without a doubt in on it together. Those two were absolutely laughable. Didn't they know the way this story would end? I would be the victor, and those two losers could rot in joint graves.

That familiar emotion came back- the only one I knew now- anger.

It's on.

38

Cora

It felt like a whirlwind, these past couple of days. While I felt sure, and absolute in our plan to kill Taylor, I couldn't help the nagging feeling in the pit of my stomach.

Every day I worried that I wouldn't have the strength or the guts to follow through with our plan. My only motivators in this entire thing were anger, and fear.

I hated Taylor more than I hated anybody in my entire life. I wanted nothing but pain and suffering for her.

Riley finally spilled her guts and told me the full truth about it all, and not just the bits and pieces that Taylor chose to reveal to me herself.

Taylor killed Daisy. My suspicions were right, and I was absolutely sick to my stomach.

All I had on my side were facts. Fact: She killed Daisy.

Fact: She wanted Riley dead... even tried to get me to do it.

Fact: She was an imminent threat to not only Riley and I… but to our families and anyone else we loved.

So, I guess that was where the fear motivator came into play. Her willingness to do whatever it took to get what she wanted, regardless of who she hurt worried me. It chilled me so deep to the bone that I was willing to do one of the worst things someone could do.

I was going to commit murder, and every time I woke up and started my day, I had to remind myself over and over again of the reasons behind doing this.

I was protecting my family, and that was something that just had to be done. I had to be the one to do it, along with Riley. We both had so much to lose if Taylor decided to lash out, and I couldn't afford that chance.

I didn't mention any of my doubts or worries to Riley. I grew up with that girl, and I knew personally that she had the biggest heart out of anyone. I knew that this was wrecking her inside as well, not to mention that Taylor was this sister who she had no idea about.

I know a part of her, maybe deep down, wanted to try for a relationship with her sister, but Taylor was the one to shut all that down with talks of murder and kidnapping.

Still, I know it didn't make it hurt any less, but possibly more. Knowing Riley, she was mindlessly pouring over what-ifs.

What if her parents hadn't abandoned their third child? Would she be different?

What if she had met Taylor before Daisy did? Would Daisy still be alive?

What if she didn't go through with the plan? What if Taylor hurt her parents?

I knew in my heart that this was what Riley was going through. I knew it, because I was going through the very same thing.

It didn't change a thing. It couldn't. Taylor had all the time in the world to change her route, to become a better person, and yet she chose a life that hurt others and that was something I couldn't condone or allow.

My mom and I weren't talking very much at the moment. I think she could tell that something was off with me and growing up she always did give me my space when she could tell I wasn't feeling right.

Right now, I felt gracious for that, as I couldn't very well ensure that I wouldn't break down and spill everything if she decided to ask me if everything was okay. I couldn't lie to my mom, and that was something that I knew I wouldn't be able to keep in if she asked.

I knew I was a walking time bomb. One wrong move or question, and it would be lights out. I feared that I would be the one to ruin this entire plan before it was even executed. I also feared that it would go off without a hitch, and I would have to live with the fact that I murdered someone in cold blood for the rest of my life regardless of how horrible that person may have been.

She was willing to kill Riley. She killed Daisy.

I knew that. I guess I just wasn't cut from the same cloth as Taylor. Human lives were not disposable to me.

In the moment the other night at the hospital, when Taylor approached me outside, the amount of rage I felt was enough to drive me to kill her. I was shaking with anger after she left. It was a mix of the built-up emotions watching Riley collapse, then getting in the ambulance, and having to wait in the waiting room.

All of that, coupled with Taylor's threats to hurt the people I loved that night, just drove me into a blind rage. I spent the better part of that night planning her murder down to the very last detail.

I had decided it. She was going to die, and even if I wasn't the one to take her last breath from her, I would be there to witness it.

The next morning was about the same… and the one after that.

However now, just a few days after the initial incident, I was having doubts. There was no room for doubts especially in a plan or situation like this. There was simply too much to lose.

You need to pull it together.

"Hey mom. I am meeting Riley today. Did you need me to stop by the store after?" I passed by my mother in the kitchen drinking a cup of coffee from her favorite emerald green mug.

"No thanks honey. Can you sit down for a second? I wanted to talk to you." She smiled and gestured to the barstool opposite her.

My nerves began to start, and I could feel my palms begin to sweat.

Don't blow this entire thing. Calm down. Lie.

I returned her smile, although I was sure mine was a lot less genuine and I sat in the chair.

"What's up?"

Her face quickly transitioned from smiley to serious, and she began to speak.

"You haven't been yourself these past few days. You seem to be coming and going at weird hours, and you barely have spoken to me. I know you're going through a lot right now especially with Riley. But... I just wanted to remind you that you do not need to take on everyone else's problems. It will break you. I love how big your heart is, but don't let it be the death of you... okay?"

I breathed a mental sigh of relief when she finished talking. I was so grateful that it wasn't some spiel trying to get me to talk about my feelings. If it had been, who knows what I would have revealed?

No. Instead, she just wanted to comfort me. My heart swelled three times its size, and everything began to come into clarity for me. This is the reason I was doing all of this. I wanted to make sure that my mother, along with everyone else I loved... would be safe.

I needed to protect them all from that monster. "Thanks mom, I needed to hear that. I love you." I stood up and walked around the counter to hug her.

I squeezed her tight, and she returned the sentiment.

"Have fun with Riley today, my love." She turned to fill up her coffee cup once more.

I swear that woman was a walking coffee addict.

Today was the day that Riley and I scoped out the spot. Like I said, it wasn't time to start doubting things or myself. I could do this. I had to do this.

The weather was especially nippy on this fine winter morning, so I needed to warm up my engine to a few bars before I felt comfortable enough driving it.

It wasn't the newest or the shiniest car on the block, so I needed to take care of it, or so my mother liked to remind me incessantly.

I texted Riley before I backed out of my driveway letting her know I was on my way. She sent back an almost immediate text replying that she was already ready and sipping on her morning cup of coffee.

I shook my head and laughed. Like my mother, and pretty much everyone else I knew, coffee practically ran throughout their veins. I felt like I needed to hold an intervention for them all and start thinking seriously about switching them to decaf.

The drive there was nice, and absolutely peaceful. I craved the peace and quiet these days, but I could never ignore the nagging voice in the back of my head telling me it was too quiet, and there was something wrong.

I didn't use to be such a worrier, but the reveal of Taylor and all that transpired afterwards definitely made me more paranoid and on my toes whenever I could.

I looked out for myself more, that was for sure.

I basked in the quiet roads this early in the morning and appreciated the fresh dusting of snow we got. I couldn't even really call it snow, it looked like someone poured a teaspoon on the grass if I'm being honest.

I didn't care though, snow was snow, and I was in love with the way it made me feel. It was the simple things after all.

I pulled into Riley's driveway, and not wanting to wake the still sleeping neighbors, opted for a quick text rather than an obnoxious honk.

She sauntered out of the front door wearing the cutest knee-high boots and scarf just a few moments later. Like me, my friend appreciated the "snow" and all the nice cold weather.

"Hey! How did you sleep?" Riley spoke as she climbed into the passenger seat.

I hesitated for a split second before answering. Did I tell my best friend in the entire world a lie, that I slept well, or did I tell her the truth... that I spent the whole night tossing and turning over this plan that was a day or so away.

"Hello... Earth to Cora." She laughed at me, clearly unaware of the battle I was having in my head.

"I slept great. You?"

And so that launched her into a ten-minute story of how she dreamt that she was a caterpillar, doomed to being stepped on by all these people, and her one mission was to make it safely across the sidewalk to a grass area.

I knew it sounded insane, and if I didn't grow up hearing similar stories my whole life, then I probably would too.

Riley always had really weird dreams and that was something that both Daisy and I teased her about.

"Hey, do you think we could stop at one of those little drive thru coffee spots?" She batted her eyelashes with the deliverance of the last word as some sort of ploy to get me to go along with her idea.

Two words. Caffeine. Addict.

"I thought you already had coffee!" I rolled my eyes, but it was all in good fun.

I was an enabler when it came to my best friend's happiness, especially if it was something small and very much in my reach to do.

"I did... but..." Riley shrugged her shoulders as if to say, and?

I laughed and made a right turn at the light ahead to make a little pit stop at one of our favorite coffee stops.

Ten minutes, and twelve dollars later, we had two large mocha lattes and we hit the road once more on our trip to the spot.

I don't know if it was the extra shot I opted to add to my coffee or my jitters, but I was not handling this well. I kept trying to tell myself... more like scream at myself to get a grip but it simply wasn't working.

It wasn't helping the fact that I hadn't been talking to my friend about it, mostly out of sheer terror for how she would react. I didn't want her to think I was trying to bail on her, because that wasn't the issue at all.

I was just having a much harder time than I think she was, or at least as much as she was letting on. I decided against my better judgement and started to tell Riley.

"Look, I wanted to talk to you about something." I decided to keep my eyes on the road, because if I looked at my best friend, I would break.

Like that will help... you're a mess!

"Okay, shoot." Riley took a swig of her coffee.

"This whole plan... just has been really wracking my nerves. Now, I don't want you to think that I'm trying to back out or anything. I just wanted to see where your head was at as well..."

I continued.

"I just figured if I was struggling, then you probably were as well. I'm sorry, I know I'm rambling, and I'm sure I'm not expressing all of this the best way."

After I finished, I continued to look straight ahead. I didn't know if Riley was looking at me or not, and I didn't want to know.

It was quiet, like eerily quiet.

I felt a pit form in my stomach, knowing with certainty that I either upset or offended her.

"Say something Riley, please."

"I feel the same way Cora, I do. This isn't who we are. The problem is that we have been put in this awful position where we are forced to choose- her life or ours. I'm sorry, but I choose us. She murdered my sister Cora."

I felt like a weight had been lifted off my shoulders. I finally got everything off my chest that I had wanted to for days, and the end result was promising. Riley wasn't mad, or angry. She was understanding... she was compassionate.

I suppose I always should have known she would be.

The house came into view, and we both drained the last of our coffees as I found an area to park. Like I knew earlier, there was nobody around for miles, and that did make me feel just the tiniest bit better.

Riley had the gun with her and plans to hide it inside the house. She didn't want it to have it on her, and I know that having it in her house didn't make her feel good at all.

It would be the right thing to get it out now. We could revisit it when it was time for the deed to be done.

She grabbed her oversized purse and I grabbed my car keys.

It was so quiet you could hear a pin drop. While I normally relished in the quiet, found it peaceful, I felt uneasy and nervous.

That was to be expected though, right?

The chill hit me like ice in my veins, and Riley and I both exchanged nervous glances as we climbed the front stairs.

Both of us had only been here a handful of times when we were younger. It was the place a lot of high school kids came to hang out but after most of us graduated it fizzled out some.

The front door was already open, but it didn't worry me in the slightest. I was sure that drifters made their way through here from time to time, shacking up for the night.

Thankfully we would only need the place momentarily, and we weren't planning on making it our permanent residence. It was because of that that I could tolerate the mildew smell coupled with the pungent smell of piss.

It was an absolute dump in this place. The thought made me chuckle to myself. What a perfect place for scum like Taylor to die in.

Riley must have had the exact same idea because she chuckled and said,
"Fitting isn't it? A trash place for a trash person?"

We both broke into a fit of giggles, and while it may have seemed cold or harsh, it was simply our way of coping.
"Where should I put the gun?" She looked around for a spot to hide it.
"Somewhere where no one would find it. Let's check upstairs. I don't see anything here, unless you plan to hide it in the eroding walls."

She shook her head and we slowly but surely climbed each step with the utmost care trying our hardest to not break a step. They were all made of wood, and decayed pretty badly.

"Be careful Cora," Riley warned as she gripped the banister for support, which wasn't very sturdy either.

At that exact moment, we both heard a loud bang upstairs. I jumped nearly two feet in the air and had to grip the banister so hard to keep myself from falling that I broke my nail down the center.

As I pressed my t-shirt into my now bleeding finger, I looked up at Riley who was now frozen on the steps.

I looked around her at the top of the stairs to see what, or who she was looking at, and I too froze in my spot when I saw Taylor's boyfriend Officer Brooks standing there, gun in hand.

I immediately grabbed my friend's hand and turned to bolt down the crumbling steps when Taylor stepped out from behind the corner, also brandishing a weapon… except she had a knife.

"Uh, uh, uh. Now where do you think you two are going?"

I knew I didn't have minutes to decide what to do, but seconds, and I ran through the millions of possibilities that could happen. I could try to stop Taylor and end up getting myself stabbed or shot in the process. That was one of the thousands that didn't end well.

It didn't stop me from charging Taylor. I made sure to shove her out of the eye view of the staircase, saving myself from being shot by her loving boyfriend.

I had planned for her to die at a later time, but I would do it right now if I had to, and that's what it was looking like.

Taylor fell back onto the rotting floor, clearly not expecting my outburst. The knife flew from her hand, skidding across the floor. I ran for that, rather than for her, and by the time my hands enclosed on the handle of the blade she was on her feet ready for a fight.

I knew I had the upper hand with my weapon, and her without, but if I had learned anything, it was to never underestimate Taylor.

I elbowed her in the face, sending her stumbling back. I went to punch her, but she dodged my fist and drove her foot into my gut. I advanced with the knife at my ready, and my hand flew forward.

Within an instant I had her back against the wall, blade at her throat.

This was it. This was the moment.
"Stop. Now. Or she dies."

I felt my heart sink, and I turned slowly to my side, blade still at Taylors throat only to see Riley now down the steps along with Officer Brooks.

His gun was pointed at the back of her head, and she was sobbing.

I knew she had her gun in her purse that she was gripping tightly, but I knew, and I think she did as well… she didn't have nearly enough time to get it out before he pulled the trigger.

It wasn't worth it.

"You don't want to do this. Can't you see that? Taylor is just using you to get what she wants. That's what she does to everyone, and its what she's doing to us. She's using Riley and Daisy to get back at their parents for what they did." I tried to reason with him, because if I could do that, then it would be game over for Taylor.

He paused, possibly considering switching teams.

I should have known that he would not side against Taylor when a smirk spread across her revolting face.

"Nah, I'm good," and with that being said, pistol whipped Riley, knocking her unconscious.

I turned to slit her throat, but she was already out from under the knife, and hit me over the head with something hard.

I was out before I hit the floor.

39

Taylor

Once I had figured out where my sister and her follower friend went that day, it wasn't too difficult to begin to piece together the string of events that were their plan to come after me.

It went from humor, to a slight annoyance, to humor again.

They probably would have figured I would be scared, or even a little angry but I was way past that. Their plan would never work. It hadn't even been attempted yet, and I had already figured out practically everything I needed to know.

They wouldn't be successful. I also had a police officer boyfriend on my side, which after digging into both of their phone records, was able to confirm what I already knew in my heart.

My sister was planning to kill me.

Maybe that would hurt slightly more if it wasn't exactly what I was doing as well, and I had actually already killed one of my sisters.

May Daisy rest in peace.

I snickered.

Ah, that was my family's issue. They had a tedious habit of continuously underestimating me. The life I had been handed had done a spectacular job of molding me into a cold-hearted killer, cunning as well.

Hell, I even feared me sometimes. I had the police force on my side. I had the experience and let's be honest- I had the guts.

That was something Riley could never say about herself.

She was a puppet, a spineless loser, unable of ever actually committing to, better yet following through with a plan.

I remember one day at the lake, she told me a sappy story about how she accidentally killed a squirrel trying to drive Cora's car once.

She broke into tears as she told the story. That girl was going to kill me? Yeah, right.

Once I had all the information I needed, it was quite easy to track them down. After all, I had the tracking device planted on the underside of Cora's car, and a wonderous little app at my ready.

I had filled Thomas in on all parts of the plan that he absolutely needed to know and left some parts out just for myself.

Hey, knowledge is power.

This was all happening a lot sooner than I ever planned, but it was probably for the best. I grew tired of these games I was playing with them, and just wanted the entire charade to be over and done with so I could collect my prize already.

What that prize was, was still my little secret to keep.

Thomas didn't even blink when I told him that not only was the plan moved up to today, but that Cora was now apart of the deal. I can't really feel sorry for the girl, as she brought it on herself if I'm being honest.

That girl wouldn't know how to stop meddling in other peoples lives if hers depended on it.

And what would you know… today it would.

As we tracked the girls to the house, we pulled around back. We entered through the back of the house and utilized that opportunity for Thomas to gain access to the upstairs part of the home.

I wouldn't even call it a home, and it certainly didn't make sense to me why my sister would pick this place to deem as a murder spot.

It was filthy, and it reeked of piss.

However, she chose it for me. Little did she know that it would be the place that she died.

Now, I had originally planned for her to die in the same way her sister, I mean… our sister did. It seemed poetic to me in a way.

She kind of screwed that for herself, I guess.

It was a tad bit ironic to me that she was planning to kill me in a dump like this, while I on the other hand had a very meaningful and poetic way planned out for her.

Who's really the bad sister?

I knew in my heart and bones that Cora would never follow through with it, so the plan all along was for me to be the one to kill Riley.

I was fine with it, but to be honest, it created a lot more work for me and I was exhausted.

Thomas picked up zero of the slack per usual, but that would all improve once I did away with him like these other two.

Now the little showdown, that I was not expecting. I have to be fair. Cora had a hell of a lot more fight in her than I ever though possible but people in this town are constantly surprising me.

Riley went down like a sack of shit, no surprise there. The girl doesn't have a fighting bone in her body, once more proving my point that I had nothing to fear in the first place.

Time after time, I have told both of them that this wasn't going to end in a fairytale sort of way where the heroines defeat the bad guy and go on with their lives.

I hadn't spent most of my life lying in wait and creating a plan to later leave any room for error. Maybe, just maybe there was a small part of me that wanted to leave Riley out of the plan, but it really only worked if she was gone… for good.

I didn't know just how much that Cora was in my sister's lives- both of them.

She was an unforeseen obstacle, but one that could be dealt with, nonetheless.

Thomas was a happy coincidence. I feared that the officer I tricked into liking me would be old, fat, and senile. I was lucky to get the younger, handsomer model.

Unfortunately, after today, he was all out of use for me…and you know what they say about throwing things out that don't bring you joy.

The girls were out cold, so Thomas and I took the liberty of tying them up to ensure they couldn't run.

I knew they would be out for a while, so I brought it on myself to rifle through Riley's bags. After all, that was what sisters did, right?

I have to say… I was impressed. I thought my sister would have chosen a smaller gun, one of those little pocket-sized ones. But no, I definitely underestimated her because it was incredibly similar to Thomas's gun.

Weird.

I have to say, the feeling of holding the weapon that was meant to kill you in your own hand was similar to that of being euphoric.

The feeling came with a sense of victory.

I walked over to Riley's slumping unconscious body as Thomas was finishing up the rope ties.

"You were never going to win. You had to know that, right?" I snickered and walked away.

I slipped Riley's gun in the waistband of my jeans, safety off of course. I wasn't an idiot.

I couldn't help but look at Cora. She could have avoided all of this. She was never a part of the plan originally, but her constant insertion into all of this made her an addition. I would say she brought it on herself, but deep down she probably knows that as well.

"Do you plan to do both?" Thomas's sudden question broke me from my thoughts.

"Yes. I mean, unless you wanted to." I had no intentions of letting him do either kill, but I would rather avoid a fight right now.

"Cora, please. I know Riley is all yours." He smiled at me, and I nod my head in agreeance.

"Get rid of Cora's car. Quickly." He nodded in agreeance and scurried out.

First things first, I need the girl's phones. I found both of them and sent different, but also similar texts to both of their parents.

In both of the texts, I essentially said that the stress of everything was getting to them, and that they would be going away for a while with the other. I also added not to worry.

They were old enough that they wouldn't be able to get the police involved even if they suspected something was wrong.

I took the batteries out of both phones and tossed them in the trash. I didn't need them to be tracked here.

The girls were beginning to come to, and I could feel the excitement began to bloom inside me. "Wakey wakey girls." I was teeming with happiness, and it showed in my singsong voice.

Riley opened her eyes first. She went from confused initially, to panic as I saw her eyes grow wide. She started to yank on her limbs, but they were all fastened up nice and tight. Thomas used to be a boy scout, and there was no way in hell those girls would be able to get free.

Like clockwork, Cora began her wake up process and did the same exact thing as Riley had done.

It was comical to watch. It truly was. I couldn't help but break into a fit of laughter, which earned me a scowl from both my sister and Cora.

Thomas didn't share the same humor I did, and that was one of the many reasons I was done with him.

I let them squirm until Thomas returned which took all of about thirty-five minutes. He wouldn't want to miss this.

He stepped in front of the girls and started to threaten Cora with his gun.

I rolled my eyes. He wasn't cut out for this. She started to cry, and tremble.

Normally I would bask in this, but as I wasn't the one doing it, I found it to be incredibly annoying and even more obnoxious.

"You know, I feel so lucky to have found you. You have truly served your purpose, and for that I will always be grateful." I started to pull the gun from the back of my waistband, right as Thomas turned around.

"What th…" I pulled the trigger, which sent Thomas's body in a heap to the floor.

Riley and Cora began to scream as Thomas's blood covered their faces and exposed skin.

I stuck the gun back in its spot, and grabbed a hold of his collar, using all my strength to pull him into the next room.

The screams continued and I laughed.

Ah, this was all working out perfectly.

"You can scream as loud as you want really, it will make no difference. Nobody can hear you. That was the beauty in choosing this place, wasn't it? There would be nobody around for miles to hear me die." I snickered and continued.

"You thought you could scheme and plan and be able to take me down. Has the irony hit yet?" I walked away from them, allowing my works to sink in.

"Screw you!"

I didn't need to turn to know that was my loving sister.

"You did screw me actually. You, and those shitty people you call parents." I made sure to deliver the last word with spite clear in my voice.

"I did nothing to you. You came here. You infiltrated my life… my sister's life… and then you killed her. You are holding onto some revenge fantasy because mommy and daddy didn't love you enough. Don't you realize how pathetic that is?"

I did not turn because I didn't want her to know how much the words were angering me at that very moment. Did they hurt? Not in the slightest. But I was two seconds away from shooting her with her own gun. If she thought she had invoked any emotion in me, even one of anger and rage, she would feel like she was winning.

"I would rather be not loved at all by them, then to just be loved significantly less than Daisy. You don't actually think you were the favorite, do you? They loved her, and her death tore them apart more than yours ever will. You know that… deep down." This time I did turn around after I spoke, simply to watch Riley's face as my words cut deep.

I was glad I did because her face turned from triumphant to meek. That was when Cora the protector decided to step up and try to hurt me as well.

Good luck with that. I don't care about anything.

"Do you hate looking in the mirror? It has got to be so hard seeing the repulsive person staring back. Its funny to me because you may be a triplet, but you're the ugliest."

I couldn't even contain my laughter after that poor attempt at an insult. The ugliest one? Of triplets? My god, Cora was far denser than I ever imagined. Her death would bring me copious amounts of joy, and I was sure of that.

It had been only ten minutes, and I was surprised when I realized that I kind of missed the constant annoying babbling that Thomas used to do. It was a little too quiet for my liking, but all's well that ends well.

"What's your plan? Just keep us here? If you're going to kill us, why not get it over with now?" Riley sneered at me.

"But waiting is the best part. To be quite honest, I don't have time to kill you right now. I have a shift in about twenty minutes and it's a good distance away. Sit tight until I get back though."

I sauntered outside and grabbed paper towels out of my car to clean the visible blood off of me. I changed quickly into my work uniform and started the engine. I used my mirror to position my wig perfectly. It would still be pretty light out when I got back, but I made a mental note to swing by the hardware store and pick up a gas lamp.

How inconsiderate were those two to choose a house, or spot, that had no indoor lighting? You could barely consider the front of the house as having a door as well. The thing was practically hanging off of its hinges.

I knew that the girls were most likely already beginning to plan their escape, which probably started with them trying to free themselves of the rope,

I had no worries at all. There was no way in hell that they were getting out of there. I just had to get through my shift today. If everything went according to plan, I wouldn't need this job anymore after today. I wouldn't need a job at all.

I drove at a pretty relaxed speed. I couldn't help it. I was practically euphoric. Everything I had worked for… everything I had planned… it was all finally starting to fall in place.

The only thing that kept me from falling apart in that horrid place, in all the horrible places I was placed in, was the distant idea of revenge. I held onto that, promising myself that my parents would pay for everything they did to me.

I know I was the villain in their story, but they were the villains in mine.

I pulled into the familiar parking lot and glanced up at the flashing neon sigh.

Thankfully the parking lot was seemingly empty. It might be a slow night which waitresses don't usually hope for as money is their source of livelihood and you get that from tips... but I had a long morning and I was more than happy to take a breather today.

"Hey honey." My boss greeted me with a warm smile when I walked in.

I would miss that.

There were two officers sitting down at a table that I recognized as Thomas's friends. They knew me as well, and I tried to dip into the employee locker room without them noticing me.

"Hey Allie!"

No such luck.

I turned around slowly, with a huge smile hanging on my face. My cheeks started to hurt.

"Hi you guys. How's it going?"

"It's good. We decided to pop in for a bite to eat before we patrol. Have you seen Thomas today? He didn't show up for his shift." The one I recognized as Randy addressed me.

Play it cool.

"Actually... I don't. Thomas and I broke up a few days ago. I haven't seen him since he left here." I shrugged my shoulders and attempted my best somber look.

I could feel the energy in the air change quickly. They both went from grinning and excited to feeling guilty that they ever asked and annoyingly sympathetic.

Randy opened his mouth to speak again, but I waved him off.

"Sorry, I just don't want to talk about it right now. It's still fresh. I have to get to work. See you guys later?" I turned around and headed into the locker room without so much as another word or glance at either of them.

Once safely inside the room, a smirk spread across my face as I hung up my purse.

Well played, Taylor. Well played.

I slammed the door shut and headed out to what would surely be a dull shift.

40

Riley

I had to fight long and hard mentally to keep the overwhelming sense of defeat at bay. I wanted to be strong for Cora, and to show her I wasn't scared.

I knew that if I even hinted at thinking we may die here, that it could very well send her off the rails.

The truth is, I was scared. Even while creating this plan originally, I feared that something would go wrong, and that it would be mine and Cora's life that paid the price.

Taylor was far more insane than I ever thought. She shot the one person who was on her side and seemed to love her unconditionally right in front of our faces.

I was unsure if it was to make a point, or if she was really that cruel. It seemed like a calculated move, especially with the nonsense she was droning on about right before she pulled the trigger. The worst part? It was my gun.

Can you believe that? The guy kidnapped me and knocked me unconscious by pistol whipping me. I should hate him, and I thought I did.

But here I was… sitting here, tied up in ropes that burned to the touch, feeling guilty because the gun I purchased was used to kill someone that I felt could have been redeemed.

I think Taylor brought out the worst in him, and if he had a chance to get away from her, he could change.

"Cora, are you okay?" I struggled to keep the fear from entering my voice.

"I think so. Are you?" Her voice was incredibly shaky, and I wished more than anything that I could free my hand and grab hers.

This was my mistake. I should have never let it get this far. Taylor was my family, like it or not and I had to be the one to deal with it. Now, I put my friend's life in danger and that was something I would have to live with for the rest of my life.

Unless she kills you.

I was going to put up a hell of a fight. Taylor was absolutely delusional if she thought for a split second that this would be easy.

I know she was jumping for joy at the thought of her being the winner, but she was sorely mistaken.

I had tried for what felt like hours now to get the hell out of these ropes. My wrists and ankles burned from the rope, and my skin had been rubbed raw. Still, I wasn't giving up, and neither was Cora.

"Yeah. We just need to get out of here."

We were shit out of luck. The way Thomas had tied us up left us pretty much immobile but if I could get to my feet, I knew I could find something in here sharp enough to cut the rope.

"I have a plan. I just need you to help me get to my feet."

We strategized and figured out that the best way to get me up would be to have Cora close to the wall touching it with her feet. Her back would be to mine, and I would push all my weight onto her, steadying myself and shimmying my way to my feet.

It wasn't a perfect plan, but it was something and that was a hell of a lot more than anything else that we had right now. This could work. It had to work, because I had a gut-wrenching feeling that we were running out of time before my sister got home.

It took us ten long minutes to get Cora positioned the exact right way, and I dove into the process of leaning on her, sliding my feet out, leaning on her, pulling my feet in, and so forth.

I was almost there. I just needed one...more...PUSH!

I was on my feet, and I nearly cried of happiness.

"We did it, Cora! Oh my god, we really did it!" I was jumping.

"Yes, we did, but we don't have much time so now you need to find something sharp, and fast," There was a sense of urgency lining her voice.

But she was right. I had no clue how much time we had, and while there were two of us and one of her, she had a weapon and we were clearly incapacitated.

This house was so run down the walls were barely there anymore. I looked for a window, and while the glass was missing from all of them, it wasn't scattered on the floor like I had hoped. I wandered into the kitchen, which took me a long time as mt feet were bound tightly.

It was more of a hop, and I looked like a disfigured rabbit.

There was a small mirror leaning against what probably was the dining room. It was practically nothing after all this time, but it had a single shard of glass hanging haphazardly out of it.

I dropped to my knees, which I would like to say was a lot more graceful than it actually was.

My hands were fastened at my back so I scooted backwards until I could feel the tip between my fingertips. It was incredibly loose and didn't need much tug and pull before it came off easily in my hands.

Using the wall as my support, I stood back up and hopped right back into the hallway where Cora was sitting, slumped.

"I got something. Put your back to me."

Once again, I dropped back to the floor sitting with my back to Cora's. Being very tedious and extremely careful, I began to maneuver the shard of glass in a seesaw motion. I could hear the tearing of course fibers, and hope swelled in my chest.

Good, now keep going.

As I continued to cut, it began to get easier which meant that it was working. It took several minutes before Cora breathed a loud sigh of relief as she now had her hands free.

She took the glass from my hands and freed her legs, then started on me.

She had barely started to cup into my wrist rope when Taylor came storming up the steps with her, I mean my, gun in her hands looking furious. "What the hell do you think you're doing?"

And then a shot was fired.

41

Cora

I tried. I was so close to freeing both of us, and then Taylor arrived. She was fuming.

The gunshot was loud, and so unexpected that it sent a shockwave through my system.

Everything that happened next was a blur, and all I could remember was everything fading to black.

The last thing I remember was hearing Riley scream my name.

I opened my eyes, still completely stunned, and saw that Riley and I were tied up... again.

Except that I was wet... spanning over the entirety of my bottom half of my body.
What the hell?

I was still in a daze, and I started to look around trying to figure out what was on me. I started to panic when I realized that it was coming from me. I craned my neck and saw a patch of blood seeping out of the side of my shirt.

It streamed down from that point to my pants and was soaking my socks in my shoes.

"Cora… don't panic." I looked to my left at Riley, who tied up was doing her best to keep me from panicking over my now very clear gunshot wound.

I was completely dazed.

I was shot?

I could see the wound, and yet I could barely feel anything.

Adrenaline. It's the best drug out there.

"Oh, please. It's a surface wound. She'll live."

I lifted my head to see a very exasperated Taylor rolling her eyes as if I was overreacting. Its not a fucking papercut. You shot me!

The rage surged and I suddenly wanted to kill her. Riley and I were able to free ourselves earlier, but now I felt really weak.

I was losing a lot of blood, and without some way to stop the bleed, I would be dead soon.

The thought didn't scare me as much as I thought it would, but the idea of dying and having Taylor get what she wanted made me want to stay alive that much more.

How funny. My rage for Taylor outweighs my will to live in general.

I was grateful that Riley wasn't hurt but feeling pretty defeated that our plan went wrong in every possible way. Originally, we tried to weigh all possible outcomes, knowing that Taylor was smart.

At this point in time, it didn't even feel like she was smart but just lucky.

There was also no way in hell she was letting either of us out of her sight again until she got what she wanted.

If I were to go out on a limb, I would say she wanted both of us dead. Maybe she would let me bleed out and die slowly as a punishment for trying to escape. That seemed very Taylor-esque.

I wanted… no, I needed Riley to escape. She needed to get the chance to live. It wasn't fair that Taylor got to win. Taylor took so much from Riley. She took her best friend away from her, and that was Daisy. If she took me, Riley would have nothing left. She needed to get out. She needed to survive.

` And Taylor needed to die.

I would use every last ounce of strength I had within me to make sure that happened.

"You're not going to get away with this." I strongly spoke, trying to keep my words from quavering despite the pain that started to throb in my side.

Taylor rolled her eyes and did a huge belly laugh.

"That's so cliché though, isn't it? That's what the good guy always says to the bad guy in every movie, and they're always right…"

She continued.

"…but this isn't a movie."

Using her gun, she smacked the handle upside Riley's head, knocking her backwards.

"What are you doing? You're trying to do what exactly? Proving that you can beat the shit out of someone who's tied up?" I practically spit when I spoke as I was so consumed with anger.

She didn't even justify my question with a response. She walked away from us and rounded the corner of what I assume to be another hallway.

"Are you okay, Riley?" My concern for my friend outweighed the now excruciating pain in my side.

I also felt extremely weak, but I didn't want to worry Riley about that. It could just be the blood loss after all.

"I'll live. What about you? That looks bad." She eyed my side up and down, a worried look plastered on her face.

She looked confused for a minute, then scooted closer to me using her legs until her back was pressed against my side. Her hands were tied, but she used all her weight, cupped her hands, and pressed it right up against where the wound was.

It hurt so bad that I bit my lip to keep from screaming, which in turn made me start bleeding more.

I looked down and while it hurt like hell, I finally stopped seeing blood gush out.

"Thank...you." I smiled even though she couldn't see me.

She leaned her head back on me for comfort. "What are we going to do?" I asked my friend.

I had not a single clue what to do. Taylor was here, so any elaborate escape plan would be completely not doable. We needed something quick and easy to get us out, before Taylor walked back over and caught us.

She also had a gun, and I'm sure the bullets fly a hell of a lot faster than we can run.

So, we were pretty much screwed, although I knew better than to say that to Riley. We needed to stay positive. Nobody knew we were out here except for each other, and that did us no good, seeing as we were both a little tied up at the moment.

Suddenly, Taylor came back in with a grin on her face and a small nylon bag in her hand.
"I just thought of the best idea."

She looked at me.
"Don't look so glum Cora, now you get to live."

She took out some gauze and other bandages and moved Riley to the side. She slowly began to bandage my wound nicely.

I was just as confused as Riley, so we both sat there in silence observing Taylor's odd behavior.

When she was clearly satisfied with her handiwork, she stood, wiped her hands on her jeans, and pulled out a pair of scissors from the bag.

She cut me free from my ropes. She took my hands in hers and stood me up. Once I was standing, she slapped some cuffs on me and led me outside towards the cars.

That was it. No explanation. No warning. She just took me and left.

I turned my head towards Riley, who was sitting there dumbfounded.

I could tell she was struggling with what to do... should she run or stay?

I had no clue what was about to happen to me, but I knew one thing for sure in my heart- Riley needed to escape.

I mouthed the word, "Run", before turning back around.

"Where are we going?" I knew full well that Taylor wouldn't tell me a damn thing. She was relishing in the fact that she was the only person who knew anything, and she liked having that power.

To no surprise, she didn't say a word. She opened the back door of her car and stuck me inside. She buckled the seat belt across me, making sure my hands were not only cuffed but now restrained as well.

She slammed the door hard, and then climbed into the front seat, starting the engine.

"Better get comfy Cora. Its going to be long ride."

She adjusted her mirror so she could see her face and then retrieved the blonde wig from the front passenger seat. She meticulously slipped it on, careful to keep any hint of her red hair hidden under it. She took the gun and slipped it in the glove compartment.

Okay, so were going somewhere in public.

Once she felt it looked convincing enough, she peeled away from the house with my best friend inside. If we came back, I wanted Riley to be gone.

As promised the drive was long. I took the time to look at my surroundings, if I needed to remember for later. But quite frankly, I hadn't recognized anything outside of the house and I had a feeling that the trend would continue.

The route she took was coming from the other side of where we had come which meant we were traveling further and further from town.

She said her plan would allow me to live. I was running through the possible scenarios in my head on a continuous loop, but I was unable to come up with anything solid.

I decided to give up on the sight seeing adventure, sit back, and enjoy what might very well be the last moments of my life.

My mind immediately drifted to my mom. My mom had given up everything to be the best mother she could for me, and the thought of leaving her behind without me felt so horrible that it physically pained my heart.

The idea that there could be that much love in my heart for one person that the thought of losing them physically pained me, while Taylor was comfortable with killing family members, and someone she supposedly loved.

I don't know if she was simply more interested in self preservation than loyalty or love, or if she was just a sociopath who lacked any empathy or emotions.

Probably all of the above.

She was silently humming along to a Christmas song on the radio, as if it was any other day.

Meanwhile, I'm sitting in the backseat of her car with a poorly patched up gunshot wound, wondering if I would ever get the chance to see the people that I loved again.

For one second I would love to know what was going on in that messed up brain of hers. I needed to know what possible plan she could have for me, that would require her to drive this far away.

It was something that was clearly important, because she was willing to leave Riley behind who could probably be escaping at any moment.
I really wished she would.

If we were going so far out of town, why would she need to disguise herself? There was no possible reason for that. She needed to keep up the charade or façade of "Allie", and I wanted to know why.

So many unanswered questions, and one very hesitant and secretive sociopath.

She looked in the rearview mirror, making direct and continuous eye contact with me.

"I can see your mind running in circles trying to figure out what very possible reason I brought you this far away. Just ask. Maybe I'll decide to be nice and give you a hint." She winked at the end, followed by a low chuckle.

She was really enjoying this, and that boiled my blood.

"Well, what's my hint? Why did you decide to keep me alive?"

I didn't break eye contact once, letting her know she didn't intimidate me.

"Well, let's just say that this is considered my own personal punishment for you and all the trouble that you caused. There's been so much death lately at my hands, and I still have more to go. This punishment is worse than death, believe me."

Worse than death? What in the world could be worse than death?

Not only was my interest peaked, but my heart rate accelerated, and my cuffed hands became sweaty.

The fear alone gave me something else to focus on besides the agony I was feeling in my side.

"Stew on that Cora… but not for too long. We're almost there." She then turned up the volume on the music, letting me know loud and clear she was done talking.

That was just great, now I could wonder endlessly about what exactly she meant when she said that she had a punishment for me that would be considered worse than death.

Just. Great.

The rest of the ride was thankfully filled with such loud music that it did a good job at drowning out the horrifying thoughts in my head. I could almost bask in the non-silence.

She, however, did not utter any more words to me but instead continued that god-awful humming. How could someone not even be singing but sound so incredibly offbeat? I would mention it to her just to be a bitch, but my life was kind of in her hands so probably best not to piss her off.

I fail to understand how things could go so horribly wrong so fast. This time today we should have been in the works for the plan. The house would have been set and ready... the gun hidden.

But as we should have known, Taylor was one step ahead.

They followed us. They were onto us, and I can only assume she saw my car at the diner the other night which meant I did a crap job of playing detective.

I was probably the one who ignited her suspicions and led both me and Riley to this dire situation.

I couldn't help but dwell on everything that Taylor had said from the thing about a punishment worse than death, to saying that she would allow me to live.

Did that mean she didn't plan to let Riley live? The only reason I could think of for her needing to kill her would be because she knows too much and is becoming a liability.

The only reason I can think of for her *wanting* to kill her would be to punish her parents she seems to hate so much.

I still don't know if there's any truth to the story, and at this rate, I'll probably never know.

Its not exactly something that you can go right out and ask you know?

Hey guys, what's for dinner? And did you have a third daughter that you treated horribly and shipped off to a mental institution? Yes, Ill take a roll, thank you.

My head was going to explode.

"We're here," Taylor sang in an overly cheerful voice, and threw the car into park.

I sat straight up and looked around. It looked like a bunch of dirt, and then I noticed the barbed wire fence. It was a large grey building, but I couldn't see any visible windows, or even a sign.

What was this place?

She got out of the front seat, and took her time opening the back door. She was building suspense, and I could just see the sheer amount of joy that it was giving her.

It only made me that more motivated to get the fuck out of here.

I wanted to ask where we were, but that would only further satisfy her. I would just try and figure it out for myself.

How would she explain the handcuffs to whoever was here? And what about the gunshot wound? None of this made any sense.

"Do you know where we are Cora?" She pulled me out of the car after unbuckling the seat and held me in place there staring at the old building.

"Uh, no?" She was annoying, and I grew irritated.

"Then you haven't been paying attention to my stories. This here, my dear, is Greenburg Mental Institution. And you, are their newest patient." She smiled creepily and bustled me towards the entrance.

42

Riley

The metallic stench of Cora's blood on my hands lingered in my nostrils long after Taylor took them both away and left in the car.

I had a million thoughts running through my head. Cora told me to run. What if I did, but Taylor killed her as some sort of revenge. I would get away, but she wouldn't? It didn't seem fair and it didn't seem right. I was at a crossroads on what to do.

There were so many possible outcomes to this and knowing Taylor at this point, I knew to expect the unexpected.

I mean tomorrow she was supposed to be dead. She would be out of our lives once and for all, but now here we were, and it was our lives that were on the line. I hadn't a single idea on what to do, and now Cora had been shot, whisked away, and I was stuck here tied up and twiddling my fucking thumbs.

I was angry at myself for being so useless and letting this psycho overpower me more than once. I mean how pathetic was I?

She hid all the glass, so I had nothing to cut myself free with, and I wouldn't know how to do it without a little of Cora's help anyways.

I know she took the gun with her… she wasn't stupid.

I could barely stand with the way this bitch tied me up. I was so frustrated I felt like screaming. It was pointless though, as there were practically no neighbors around and it would do fuck all to cheer me up.

In actuality, I was screwed, and all I was doing here was trying desperately to convince myself otherwise.

At least when it came down to the time to kill me, I knew in my heart that I would fight like hell. I wouldn't make it easy for her.

I looked down at my new tennis shoes, which were now covered in my best friend's blood. The white laces were drenched, and the smell was absolutely overpowering.

And then it hit me.

When we were both "kidnapped" together, Taylor had used her shoelaces tied together to saw through the zip ties. Granted, those were smaller and less thick, but it was worth a shot.

My mom was always so scared by the constant threat of kidnapping and trafficking and always made sure that she forwarded those videos to both Daisy and myself, so I slightly remember it too.

In the video, the girl was wearing a pair of tennis shoes much like myself, and she tied the two shoelaces around the rope encircling her hands. She tripled knotted it to ensure that it would come undone and began to move her feet back and forth in a rapid motion which after a while cut through the material dude to the rapid motion mixed with the fibers being rubbed hard.

It was a long shot, especially with rope this coarse, but I worried I had no other choice.

I needed to try it.

I lined my two shoes up next to each other. I used my free fingertips to loosely grab the lace from each shoe and pulled it over my wrist. It was incredibly hard, but I was able to get them interlocked.

From there, I knotted it. Then I knotted it again. And again.

Once I was sure that there was absolutely no way that the laces would separate, I got to work. I began moving my feet faster and faster until I had to take a break due to exhaustion.

It was yanking hard on my wrists, and I didn't see it making any leeway. Nevertheless, I wasn't a quitter, and this was quite literally my life on the line.

So, I kept going. I moved my feet harder and faster than I ever did, even when I was stuck running the mile for fitness class.

I stopped momentarily to check my progress and felt disappointed when there was still no damage done to the rope.

It was in that moment that I begin to cry. The tears made me angry, mostly at myself, which in turn made me cry harder.

I was mad that I could be so weak. The only thing on my mind right now should be getting the hell out of here and living.

But instead, I was sitting here weak and docile... feeling sorry for myself. I felt like the most pathetic person in the world and I was in disbelief of myself.

I wouldn't allow it. I was going to die anyways. She took Cora somewhere because she said she would allow her to live.

So that meant I was going to die. The only way I could avoid that fate was to escape and the possibility of doing so was looking quite dismal at this point.

Okay, this shoelace trick was a bust. I suppose it would work for thinner rope and zip ties, but this rope was far too thick and far too coarse.

I wasn't going to give up. I simply just needed to find another way out of here.

The only thing I could do being tied up the way I was, was roll on my side. I definitely wouldn't make it very far from here if all I was doing was rolls. All the sharp objects were gone, then gun was gone- not that it would help me anyways, and I couldn't stand.

It was hard to focus on escape strategies with Cora's blood stench mixed with Officer Brooks. He had begun to smell, and Taylor had yet to move his body.

Even though he was in another room, the smell was overpowering, and it felt as if it was stuck in my nostrils.

What if Officer Brooks had something on him? He was in his uniform. Surely, he must have something I could use to get the hell out of this. Taylor took his cuffs to use on Cora, so that means he has his belt on.

So now I would have to belly roll into a room, and rifle through a dead man's belongings, on his body.

This should be easy.

43

Taylor

The look on Cora's face when I revealed where we were was one that I wish I could freeze and frame to look at every day of my life.

It was absolutely priceless.

It was a mix of fear, concern, confusion, and many more that all gathered together in a wonderful symphony which brought that much more joy to my life.

Cora had become a problem time after time again, and I needed her gone. If I was to ever fully complete my plan, she needed to be out of the way. I knew she and Riley both knew it at this point. She had simply become a liability, or more so a loose end per say.

It really was nothing personal. I will admit that I did extensive research into my sisters' lives before the fact and had a slight idea of their best friend Cora. What I didn't know was how hard she would fight for them. It was entertaining at first, but it didn't take long before it transitioned into an annoyance.

This was never part of the plan though. I was simply going to kill Cora, Riley, and then move on to Phase 2. But this way, Cora gets to live, and I get to live with the satisfaction of knowing I was the one who put her in this place.

I was the one who made her suffer the way I suffered, and that was just the cherry on top of a really shitty day.

She had already moved from the shock to blithering apologies and begging. I knew it would come at some point, as they all begged when they knew it was too late.

Daisy sure did.

"God, would you shut up already? All your babbling is only going to further my case with them. If I were you, I would shut the hell up."

My outburst momentarily shut Cora up, and I basked in the sweet peace of silence.

That girl really had a motor mouth on her, and most conversations with her in general tended to be one sided, as she would fill the silence for both of you.

I knew this from personal experience.

We reached the front doors, and were greeted by a security guard, and a nurse.

The chills that went down my spine made my hands start to sweat, but I reminded myself that I wasn't going to be a patient, and that I could relax.

However, it was hard to do so, especially when the very vivid memories of being here were all coming rushing back one by one.

From being checked in, to being doped up with medication I didn't need, to being stuck with people who were actually crazy, to being poked and prodded and later electrocuted.

I felt paralyzed, until I gave myself one big mental push.

You have a job to do Taylor. Get in and get out so you can start living your real life. The one you were always meant to live in the first place.

"New check in?" The nurse was very brusque, and I remember her well from my time here.

"Yes. C-Caila Sanders. This is my cousin. She has had a mental break coming for quite some time, and today she went after me and my husband with a gun. As you can see, she was the one who ended up hurt." I gestured towards the wound.

The nurse nodded and wrote some things down on her clipboard.

"Any identification?"

Think fast.

"No, she threw all her stuff away some time last week I'm assuming. She was planning to run away."

Not bad at all. You could win an Emmy.

"Okay, well we will get her checked in, have you sign some papers giving consent, and she will be patched up."

Cora began to scream and freak out at that moment, despite being eerily quiet during the whole exchange prior.

"She's lying! My name is Cora. I was kidnapped! She has my friend Riley hostage, and she was a patient here! She's a triplet, and that's a wig!" She pointed at my blonde hair, and I had to keep myself from bursting into laughter.

Putting it all into one long winded message like that really made it sound crazy, especially with no context or backstory behind it. I told her earlier that she was better staying quiet, and I guess spouting all of that was what she had decided to do instead.

My point was further proven when the nurse eyed her up and down warily, looking at her like she was an insane person.

"I'm sorry. As you can see, she is very confused." I shrugged towards the nurse.

"Well, they all usually are. I didn't catch your name."

She stretched out her hand to shake mine, and I had to fight the tremor that was reaching my palm.

I stuck my hand out and shook hers.

"Allie Sanders. Nice to meet you."

The nurse opened the big metal door and led us inside. The waiting room brought back more memories I didn't want to resurface.

The one where I was a little kid being brought here by my parents… left for years without so much as a visit from them.

I wish I could say the memory hurt, but it didn't. All it did was make me angry and realize just again why I was here. I had a plan to execute and getting Cora off my back was just one of the steps I needed to complete first.

The nurse waved over two muscular male nurses who each took one of Cora's arms. "You're not listening! My name is Cora!" She screamed as they dragged her the entire way through the doors.

The nurse then came back over and sat next to me as she handed me the paperwork. She reached out and touched my arm.

"You're doing the best thing for her you know. I know it can be hard." She actually seemed empathetic which was a weird change from the demeanor she presented towards me as a patient here.

"I know. I just want to make sure she can get better. How is your security here? Has anybody ever been able to escape?" I was teetering on a dangerous line, but I felt bold in the moment.

She looked thoughtful for a second, acting as if she was trying to remember, but I knew the truth. She was contemplating whether or not to be honest with me.

"Nope. Our security is pretty efficient in doing their jobs." She smiled fakely.

"Good to know. Where do I sign?"

She pointed out all of the places I had to initial and sign, and yet all I could focus on were her long pointy red fingernails. She used to point and scream at the patients, myself included, and I know that it rang true for more than just myself when I say that I would never forget them.

It took a lot longer than expected to sign all the paperwork. The stack she handed me resembled a phone book more than anything, and a lot of the questions and concerns were unappealing to me. I didn't care what happened to Cora, I just wanted to get out of here.

The thought that was eating me alive for the past twenty minutes was the thought of my parents in here doing the exact same thing all those years ago.

Did they face the same thought process? Did they not read the paperwork as I had, and simply wanted to rush through it so they could cut all ties and move on with their lives?

The thought was horrifying to me. I couldn't imagine being that heartless as to not care about what happened to someone you brought into the world.

I only hurt people who deserved it. My parents hurt people who didn't align with what they wanted. The idea that these people raised two other children is scary, and yet they turned out to be really good people. They were annoying, but good people.

It sucks that they were the ones who had to pay for their parent's mistakes all those years ago.

I was sure that Riley was brainstorming on how to escape, so I felt very tired of the ridiculously long paper signing process. I wanted to be done so I could leave this hellhole and never look back.

Cora's mom would think that her daughter picked up and left.

That would be the story that Riley would sell to them anyway.

It would be hard at first, but I think with Riley's convincing, she would be more susceptible to the idea.

Finally, after an eternity, the nurse shook my hand once more and assured me that they would do everything in their power to get Cora, I mean, Caila back to her normal self in no time.

"Good. I just want her to get better." I smiled at the nurse, who once again looked uncharacteristically empathetic.

"Of course, dear. You have a good holiday." She touched my shoulder and sauntered towards the double doors, no doubt to engage in a screaming match with one of the docile patients.

I hightailed it out of the front door, not realizing I was holding my breath until I reached the front door of my car. I unlocked it, slid in, and exhaled a huge breath.

My hands were shaking uncontrollably at this point, and I was pretty surprised that this place had that much of an effect on me still. It was kind of ridiculous in a way, but very understandable. I spent many years here, being told repeatedly that I was a waste of space, and chronically ill. The treatments were severe and clearly ineffective. This place was more a torture spot than a mental rehabilitation center.

It should be shut down for the trauma.

After seeing the impact this place had on me, its questionable why I would choose to inflict the same on anybody else, namely Cora.

I didn't want to kill her. She had so much life to live still, and even though she had become a massive burden on me, I simply relocated her. I made her someone else's problem.

I had escaped, and if she put her mind to it, and planned extensively than I had no doubt that she would be able to do the same.

Although I was sure that they may have beefed up security enforcements since I left.

Good riddance. I look forward to never coming here again.

I started up my car, sitting in there basking in the heater blasting on my face for a while longer. I had eliminated 3 of my problems at this point in time, and I knew the fourth would be waiting for me when I returned.

I didn't worry about the possibility of her escaping. The rope was incredibly thick, and without anything to cut it on, she was stuck there whether she liked it or not.

I took the weapons, and the way I tied her up was a surefire way to keep her immobile for when I returned. I liked excitement as much as the next person, but I didn't feel like a physical blowout would be in the best-case scenario for when I returned.

I wanted to simply put an end to her life, and then begin anew.

Easy, peezy, no strings attached.

The drive would take a while, and I was feeling a tad bit rundown. I stopped for coffee on the way back home and savored every deliciously sweet sip. I preferred my coffee with tons of flavor and crème, as I already had enough black in my life.

I even had the barista add a few pumps of peppermint syrup, just to get into the holiday spirit.

My GPS said I had about twenty-five more minutes to go, and I really had to pee. I stopped at a gas station, grabbing a water and a shitty cookie.

I was really enjoying my "me" time.

Once I killed Riley, the scheming that I had been doing for months on end would finally cease to exist, and I would be able to bask in endless amounts of me time.

I looked forward to that, and it's what kept me motivated and strong throughout this whole experience. Even though I couldn't exactly blame Riley and Daisy for our parent's mistreatment of me, I envied them. They lived the life that growing up I had always wanted.

An eye for an eye seemed like the perfect fit for this situation, and that was why they had to die. I know that taking not one, but both of them from my parents would be the best way to hurt them.

They valued those two girls more than they valued their own life, and I used that to my advantage.

I pulled up to the house, and parked. I scarfed down the rest of my cookie because I could use the energy. I grabbed the wig by the back and yanked it off, fluffing my red hair.

I opened the glove compartment, retrieving Riley's gun. I slowly opened the door, climbed out and braced myself for the end of what would be the longest chapter of my life.

This was it. This was the moment that would finally change everything for me.

I slipped the gun into my waistband and began to walk towards the house. Riley wasn't where I left her, but I knew she wouldn't have gotten very far. "Riley... where are you?"

I heard movement in the next room over. "Do you want to make this hard or easy?"

My sister started to charge towards me, free of her bindings.

She caught me off guard, knocking me to the floor.

I grabbed a hold of her shoulder and shoved her backwards, and to the side so I could get a better foothold.

"Hard. You got it."

44

Cora

Nobody was listening to me… not the guards, not the nurse, and certainly not any of the doctors.

I would have never imagined Taylor to come up with something this cruel. It far exceeds any previous idea I had of just how insane she really was. This proved the lengths she would go.

She had no plan of ever getting me out of here. I was stuck, and not one single person knew where I was. I doubt she would tell Riley, and even then, how would Riley be able to get me out?

Knowing the idiots that work here, they would probably assume that Riley was Taylor and lock her up right inside here with me.

I had probably only been here for an hour or so, but it felt like days. They already had me hopped up on all kinds of medication, which left me feeling exhausted yet energetic at the same time, if that was even possible.

The doctors diagnosed me as schizophrenic, with a manic disorder, and all I could do was shout at them. That only made them believe I was crazy a little more than they already did, but I had no other way to make them realize what was going on.

That was the brilliance of Taylor's plan. She knew it would work, and that was precisely why she did it. She was absolutely right about what she said earlier. This was a fate worse than death.

They stuck me in some cold room with a single bed, a sink, and a wobbly wooden chair. There were no windows, and only one single door to enter and exit.

I knew there were bars on the outside of the door, or locks, so I didn't even attempt to get out of there. They simply made me change into a gown, gave me some pills, diagnosed me, and left me to my own demise.

Not that I could get anything done in here. It was like a prison cell, only worse. I hadn't actually done anything to get put in here.

I heard the bolt lock slide, and I sat straight up. The doctor came strolling in with two nurses following very closely behind him.

He had his hand behind his back carrying something he didn't want me to see. Suddenly he stopped, and the two nurses continued advancing.

They each sat next to me on the bed, grabbed one arm, and the doctor quickly strode over and slid a needle into my arm. I could feel the liquid from the needle spreading fast through my veins. All of a sudden, I felt very fatigued and my body felt heavy. "Don't worry. This will make you feel all better Caila."

His voice sounded miles away as my eyes slid shut and my head hit the thin pillow.

I don't want to be here.

45

Riley

I rolled my body over once, and again, and repeated the same process until I reached the dark hallway.

There were a lot of rooms, and my only way to navigate was the sense of smell, and by the rotting smell coming from my left, I could only deduce that was where Thomas's body was at.

So, I swung my body left on the final turn, and one look to my side confirmed it. Thomas was right there.

I felt sick to my stomach at the mere sight of him laying there. His mouth was open slack, and his eyes were wide open staring at the ceiling. I could see where the gunshot wound had stemmed from, and the dried blood pool that surrounded it and him.

God, Taylor really did a number on him. My heart hurt for him and his family despite everything he had done to me and put me through. I felt all along that he was simply a pawn in Taylor's game. I don't think he could have ever done things as evil as he did, had he not had her in his life.

I mean he was an officer of the law, for God's sake. His one mission was to protect the people of this town, and all it took was one pretty redhead to sway him from everything he should've believed in and fought for.

In the end, he only dug his own grave as she easily took him out when she felt he wasn't of use to her anymore.

That's all what any of us were to Taylor. We were all simply mere pawns in her bigger game. I was clearly the biggest pawn, and why she kept me alive until last. It didn't matter, and neither did the sibling connection we shared. Taylor may have been a good person at one point, but either my parent's lack of love, or the mental institution, or both are what fucked her up.

She was a much different person than I think she would have ever turned out had she stayed at home with us. I still didn't understand my parent's reasoning behind sending her away and keeping her identity a secret.

I probably never would. I would also probably never get the chance to see my parents again, so I didn't want my last thoughts of them to be negative and biased with a one-sided story accusation.

The stench was overpowering my nostrils and making my eyes tear up. I couldn't stand it any longer. I saw his belt on and clearly the gun was gone.

A lot of the stuff wasn't on there, like pepper spray which would be pretty useless getting me out of the rope, but something that would aid to my benefit in taking down Taylor.

I did see a multitool attached by a clip. Like pretty much everything I did at this point, I had to scoot almost too close for comfort to his cold hard body.

I reached as far as I could until I could feel my fingertips connect with the edge of it. I still was having trouble pulling it from the belt. I would have to get much closer if I wanted any chance of removing it.

I pulled my body slightly up onto his upper leg and stretched for the tool. I felt my fingers grab it, and then I was fully able to grasp it with my hands, pulling towards myself. I heard a light snapping noise when it disconnected from the belt, and I breathed a sigh of relief.

This wasn't over yet. I still had a chance.

I fumbled with the tool in my hand, pulling out every tool until I found the tiny blade. It wasn't that sharp at all, so this would probably take a while.

I started sawing my wrist area first, slowly moving the tiny blade back and forth being extra careful as to not snap it.

It was likely a lot more durable than I gave credit for, but this was no time for slip ups.

It was a tedious motion- back and forth, back and forth... back and forth.

It must have been going on for fifteen minutes, and then twenty, and then nearly thirty before I saw the rope start to give way. It wasn't more than a minute later when the entire rope snapped in half, freeing my hands.

I was so excited that I could have started jumping for joy, but I still had my ankles to get through. This would be a lot easier as I could have more range of motion for my hands to work. There was no measure of the time I had left, so I just had to do my best.

I started in, back and forth, going as hard as I could by pressing the knife down with a great deal of pressure when cutting. It went to my benefit, and I saw the rope start to break about five minutes into it.

Ten minutes later, and I was free. My wrists and ankles were red and chafed from the rope rubbing from the past day.

I rubbed them mindlessly as I heard a car pulling up. I was immediately nervous, and then realized I was faced with a major decision.

Did I run? Or did I stay and fight?

A sudden surge of confidence and fire coursed through my veins, and I had the urge to fight. She didn't deserve to get away with this scot free. I came to this house on a mission, and I wasn't leaving until it was done.

The confidence slightly weened when I realized I had not a single weapon to defend myself with besides a very dull and very small knife from a multipurpose tool while Taylor had a gun.

I heard the car engine running, but no movement and I had yet to hear a car door. She was sitting there, but why?

I had no time to look, because I had to hide. The only advantage I had at this point in time was the element of surprise, and even after being gone for hours, she had most likely deduced that I would try to escape.

She probably had no idea that I would actually succeed, but little did she know that I planned to succeed in my original plan as well.

Some way, somehow, I would kill Taylor.

Then, I would go and find my friend that she took off to God knows where.

Finally, I would make sure that Officer Brooks' family knew where the body was. I had already decided that I would leave his name out of Taylor's antics. For the most part, he was a decent cop, and deserved to be remembered as such.

The car door being slammed broke me from my thoughts and launched me into reality. I had to overcome the greatest obstacle yet- Taylor.

The sister I never knew I had… but now I felt grateful for that. I would never want someone like her in my life. If everything went according to plan, I would never have to again, nor would anybody else.

I heard her ascending the front steps, and rather loudly I might add. She wanted me to know that she was here.

She called out to me.

"Riley… where are you?"

I didn't answer her, staying hidden and out of sight. She hadn't yet come into my eye view.

"Do you want to make this hard or easy?"

I finally saw her from where I was squatting at. I slowly rose, careful to not make any noise and started charging full speed ahead right at her.

Her eyes snapped up towards me as I was almost near her, and I could tell she wasn't expecting that.

I was able to knock her backwards onto her ass. Within a split second, we were both on the floor rolling around, neither able to get a good grip on the other until she was able to grab my shoulder and pin me to my back.

"Hard. You got it."

She raised her fist to punch me in the face, and I narrowly avoided it by jerking to the side. Her first hit the wooden floor, and she yanked her hand back in pain. I used her momentary distraction to my advantage and knocked her backwards once more.

This time, the gun slid from her hand. I started to crawl towards it, and I slid my hands around the handle of it when I felt pain shoot through my fingers as Taylor was already standing, and on my hand.

I grabbed my hand, flexing my fingers to make sure I could move them. Taylor kicked me in the face, sending me backwards and onto the wooden floor.

I pulled myself up, as she stood there patiently waiting.

She was enjoying this far too much, or she would have shot me already.

"Any last words Riley?"

She made sure the gun was fully loaded as she waited for me to speak.

I wouldn't dare give her the satisfaction.

I ran full throttle towards her once more, and once again she bested me, launching me forward and onto my back. I tried to stand, but she sat right on top of me bearing all her weight onto me.

"Nothing to say, huh? What? Cat got your tongue?"

She snickered, and I felt myself consumed with hatred.

"Go. To. Hell," I said angrily and then I spit in her face.

She barely flinched but wiped her face clean using her sleeve and aimed the gun in between my eyes.

"I wish this could have ended differently. You were such a good sister." She smiled, but it was lacking any real or genuine sincerity.

"You weren't. I can see why our parents sent you away. You're a monster." I couldn't even bear to look at her, knowing her face would be the last I saw before I died.

"Goodbye, Riley."

I closed my eyes and thought once more of my parents, as I heard the gun go off. Within seconds the pain, the sounds, the lights, and everything else that made me myself was gone. It was just darkness.

I faded away into an empty nothingness.

46

Taylor

I watched as my sister's body turned lifeless and fell slack.

I sat back, leaned on the wall, and just stared at her. It was all done. I had done everything that I sat out to do all those years ago. All the planning that went on in my small cell had finally come full circle.

I had gotten the chance to see my plan come to life, faced some obstacles, dealt with them accordingly, and was now getting the chance to bask in the completion and absolute success of it all.

I was euphoric.

I couldn't celebrate my success for too long, because I had to dispose of Thomas and Riley's bodies. His had already begun to smell, and I could barely tolerate his stench when he was alive, much less now that he's dead.

I walked out to my car, opening the trunk and retrieving the shovel I brought with me when I came.

The good news was that I would only have to dig two holes rather than three. The absence of hard work was always something to celebrate.

I walked back into the house, past my sister and out the back door into the large open field they considered a back yard for this place.

I picked a good area with soft topper soil and started at it. They were both about the same height, and I wanted them buried pretty far down.

I started in on the first hole using a painfully rhythmic pace. It was almost punishing with the ways my arms began to feel after a short while of shoveling dirt.

It took a little over two hours according to my watch, and I returned to the car, retrieved two of the tarps and went back into the house. I laid Riley's body on one and dragged it by the edge all the way over to the holes. I used the rope I had leftover, to roll her all the way up inside of it, using the rope to secure her.

Standing up, I used all of my weight and strength combined to push her into the hole. She dropped with a loud thud, but it was a perfect fit if I do say so myself.

I repeated the process with Thomas, although he proved to be quite a little more difficult given the extra forty pounds of muscle and extra foot of height that he had on him compared to my small sister.

Nevertheless, I was able to get both of them in their respective holes. I started to shovel the earlier removed dirt back on top of them.

I would pack every layer with the backside of the shovel, ensuring that even in weather changes, they would be safely tucked under the soil.

Once my sister was covered about halfway, I threw the shovel and the gun in there with her, as well as any of the other belongings. I then filled the rest of the hole with the dirt having my hands and feet act as a makeshift shovel.

When I was finished, I was absolutely filthy and covered in dirt, now turned to mud with the mixture of my sweat incorporated.

I admired my handiwork. If you were a visitor or a passerby, then you would have virtually no idea of the events that occurred here, or that there were two people buried at least five feet below the surface.

I headed back to the house to clean up the mess before heading to the gym to get myself cleaned up. There was blood everywhere. While I didn't care to make it spotless, I needed to make the blood at least not visible to the naked eye. I doubt anybody would come looking for the girls or Thomas here, but I didn't want them to walk in and see a crime scene.

I had Lysol wipes in my car along with a few water bottles. It was wood, so I knew it wouldn't do too well with trying to get it out.

Getting the appearance of blood off of this old wood wasn't that difficult until I went to the area where Thomas's body lay for a day. It had pooled in one spot and then dried.

It was nothing a little elbow grease couldn't fix. When it was all said and done, I gave one more look around to ensure that I wasn't leaving anything of importance behind.

The drive to the gym was almost surreal, and I looked back on the entire journey. From sitting in my cell, to escaping, to meeting Thomas, befriending Daisy, killing Daisy, meeting Riley and Cora, kidnapping Riley, and the rest goes on and on.

It was quite the story, and it was one that I would hold near and dear to my heart forever.

I grabbed my gym bag with Riley's clothes. She had a pair of sweats, along with a pair of tennis shoes from when we all hung out one night by the lake and she got wet. She decided after that might, she would keep some in my car if she ever needed to change spontaneously.

This was perfect for me.

I grabbed the sweats, shoes, and a fresh t-shirt of mine, added it to my bag, and headed into the gym.

The gym workers paid me no mind and didn't even look at my disheveled appearance twice as they scanned my card.

This was the cheapest gym to get a membership for, so I had no doubt that they got a barrage of homeless people coming everyday just to have a shower and feel better.

I didn't care to be associated physically with a homeless person, but if it could get me zero odd looks then I was here for it.

It was the quickest shower I had ever had in my life, and yet the feeling of being clean was still as good as ever.

I slid on the fresh clothes, washed, and then dried my hair. I took one look in the mirror. I looked and felt human again.

I got into my car for the last time and drove to a spot I hadn't been in years.

You never forget, which is something I'm starting to realize.

But first, I needed to make a pit stop at the lake.

I pulled through this spot that was adjacent to the one that Cora and Riley had shown me. This one had a lack of trees, so I was able to drive my van pretty close to the water. I kept a good distance, however.

It was a somber moment for me. I would have to shed every ounce of my old life in order to be ready for my new one.

With that being acknowledged once more, I climbed out of my car, reached over and took off the brake.

The car slowly inched forward, picking up speed before it hit the water and started to sink as it inched further towards the center of the lake.

There were bubbles, and then it was gone. It was completely submerged.

The lake wasn't far from my destination, so I took one final look, and then started on my way.

Driving so often made me forget the simple pleasures that walking brings. There's the cool air, the smell of nature around you, and all the sights and sounds you experience.

My destination came into view.

The butterflies in my stomach were moving at rapid speed, and I felt nervous.

I slowly walked up the steps and knocked on the door in front of me.

It swung open almost immediately, and the sight of my parents standing there took me back to memories of being young.

My mom pulled me into a tight hug, and my dad joined in.

"Riley, where have you been?!" My mom was shocked to see me, clearly.

"I'm sorry, I just had some things to figure out." I tried to be as vague as possible.

"Well, we are just glad that you are home Riley," My dad said as he hugged me tighter.

Me too, guys. Me too.

Made in the USA
Lexington, KY
08 December 2019